PROMISES TO KEEP

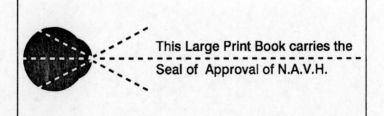

PROMISES TO KEEP

ANN TATLOCK

THORNDIKE PRESS
A part of Gale, Cengage Learning

Detroit • New York • San Francisco • New Haven, Conn • Waterville, Maine • London

GALE
CENGAGE Learning®

Copyright © 2011 Ann Tatlock.
Thorndike Press, a part of Gale, Cengage Learning.

ALL RIGHTS RESERVED
Thorndike Press® Large Print Christian Fiction.
The text of this Large Print edition is unabridged.
Other aspects of the book may vary from the original edition.
Set in 16 pt. Plantin.

LIBRARY OF CONGRESS CATALOGING-IN-PUBLICATION DATA

Tatlock, Ann.
    Promises to keep / by Ann Tatlock.
        pages ; cm. — (Thorndike Press large print Christian fiction)
        ISBN 978-1-4104-5138-5 (hardcover) — ISBN 1-4104-5138-0 (hardcover)
    1. Families—Fiction. 2. Illinois—Fiction. 3. Large type books. I. Title.
PS3570.A85P76 2012
813'.54—dc23   2012026797

Published in 2012 by arrangement with Bethany House Publishers, a division of Baker Publishing Group.

Printed in Mexico
1 2 3 4 5 6 7 16 15 14 13 12

To Mike and Kris Sullivan
Who have blessed me more than
I can say

CHAPTER 1

We hadn't lived in the house on McDowell Street for even a week when we found a stranger on the porch, reading the morning paper. Wally saw her first, since it was his job to fetch the newspaper from the low-lying branches of the blue spruce, where the paper boy always tossed it. I was in the kitchen setting the table, and from there I could see Wally — tall and lanky and bare-chested in the summer heat — move down the hall toward the front door. He was grumbling about the rain as the soles of his feet slapped against the hardwood floor. He reached for the doorknob, then stopped abruptly. In the next moment he hollered back toward the kitchen, "Mom, there's an old lady out on the porch."

Mom was frying bacon at the stove. She jabbed at the sizzling pan with a spatula and hollered back, "What's she want? Is she selling something?"

"I don't think so," Wally said. "She's just sitting there reading the paper."

"*Our* paper?"

"Well, yeah. I think it's our paper."

"What now?" Mom muttered as she moved the frying pan off the burner and untied her apron. When she turned around, I saw the flash of fear in her eyes. It was a look I was used to; it showed up on Mom's face whenever she didn't know what was coming next, which happened a lot in our old house in Minnesota. But not because of strangers.

Mom laid the apron over a chair, smoothed back her blond hair, and ran the palms of her hands over the wrinkles in her housedress. At the same time she tried to smooth the wrinkles in her brow enough to look confident. I followed her from the kitchen to the front door, where Wally stood so close to the window the tip of his nose touched the glass. "Can you believe it?" he said quietly. "She's just sitting there like she owns the place or something."

Mom raised one hand to her lips in quiet hesitation. Meanwhile, I slipped to the living room window and peered out from behind the curtain, finding myself only inches from our uninvited guest. At first glance she was one huge floral-print dress

8

straining the straps of the folding lawn chair on the porch. Her legs were propped up on the railing, and her bulky black tie shoes dangled like dead weight over the lilac bush below. I couldn't see much of her face, just a small slice of fleshy cheek and the bulbous end of a generous nose, a pair of gray-rimmed glasses and a mass of white hair knotted at the back of her head. She was reading the Sunday comics, and something must have tickled her because she laughed out loud.

That howl of glee sent enough of a jolt through Mom to get her going. She gently pulled Wally away from the door and swung it open. She pushed open the screen door and stepped outside. I saw the old woman's head bob once, as though to acknowledge Mom's presence.

"Can I help you?" Mom asked. Her voice was strained, the way it sounded when she was trying not to yell at one of us kids. She waited a few seconds. Then, a little more exasperated, she repeated, "Can I help you with something?"

The stranger folded the paper and settled it in her lap. "No, dear, I don't think so." The corner of her mouth turned up in a small smile. "But thank you just the same."

Mom stiffened at that, and all her features

seemed to move toward the center of her face. "Well," she said, "may I ask what you're doing on my porch?"

"Just sitting a while," the old woman said, as though she'd been found passing the time of day on a public bench. "Anyway," she went on, "it's not your porch. It's mine."

"Uh-oh," Wally whispered in my direction. "She's one of those crazies. You'd better go keep an eye on Valerie."

But I didn't want to go keep an eye on Valerie. I wanted to stay right where I was and watch Mom talk with the crazy lady.

Mom looked off toward the street like she was hoping someone would walk by and help her, but it was early Sunday morning and the streets were quiet, save for one lone soot-colored cat slinking along the sidewalk in the misty rain.

Finally Mom turned back to the stranger and said, "I'm afraid I'm going to have to ask you to leave, and if you don't, I will call the police."

The old lady pulled her feet off the railing, and I thought maybe she was going to stand up and leave, but she didn't. Instead, she said quietly, "Well now, I wish you wouldn't do that."

"You don't give me any choice. You're trespassing on private property."

"I might say the same for you."

Mom's eyes widened. "What do you mean by that?"

"The law might say you own this house, but it'll always be mine."

"Mom," Wally hollered though the screen, "you want me to call the cops?"

Mom latched her hands together at her waist and squeezed her fingers together. "Not yet, Wally. Just hold on." To the woman, she said, "I want to give you the chance to leave peacefully."

The old woman wasn't looking at Mom anymore. Now she was looking out at the street, but I had the feeling she wasn't seeing the street but something else altogether.

When she spoke, her voice was low and even. "My husband built this house for me in 1917. Built it with his own hands. And you see these two hands here?"

The woman held up her hands, large as any man's. Mom nodded reluctantly.

"These hands helped him. I laid flooring, plastered tile, painted the rooms, hung wallpaper. We built this place together, Ross and I."

A small muscle worked in Mom's jaw. "I see."

"I came here as a bride, twenty years old. Had my babies here. Lived here all my mar-

11

ried life. Watched my husband die in our bedroom upstairs."

"Oh, great," Wally said, glancing at me. "Some old guy croaked upstairs."

Though he said it loud enough for the woman to hear, she ignored him and kept on talking. "My heart is in every piece of wood and every nail. For that matter, so is my sweat. I believe they call that sweat equity. There's so much of me in this house, you'll never get it out. You might live here now, but this house — it'll always belong to me."

Mom was chewing her lower lip by now, and her eyes were small. Her knuckles had turned white because she was squeezing her hands together so hard. I knew exactly what she was thinking. I knew she was thinking about our old life in Minneapolis and how this place in Mills River, Illinois, was our new life, and she may have even been thinking of those words she said to me that first night after we moved in: *"We're safe now, Roz. We don't have to be afraid anymore."* She had worked and planned for a long time, until finally, with the help of her father, Grandpa Lehman, she'd got us out of Minnesota and away from Daddy. And now, only days into our new life, some crazy woman showed up making trouble.

"I lived here fifty years," she went on. "Fifty years this place was mine until I slipped on some ice last January and broke my hip. I landed in the hospital, and while I was down and out, the boys saw their chance. Maybe not Lyle so much, but Johnny and Paul . . ."

She shook her head. "Those rascals saw their chance. I told Ross to leave the house to me alone and not divide it up four ways between me and the boys, because I knew what they'd do with it eventually. Soon as Ross died they started talking about selling the place, saying I shouldn't be living here by myself. My falling on the ice seemed to prove their point, and from the hospital I was taken to —"

Her sentence hung unfinished as she pulled herself up from the chair. The newspaper dropped from her lap to the porch. Both she and Mom stared out at the street as a Pontiac station wagon — brown with a white roof, wings reaching back toward the taillights — coasted up to the front of the house and parked. A short stocky man in a raincoat and fedora stepped out of the car and made his way up the sidewalk. "I thought I'd find you here, Mother," he said, approaching the porch steps.

"What'd you expect, Johnny?" She drew

herself up straighter and lifted her chin. "This is my home. Where else should I be?"

"This isn't your home anymore," he said, coming right up onto the porch. He looked at Mom and took off his wet hat in a gesture of respect. "Beg your pardon, ma'am," he said. "I'm very sorry about this. I've come to take Mother back to the home."

"The home?" Mom asked.

"St. Claire's Home for the Aged."

"I'm sorry, I — We're new in town. I —"

"I don't belong in any nursing home," the old woman yelled, taking a step backward. "My hip has healed, and I'm as strong as I've ever been."

The man held out his hand. "Now, Mother —"

"You defied me, Johnny Monroe. My last wish was to die in this house —"

"Now, Mother, don't make trouble. We did what we thought was best —"

"And I aim to die in this house, whether you like it or not!"

"Oh, great," Wally said again with another glance at me. I shivered.

The man turned back to Mom. "I'm very sorry," he repeated. "I'll see to it this doesn't happen again. Come on, Mother. Let's go without making a scene."

"No one was making a scene until you

came along," the old woman said.

Mom stepped to the door and nodded toward me. "Roz, go get Valerie out of her crib. Take her to the kitchen and give her some cereal."

For the first time I realized Valerie was crying and had probably been crying for several minutes. But I didn't go to her. I couldn't take my eyes off the old woman and her son. One moment they were exchanging heated words and the next he had his arm around her shoulder and she was allowing him to lead her toward the porch steps.

Mom, to my surprise, unlaced her fingers and laid one hand gently on the old woman's arm. "Wait," she said.

The two strangers stopped and looked at Mom expectantly. "I —" Mom shook her head. She looked flustered. "What's your name?"

The old woman's eyes seemed to travel all over Mom's face, looking for a place to rest. Finally she said, "My name is Tillie Monroe." She said it with dignity, as though the name itself commanded respect.

Mom nodded slightly. "Well, Mrs. Monroe, I-I'm very sorry. Really I am."

For a moment no one spoke. The old woman's lips trembled, but she didn't have any words for Mom in response. Then Johnny Monroe lifted his hat once again, bid Mom a good day, and led Tillie Monroe down the steps.

Mom, Wally, and I watched as the two of them walked together in the drizzling rain toward the car.

Mom stepped into the house, shut the door, and locked it. She looked at Wally and then at me. For some reason Valerie had stopped crying, and the house was quiet. "Well," Mom said, "it's a shame, but I'm sure her children knew what they were doing when they put her in the home. I don't think this will happen again. Let's go eat breakfast. Roz, go get Val up and get her ready to eat."

Wally looked out the window. "You still want the paper, Mom?" From where we stood, we could see that a gust of wind had picked it up and scattered it in wet clumps across the yard.

"I guess we can do without the paper today," she said. "Never much good news anyway, is there?" She offered Wally a tiny smile and moved down the hall to the kitchen.

I lingered a moment and watched as the station wagon pulled away from the curb. The strange woman's profile was framed in

16

the passenger window, and for a moment I almost felt sorry for the old lady who was being hauled back to the home against her will. It seemed a sad way to finish up a life.

"Roz," Mom called from the kitchen, "I'm waiting on you to get Valerie. Breakfast is ready."

"Can you believe our luck?" Wally said as he ambled down the hallway, his fists thrust deep in the pockets of his shorts. "We move into the one house in town where some crazy old lady wants to come and die."

"Never mind, Wally," Mom said. "She's gone now, and I'm sure the nursing home will take extra precautions so she doesn't get out again."

Extra precautions or no, I had a feeling we hadn't seen the last of Tillie Monroe.

CHAPTER 2

The next morning the sun shone brightly, and Mom was in a rare good mood, humming as she stirred the oatmeal. I put Valerie in her high chair and was tying a bib around her neck while Wally, still in his pajamas, stumbled to the refrigerator and took a long swig of milk straight from the bottle.

"I've asked you not to do that, Wally," Mom said. "Now, go put some clothes on and run outside and get the paper."

Without a word my brother went back upstairs and came down wearing shorts and a T-shirt. "Do you think she's out there?" he called from the hall.

"Let's hope not," Mom said.

But a moment later Wally's voice reached us from the front door. "Mom, you're not going to believe it."

He didn't have to tell us; we knew from the tone of his voice. Mom moved down the hall, looked out at the porch, and sighed. Putting a hand on her hip, she opened the door and said to Tillie Monroe, "Well, as long as you're here, you might as well come in and have a cup of coffee."

Tillie stood up and nodded. "Now you're talking."

She didn't need to be shown the way to the kitchen; she strode right to it, her great legs scissoring down the uncarpeted hall, Mom and Wally following behind. I saw her coming like a tank rolling into a surrendered city, and I put one hand on Valerie's shoulder protectively. With her big black shoes pounding against the kitchen's linoleum floor, she marched to the table, pulled out a chair, and sat her ample self down with a grunt.

She had the morning paper in one hand, which she dropped on the table, front page up. "Westmoreland is asking for a hundred thousand more troops," she exclaimed. "Can you believe it? He says we're winning the war in Vietnam, as though any sane person is going to believe that."

I stared at her wide-eyed, uncertain who she was talking to but fairly certain it wasn't me. In fact, she didn't seem to notice I was there. Instead, she locked on to Wally with a grave stare. "How old are you, boy?" she asked.

Wally hesitated, and his eyes narrowed. Finally he muttered, "Seventeen."

"There's still time, then. You got any relatives in Canada?"

"Not that I know of."

"Shame," Tillie said, clicking her tongue. "They'll call you up and ship you out —"

"I'll enlist before they ever call me up," Wally interrupted. "I can't wait to go."

"Merciful heavens!" Tillie Monroe cried, slapping the newspaper with an open hand. "Are you out of your young mind? We had no business getting involved in this pathetic excuse for a war in the first place."

Across the kitchen, Mom looked stricken. She had poured two cups of coffee from the percolator and was carrying them on saucers to the table. She placed one cup in front of our guest.

"Let's not talk about the war right now," she said as she sat. "Do you take sugar and cream, Mrs. Monroe?"

Tillie Monroe nodded and accepted the sugar bowl and creamer that Mom slid toward her. "Thank you kindly, Mrs. . . ." She looked at Mom and cocked her head. "I don't guess we've properly introduced ourselves. You know my name, but you haven't told me yours."

Mom took a sip of coffee and settled the

cup back in the saucer. I could tell from the look on her face she was sorry she'd invited the woman in. She watched as Tillie Monroe added three spoonfuls of sugar to her coffee and enough cream to fill her cup right up to the lip and then some. When she stirred the coffee, it splashed over into the saucer.

Mom shook her head, sighed quietly, then said, "I'm Janis Anthony, and these are my children —"

"The boy's named Wally, right?" Tillie Monroe interrupted, still making waves in the coffee cup.

"Why, yes —"

"I heard you call him by that name yesterday." She seemed then to finally realize I was in the room. By then I had dished up a bowl of oatmeal for Valerie and another one for myself. I'd taken the seat at the table on the other side of her, opposite Mom. Wally was eating his cereal standing up, leaning against the counter. In my peripheral vision I saw Tillie's round face turn to me, and I suddenly felt myself caught in the crosshairs of some great machine gun. "And what's your name, little girl?" she asked.

The spoon in my hand came to a dead stop two inches from my open mouth. A distinct dislike for this intruder snaked its way up from the soles of my feet and into every nook and cranny of my body. I resented being called a little girl. Valerie at two was a little girl. I was eleven. Already I was shedding my little girl appearance and was proud of that fact. Every night and every morning I brushed my long wheat-colored hair until it shone, and whenever Mom was out of the house, I snuck into her bathroom to experiment with her makeup. Back in Minnesota Eddie Arrington had told me I was pretty, and I'd dared to dream that maybe someday he and I would end up dating, but our move to Mills River had put a swift end to any thoughts of Eddie.

As my oatmeal-laden spoon descended in retreat toward the bowl and my eyes rolled left toward Tillie, the old woman was already attacking me with a barrage of questions. "Well?" she asked. "What's the matter? Cat got your tongue?"

"Tell her your name, honey," Mom urged impatiently.

"My name," I said slowly, "is Roz."

"Ross?" she sputtered. "That was my husband's name. Ross Monroe. What kind of name is that for a little girl?"

Wally choked on some oatmeal, trying not to laugh, and that made me even angrier. Speaking even more slowly, as though to someone stupid, I said, "It's not Ross. It's

Rozzzz." I drew out the *z* for so long I sounded like a bumblebee in flight. When I stopped buzzing, I added, "With a *z*. It's short for Rosalind."

She looked at me a moment, her blue eyes staring out from behind those gray horn-rimmed glasses. She seemed to be deep in thought. Then she asked, "You spell Rosalind with a *z*?"

"No." I shook my head. "With an *s*."

"Then why do you spell Roz with a *z*?"

An unmistakable sensation of heat moved up my neck and fanned out across my cheeks. In my mind I was picturing Tillie Monroe with oatmeal splashed across her floral print dress, and Mom must have somehow seen the image projected on my face, because she stood abruptly and said, "Can I pour you some more coffee, Mrs. Monroe?"

Mom's question managed to pull the old woman's attention away from me and on to more pressing issues. "Yes, please," she said, lifting her cup to Mom. "And a bowl of oatmeal too, if you don't mind. Heavy on the brown sugar, with a dab of butter and cream."

Mom, with a barely concealed lift of her brows, moved away from the table to fill Tillie's order. Tillie sat back in her chair

23

and let off a sigh of satisfaction. She opened the napkin at her place and laid it across her lap, then looked around the room and asked, "So where's the mister?"

Mom lurched stiffly at the question, as though she'd been slapped across the shoulder blades with a broom handle. Before she could answer, Wally spoke up. "There is no mister. Not that it's any of your business."

"Now, Wally —" Mom started.

Tillie interrupted with a wave of her hand. "Say no more," she said. "The boy's right. Whatever happened between you and the former man of the house is not my business."

The room became quiet. Valerie had finished her oatmeal and was getting fidgety, so I took her out of the high chair and settled her in my lap. She leaned her head against my shoulder and stuck her thumb into her mouth. We were trying to break her of the habit, but I figured if it kept her quiet, she could go ahead and suck her thumb for now.

Mom came back to the table with the bowl of oatmeal and the second cup of coffee. Tillie nodded. She looked around the room again, taking in each of us one at a time. "Well, if anyone has to live in my house, it might as well be nice folks like you."

Wally crossed his arms. "It's not your house anymore."

"Wally —"

"Well, it isn't, Mom. She can't come barging in here like she owns the place, ordering you around and —"

"Wally, please —"

Tillie lifted a hand again, the conversational traffic cop. "Young man, I know how you feel —"

"No you don't —"

"You think I'm some demented old lady who can't accept the fact that her home has been sold."

"Well, yeah —"

"Sold right out from under her by her own sons —"

"Now, Mrs. Monroe," Mom broke in, "we had no idea. I mean, the house was vacant. It was on the market."

"Of course it was. But against my wishes. I wanted to die in this house, and obviously, I'm not dead yet."

"Nevertheless, Mrs. Monroe, the house *has* been sold. To me. I am the legal owner now."

"But, you see, there's only this one more thing I have to do. Only one. And it won't be long now. I can promise you that."

Tillie Monroe and Mom stared at each other for what seemed a long time. Tillie's gaze was one of determined pleading; Mom's, complete bewilderment. Finally Mom asked, "How can you say such a thing?"

"I have one foot over there already, and this is my jumping-off spot. I want to go straight from here to heaven."

Mom opened her mouth to speak, but before she could say anything, the doorbell rang.

"That would be Johnny," Tillie announced. She turned slightly in her chair and hollered over her shoulder, "Come on in, Johnny. We're having breakfast. You might as well join us for a cup of coffee."

The same exasperated little man who came for his mother the day before now let himself into the house and hurried down the hall. Amid a hail of oaths, he entered the kitchen, begged Mom's pardon for the intrusion and the swearing, and proceeded to berate his mother for once again escaping the confines of St. Claire's Home for the Aged. For the first time I understood the saying "spitting mad," as I watched tiny drops of spittle fly from his mouth and rain down like missiles over Tillie's head.

"Now, Johnny, calm yourself," Tillie demanded. "You're ruining my breakfast."

Mom stood. "Can I get you a cup of coffee, Mr. Monroe?"

Flustered, Mr. Monroe shook his head. "I'm already late for work. Mother, come on. We're going *now*."

Tillie's eyebrows hung low over her eyes. "But I haven't finished my oatmeal, and I'm hungry."

"Why don't you let her finish," Mom suggested, "while I pour you a cup of coffee?"

The man loosened his tie and took a deep breath. He looked at his mother and back at Mom. "Oh, all right." Holding out a hand, he added, "I'm John Monroe, by the way. I'm very glad to meet you."

Mom shook his hand. "Janis Anthony. Please, have a seat."

"Thank you," he said, taking the seat Mom had just vacated. "I'm really very sorry about all this. Very sorry."

"Can it, Johnny," Tillie muttered as she shoveled oatmeal into her mouth. Temporarily depositing the cereal into one cheek, she said, "There's nothing to be sorry about. I'm just taking care of business. I'm sure Mrs. Anthony can understand that."

"Well, I —" Mom started, but John Monroe interrupted.

"Mother, you can finish your oatmeal, but this is the last time you're setting foot in this house."

"Not if I have anything to say about it."

"But that's just it, Mother. You don't have anything to say about it."

"And that's what's always been the matter with you, Johnny. You're not like your father at all. You've always had to have the last word."

"Now, you know I only want what's best for you."

"Hogwash, Johnny. You wanted to get your share of the money out of this house, and you know it."

"Mother, I —"

"Cream and sugar, Mr. Monroe?"

"Yes, thank you, Mrs. Anthony."

"All I ever wanted was just to be allowed to finish up here." Tillie Monroe had both her hands clenched into fists on the table-top. The one hand clutched her spoon like a flag on a rampart. "This is where my heart is, Johnny. And there's so little time left. It's really not too much to ask, is it?"

I was surprised to see tears in her eyes. Mom turned toward the sink, and Wally looked down at his feet. A sense of awkward-ness hung in the air, as though a scene were being played out that we weren't supposed to be watching. To my chagrin Valerie chose that moment to pull her thumb out of her mouth and laugh.

Tillie looked at her and smiled. She laid a solid old hand on Valerie's head and stroked her hair. "That's right, honey," she said. "No use crying when you can just as well laugh."

With that, she finished the last few bites of her oatmeal and left the house without another word.

CHAPTER 3

Grandpa Lehman and his wife, Marie, lived four blocks away in an old Victorian house with a mansard roof and flower boxes beneath the first-floor windows. It was not the house he'd shared with his first wife, Luella, my grandmother. Grams died when I was six, and not long after that Gramps was offered a job in Chicago, which took him away from our native Minnesota. He wanted to go. With Luella gone, he said he needed the chance to make a fresh start. He decided Chicago was too corrupt to live in, though, so he settled in Mills River, a small town on the train line, about a half hour outside of the city in DuPage County. Though alone, he bought a house in Mills River big enough to hold three generations; he was somewhat claustrophobic and always liked to have a lot of room to live in.

He wasn't alone for long, though. After less than a year in Mills River, he met Marie and married again. She moved into the house and brought along her maid, her cook, and her part-time gardener, which meant that Gramps never again had to wander around that big old house by himself. Mom said that's how it was with men; they didn't like to be alone. As for women, she added, they often prayed to be alone, but finding solitude was sometimes a whole lot harder than finding a mate.

Grandpa was a chemical engineer, though I've never been sure what he actually did for a living. When I was a child, I thought he painted shoes. That idea was born on a winter day in Minnesota when Gramps and I were snuggled together on a couch in his home, studying the illustrated cover of a magazine. The picture was a cartoonish depiction of a huge machine with robotic arms and all sorts of cogs and wheels and rubber belts. As complicated as it was in its mechanism, it apparently had only one purpose — to paint shoes. I stared at the ladies' high-heeled pump, newly splashed with red, rolling off the final assembly belt, and pointing to it, I said to Gramps, "Is that what you do at work?"

Gramps smiled and had a funny little twinkle in his eye when he said, "Well, yes, something like that."

Of course he knew a five-year-old wouldn't understand his job as a chemical engineer, so he gave the easy answer. But even years later I still imagined the morning train carrying Gramps into Chicago, where he worked with the big machine that painted shoes.

Marie owned a women's clothing store on Grand Avenue, the main shopping street that cut through the center of Mills River. She'd grown up in a working-class family and, with no chance for college, had started out as a buyer at the store straight out of high school. But Marie O'Connell was a hard worker and a shrewd businesswoman, and on top of that she had a gift for naming winning horses, placing her bets with her uncle, the bookie, in Chicago. Mom told me in confidence that it wasn't the best way to make your fortune, but Marie was lucky and seemed to have done very well. At any rate, she'd eventually managed to buy out the original owners of the store, which officially became Marie's Apparel in 1949.

When Mom was making final plans to move away from Minnesota, Marie offered her a position at the store, replacing one of the clerks who left to get married. Mom, she said, would work the counter in Accessories, where she'd oversee the selling of hats, gloves, ladies' handkerchiefs, and handbags.

Mom was less than enthusiastic at the thought of working retail, but she was willing, since she couldn't expect Gramps to support us once we were settled in Mills River. If she had to work somewhere, it might as well be with Marie.

That first Saturday afternoon after we'd settled into our new house, Mom and I and Valerie walked over to Grandpa's so Mom could talk with Marie about getting started at the store. Gramps had given Mom a car, a ten-year-old Chevy with a hundred thousand miles on it, but Mom said every penny counted now, and we would walk to as many places as we could to save on gas. She pulled Valerie in our red Radio Flyer wagon, something that Gramps had thought to give us when he furnished our house before we came down. We had escaped Minnesota with little more than the clothes on our backs, but at least we knew Gramps had made a home for us on the other end.

We were hot and sticky when we reached Grandpa's house on Savoy Street, and I was glad to step inside the air-conditioned rooms. Gramps swept me up in his arms, lifting my feet right off the floor, and locked me in a hug that nearly knocked the wind out of me.

"How's my girl?" he said when he set me back down.

"I'm good, Gramps!" I replied happily.

He kissed Mom's cheek and picked Valerie up and blew a raspberry on her neck to make her giggle. Gramps was a fun-loving guy, a practical jokester, a storyteller, a man who loved to laugh and who could outlaugh anyone hands down, even when he was amused by his own jokes. Mom always said he missed his calling, that he should have been a stand-up comedian, but Gramps only laughed at that, saying show business was no business for anyone with more than a lick of sense and seven mouths to feed.

Gramps no longer had seven mouths to feed; all his children were grown and scattered across the country. Except, that is, for his daughter Janis, whom he had lately rescued and reeled back into the fold — or at least close to it. Once Gramps had learned that Mom wanted to leave Daddy, he and Mom hatched a plan, and here we were, only four blocks away in a house that Gramps had helped Mom buy.

I'm not so sure Marie was as happy to have us around as Gramps was. She got along with Mom all right, but she mostly ignored us kids, as though we were as interesting as toadstools that sprang up in her path overnight. She had no children of her own and didn't seem to like kids and in fact had never been married before Gramps. She was nearly twenty years his junior but was still, as far as I could see, pretty far gone into spinsterhood when she and Gramps exchanged vows. I wasn't sure why Gramps had married her, or she him, for that matter. They seemed mismatched somehow. Certainly Marie wasn't like my grandmother, who was warm and loving and always doting on us grandkids as though we were the greatest thing in the world.

But I had already learned to stop wondering why anyone married anyone else. Grown-ups made a lot of decisions I didn't understand, and I half believed that most people were rendered senseless by the age of twenty-one.

"Where's Wally?" Marie asked as she came down the hall to greet us. She gave Mom a stiff hug, didn't bother to look down at Valerie and me.

"He's out looking for part-time work," Mom explained.

"That's my boy," Gramps said. "A true Lehman, willing to work hard."

"But he's not a Lehman," I protested. "He's a Sanderson." The moment I said it,

35

I was sorry. Mom always looked sad when anyone mentioned the name of her first husband, Wally's dad.

Gramps took my hand. "Let's move into the dining room, Rozzy. Betty's made one of her famous pound cakes. Extra good with a little chocolate sauce!"

Betty was their cook, and when she came into the dining room pushing a little cart with the pound cake on it, I understood for the first time that Gramps and Marie were more than comfortable. I think I understood too, to some extent, that that didn't necessarily mean Mom's life was going to be easy. She had to make her own way, just as Gramps and Marie had done. While they could have easily invited us to live in this huge house with them, that had never been part of the plan. Mom was to have her own house, her own job, her own life apart from theirs.

The grown-ups drank coffee that Betty poured from a silver coffeepot, the long black stream flowing from the narrow spout into dainty china cups. Valerie and I drank tall cold glasses of milk to wash down the pound cake drizzled with chocolate sauce. Valerie sat in the chair next to me, on top of a pillow on top of a phone book because the house wasn't equipped for children.

"Well, Janis," Marie said, "it's been almost a month since Tricia left to get married, so we'll be glad to finally have someone permanent in Accessories again." She stirred her coffee slowly, having added cream and two lumps of sugar that she'd dropped into the cup with silver tongs. She lifted her eyes to Mom momentarily and offered a brief smile.

Mom settled her cup in the saucer and dabbed at her mouth with a linen napkin. "Thank you again for saving the position for me, Marie," Mom said. "I really appreciate all the help the two of you have given me."

Gramps reached out and patted Mom's hand. Marie said, "Of course, dear. Anything for family, right?"

"Everything's going to be just fine," Gramps said reassuringly. He nodded and popped a generous piece of pound cake into his mouth.

"Now, you say you haven't worked retail before?" Marie asked.

Mom shook her head. "I was in secretarial work — years ago, before I was married. But I'm sure it won't be a problem. . . . I'll catch on quickly."

"I'm sure, dear." Marie lifted a hand to her hair and patted an imaginary loose strand. Every inch of her enormous beehive

was in perfect alignment. Her hair fasci-
nated me. Now and in the years to come, I
was to spend hours in her presence studying the sculpture created out of her tresses;
one, for something to do when I was with
her, and two, because I couldn't imagine
the amount of time it took to cut, comb,
curl, tease, and spray it all into place. To
me, it was a work of art. But that was Marie
— perfect hair, perfect makeup, perfect
nails, perfect clothes. She really was quite
beautiful, and maybe that was why Gramps
married her.

"You do know," she continued with a
glance at Mom, "you'll be working five days
a week, including every other Saturday."

"Yes, you mentioned that," Mom said.

"So you've made arrangements for . . ."
She nodded toward me and Valerie, as
though she didn't care to say our names.

"Not yet, no."

"But of course you can't bring them to
the store."

"No, of course not. Until school starts,
Wally can look after the girls while I'm at
work."

"And after school starts? What will you do
about Valerie then?"

"Well . . ." Mom looked at Gramps and
back at Marie. "I don't know yet. There's

been so much to think about."

"You'll have to hire a sitter of some sort."

"Yes." Mom didn't look up from her half-eaten piece of cake.

"I'm sure there must be plenty of women out there willing to watch one more child, along with their own."

Mom nodded. "Yes, I'm sure. I'll find someone."

I don't remember how long we stayed at Grandpa's house that afternoon. It seemed like an impossibly long time. Eventually Valerie and I left the dining room and tried to entertain ourselves by searching for four-leaf clovers in the backyard and playing catch with a tennis ball we found in the garden.

At long last Mom called us inside and said we were going home. Valerie climbed into the wagon, curled up, and closed her eyes. Mom looked straight ahead and didn't speak while we walked. I could tell by the way she kept lifting a hand to her face that she was crying. She cried a lot in those days, always silently. She tried not to let any of us know.

"I can pull the wagon if you want, Mom," I offered.

"Thanks, honey," she said, "but I'm all right. I'm trying to decide what I should make for supper. I forgot to take the chicken out of the freezer."

"We can just have a bowl of cereal or something. I'm really not hungry," I lied.

"Don't be silly, Roz," she said. "A bowl of cereal is hardly enough for supper."

The hand went up to her face again and touched her cheek. She wiped her fingers on her skirt quickly, as though she were smoothing a wrinkle or brushing away a bug. I wondered how many tears had been caught in the fabric of her clothes over the years.

"Mom," I said, "you know, I can take care of Valerie. I mean, while you're at work. I don't have to go to school. It's more important that I help you with Val."

Mom laughed lightly at that. "Nice try, Roz, but you're going to school. We'll both be in trouble with the law if you don't."

"But, Mom —"

"Don't worry. I'll find someone to take care of her."

"But who, Mom? We don't know anyone around here yet."

"Maybe I'll put an ad in the paper. I don't know." She lifted her shoulders in a shrug. "I've got three weeks to worry about that. Right now I've got other things to think about."

Yeah, and I knew what she was thinking. Or at least I imagined I did. If she were still married to Dr. Frank Sanderson, everything would be different. Everything would be good. Valerie and I wouldn't be here, because she would never have married Alan Anthony, but that would be all right. She and Frank Sanderson and Wally would be together as a family, and they would be happy.

I thought about that a lot. And I figured if I thought about it, Mom probably did too. Maybe she even thought about it more than I did.

We turned down McDowell Street, and I saw our house, the two-story white clapboard with the black shutters sitting squarely in the middle of the block. It was already becoming familiar, and I was thinking of it as home. With four large rooms downstairs and four bedrooms upstairs, we had far more space than we'd had in our track house in the suburbs of Minneapolis. I forgot about Frank Sanderson as I found myself enjoying the walk to our new home.

When we stepped up to the porch, Wally met us at the door looking sheepish. He pursed his lips and nodded toward the kitchen, from which the unmistakable aroma of fried chicken reached us. Stuffing

41

his hands deep into the pockets of his shorts, he explained, "She showed up again, so I let her in."

We knew who he was talking about, though we hadn't seen her in five days and hadn't expected to see her again.

Mom, carrying Valerie, frowned and blinked a couple of times before heading down the hall. I followed close behind, wanting to see what was about to happen.

Tillie, wearing Mom's apron, was at the stove pounding away at a large pot of potatoes with the wooden-handled masher. On another burner a skillet sizzled with the browned and crispy pieces of chicken that Mom had forgotten to thaw. Tillie must have been there for a while.

Her face was wet with perspiration, and her gray bun was frayed, wispy strands of hair flying every which way each time she hammered the potatoes. When she finally noticed we were there, she smiled at us, and her blue eyes sparkled behind her glasses. She stopped pounding, pushed a strand of matted hair off her forehead with the back of her hand, and said, "There you are. Come on in and wash your hands. Supper's almost ready."

I looked at Mom and she looked at me,

and that was how Tillie Monroe came to live with us that summer of 1967.

CHAPTER 4

Mills River, Illinois, was a small town stuck in time. The streets and cross streets of well-kept houses and downtown storefronts refused to budge beyond 1950. While the rest of the country had rolled headlong into the turmoil of the sixties — fiery race riots, violent war protests, the nightmare of psychedelic drug use — Mills River remained a stronghold of postwar civility and quiet prosperity.

Somehow Gramps had landed in just the right place after Grandma died, and eventually Mom followed. Gramps had needed a new life of sorts; Mom needed simply to be free to live. A life of constant fear, she said, was as close as you could get to being dead while still breathing. She was tired of the walking-dead kind of existence.

At eleven years of age I didn't quite understand. Oh yes, Daddy had his faults. That much I knew. Sometimes he drank too much, and the alcohol seemed to ignite some deep well of anger inside him. He could be violent; oh yes, I knew that too. I'd seen it all — seen the fists, heard the curses, saw the aftermath of his fury in the bruises on Mom's face. And whenever that happened, I was afraid. But I tried to shut it all out as simply as I shut my eyes, pretending that if I couldn't see it, it wasn't there. Because Daddy had a good side too, and there were times when he was all smiles and fun and laughter and even love. He said he loved us, and I believed him.

I was thinking about Daddy that summer morning when Tillie and I were walking to Jewel Food Store, with Tillie pulling Valerie behind us in the wagon. Not yet used to the stranger beside me, I was startled when she asked, "Do you miss him?"

I looked up at her sharply. "Who?"

"Your father," she said. "Weren't you thinking about your father?"

"How did you know?"

She lifted her broad shoulders in a shrug. "I just figured."

I looked straight ahead again, down the treelined street that led into the center of town. I didn't know how to answer. Finally I simply said no. Which was a lie, because I did miss him; or rather, I missed the good part of him.

Tillie shook her head. "Pity, three children growing up without their father."

I felt my fingers curl into fists. "You don't know anything about it."

"No," she agreed. "I don't. Still, it's a pity."

I didn't want to talk about my father, not with her. I wasn't sure I wanted to think about him or even *should* be thinking about him, since Mom had said we were leaving the past behind and making a fresh start.

In truth, though, I was haunted by Daddy's tears on the day we left Minnesota. Mom didn't say a word while she carried our few suitcases to the car, Daddy dancing around her like a man on fire.

"At least," Daddy said, his hands outstretched, "at least tell me where you're taking my kids."

He looked at me then, his eyes wild, sweat pouring down his face. Our eyes locked, and I couldn't stop my own tears. I wanted to cry out, *Daddy! Tell Mom you'll change. Just promise you'll stop drinking, and maybe Mom will stay!*

But I didn't say anything. It wouldn't do any good. Mom had made up her mind, and we were going.

We all piled into the car. Mom buckled

Valerie into the front seat beside her and turned the key in the ignition. Daddy banged on the roof of the car with one fist and then, as though surrendered, he stumbled blindly up the walkway to the porch and dropped down to the steps. He buried his face in his hands, and his shoulders heaved as he wept.

"Look at him now, the old fool," Wally muttered. "He's finally getting what he deserves."

At least we should have left when Daddy wasn't home, I thought. If we had to leave, we should have left without this wrenching away, without this scene of separation that left Daddy broken and crying on the steps.

Mom must have been worried that Daddy would try to keep us from going, because she'd asked Uncle Joe to be there when we left. Uncle Joe was Daddy's brother, and he was the only one on Daddy's side of the family who understood why Mom was leaving. Just as Mom started the car, Uncle Joe leaned in the open window and wished her luck. "My only regret," he said, "is that I didn't help you do this a long time ago."

"Well, Joe," Mom said, "I appreciate what you've done for me over the years."

"It was never enough."

"It was more than most."

Uncle Joe looked up at Daddy, his face a billboard of contempt. "I'm finished too," he said. "I'm washing my hands of him. If I never hear from Alan again, it'll be too soon."

He bent down and kissed Mom on the cheek, said good-bye to us kids, and stepped away from the car. When Mom put the car in gear and pulled away from the curb, I saw her glance in the rearview mirror and smile, a small victorious smile. But even then I didn't understand.

Years would pass before I understood this to be Mom's first and final act of defiance in her marriage to Alan Anthony. She didn't want to slip away unseen, like a coward. She wanted Daddy to watch us go. And she wanted to watch him crumble. She knew that at nine o'clock in the morning he wouldn't yet be drunk, so he wouldn't have the fuel required to fire up his anger. Not his violent I-swear-I'm-going-to-kill-you anger, anyway. She knew he'd be little more than a pathetic spectacle on the morning she finally summoned the courage to leave and to take us with her. She didn't want to miss that, her moment of triumph after thirteen years of misery.

After that one glance in the mirror, Mom didn't look back again. But I did. This would be the last time I'd ever see my father, so I kept on watching until I couldn't see him anymore. The image of him weeping on the steps was branded on my brain, sizzling red hot and smoking until, at length, these few weeks later, it had begun to solidify into a scar.

Tillie and I finally reached Grand Avenue, the wagon bumping over the cracks of the sidewalk behind us. When we came to Marie's Apparel, I stopped and looked in the window, cupping my face with my hands. I hoped to catch a glimpse of Mom, who'd been working there almost a week now, selling handbags and handkerchiefs to the ladies of Mills River.

"Mommy?" Valerie asked.

"She's in there somewhere," I said, "but I can't see her."

Tillie went on pulling the wagon but called back over her shoulder, "Did you need to ask her something, Roz?"

"No. I just thought I'd wave if I saw her."

Tillie shook her head, clicked her tongue. "Pity, such a sweet young lady as your mother having to work. Women should be able to stay home and take care of their children."

I hurried to catch up with her. "You know, you don't have to pity us, Tillie."

"I know I don't," she said, "but I do."

"Well, how come?"

"Because you don't have a man to take care of you."

"We don't need a man to take care of us. Anyway, we have Wally. He's working."

"Wally's a boy."

"He's almost eighteen."

"He's still a boy. He has a long way to go before he's a man."

"Why do we need a man? Women can do anything men can do."

"You sound like you've been reading Betty Friedan."

"Who's that?" I asked.

"She's one of those women's libbers —" Tillie stopped herself and chuckled. "Never mind. Still, you know, this isn't how it was meant to be. Men leaving their families, women having to work while raising their children alone. Something crazy's happening to our country, and I don't like it."

"Daddy didn't leave us, you know. Mom left him."

Tillie seemed to think about that a moment. Then she said, "Well, either which way, I think it's a tragedy when men and women don't stay together. But then, I don't know what happened between your mother and father, and it's none of my business, is it?"

"No, it isn't."

"But someday you'll tell me about it. When you're ready."

"What makes you think I'll ever tell you about it?"

"Because that's what family does, confide in each other."

"We're not family."

"No, not yet."

"We'll never be related."

"It isn't blood that makes you family, Roz."

"Maybe not. But living in the same house doesn't make you family either."

Tillie shrugged and said, as though it were pertinent, "Well, someday your mother will marry someone else."

"What makes you say that?"

"Because she's young and pretty, and I can't imagine her living the rest of her life alone."

It had never occurred to me that Mom might remarry. I didn't like the thought. We already had one stranger living in our house; I didn't want another, especially a man.

At the intersection of Grand Avenue and Third Street we turned right on Third and walked one more block to Jewel Food Store. By the time we reached the front doors, I was tired and hot and ready for the cool of the air-conditioned aisles. We hadn't brought the car, not because Tillie didn't drive, because she did, but because she wanted to help Mom save on gas money. In fact, Mom had told her to take the car. "Someone your age shouldn't be walking in this heat," Mom said.

"I may be full of years," Tillie countered, "but that doesn't mean I've lost my gumption."

I wasn't full of years myself, but I found the heat exhausting. "Can we rest inside a minute, Tillie?" I asked.

"Plenty of time for that when we get home," she said.

She parked the wagon by the door and helped Valerie out.

"We can't just leave the wagon here, can we?" I moved to catch up with Tillie, who was already marching into the store, Valerie in tow.

"This is Mills River," she said. "No one's going to steal it." She grabbed a shopping cart and lifted Valerie into the child's seat in front. Before she had gone more than a few feet, she raised a hand toward one of the silver-haired cashiers. "Good morning, Hazel."

"Why, Tillie," the woman said, slapping

her thigh, "I'd heard you got out."

"Merciful heavens, honey, you make it sound like I've been in jail."

"Knowing you, Tillie, that's exactly what it was."

Tillie rubbed her fleshy chin. "You've got a point there, Hazel. Five months cooped up in that place, it's a wonder I didn't lose my mind. But I'm out now, and I'm back in my own home, where I intend to die when the time is right."

"Good for you. You know I've always admired your spunk."

"Yes, well, I'm just doing what I've got to do. By the way, I've got houseguests now, and here are two of them, Rosalind and Valerie." Tillie waved a hand, first toward me and then toward Valerie in the cart. "I'm taking care of them while their mother works, poor thing."

Hazel beamed at me. "Well now, how do you do?"

I raised my hand in a small gesture of greeting even as my eyes became angry slits. I wanted to explain that Tillie was *our* houseguest and not the other way around, and that my mother was not a poor thing for having to work, which I figured Hazel would understand, since she herself was there behind the cash register, but I was a child and Hazel was an adult, so I kept quiet.

"Listen, Tillie, when you check out, come on through my line. I've got some extra coupons you can use," Hazel said.

"Appreciate it, honey. We're just picking up a few things, so I'll be back around in a minute."

From there, we headed toward the meat department at the back of the store. "Fred!" Tillie hollered.

A thick-waisted man in a bloody apron paused with his knife poised over a slab of beef. "Ah, Mrs. Monroe! You're back with us!" When he smiled, his great jowls quivered and his mustache curled over his front teeth. "I knew that place couldn't hold you. I told everyone, I said, 'That Tillie Monroe, she doesn't belong in the old folks home.' " He waved his butcher knife in the air for emphasis.

"You were right, Fred. I was a fish out of water there. I couldn't breathe."

Fred nodded knowingly. "Some people, okay, they go to the old folks home and they make their peace with it, and maybe they're even happy there, but not you. No sir. Not Tillie Monroe. I told everyone, I said, 'That Mrs. Monroe, she'll never be old. Never.' "

"I'm glad you see it that way, Fred. If only

54

my sons did."

"That Johnny!" The butcher knife sliced the air in one quick motion. "I said to him, 'Johnny, how could you do that to your own mother?' "

"Good question, Fred."

"He said he had only your best interest at heart."

"So he pulled that one on you too, huh?"

Fred slammed the butcher knife into the beef and came to meet us at the counter. He was shaking his head. "I don't know, Mrs. Monroe, but if I had a nice lady like you for a mother, I sure wouldn't stick her in some old folks home."

"Thank you, Fred. If Johnny tries to do it again, I'll disown him and adopt you."

Fred smiled, looking genuinely pleased. "And how's the hip, Mrs. Monroe?"

"Good as new," she said. "It only aches when it's going to rain. I've got a built-in barometer now, which comes in rather handy."

The butcher responded with a belly laugh. "You were always one to find the silver lining! If only we were all so inclined. Most of my customers, they come in here moaning and complaining, not a good word about anything. Well, you know how it is, Mrs. Monroe."

"That I do. I never put much stock in complaining." She nodded toward the industrial-sized butcher block. "I see you've hired an apprentice."

Fred looked over his shoulder, then back at Tillie. "He's a good boy, a good hard worker."

"I'm glad to hear that, Fred. These two girls here are his sisters."

I heard Tillie introduce me, but I was busy staring at Wally. He wore a large bibbed apron that was colored with blood, streaks of dark red splattered across a white canvas. I wrinkled my nose at the sight of it. Wally saw me and held up both hands so I could see his palms; they glistened with the same sticky redness. He smiled. I frowned.

"Wally," Tillie hollered, "come on over here and wrap up five of your best pork chops for me. We'll have those for supper tonight."

Wally sauntered over, wiping his hands on the apron. He didn't speak, but he picked out five pork chops from the refrigerated display case and wrapped them in sheets of white paper. He handed them to Fred, who handed them to Tillie.

As she took the chops, Tillie said, "You know, Wally, you could at least say hello to

56

us, instead of pretending you don't know us."

Wally shrugged as he moved back to the butcher block. I knew how he felt about Tillie.

Fred glanced at Wally, then turned back to Tillie with that look that said, *Kids. What can you do with them?* "So listen, while I got him here under my thumb, we'll work on the manners, all right? He's a good kid, just a little rough around the edges. Now, tell you what, Mrs. Monroe, you accept the chops as a gift, a housewarming gift from everyone at Jewel to you."

"Well, thank you, Fred. That's very kind of you."

"Now that you're back in your house, you need to celebrate, right?"

"Come to think of it, I believe you're right. If I were a drinking gal, I'd buy some champagne."

"If you buy some champagne, I can promise you, plenty of people will come and celebrate with you."

Tillie and the butcher laughed loudly, but I was ready to leave. I didn't like seeing Wally covered in blood. Something about it gave me a feeling of dread.

Valerie must have sensed the same thing, because she started to fuss, which thankfully pulled Tillie's attention away from Fred. We hurried through the rest of our shopping, checked out with Hazel, who plied Tillie with coupons, then loaded the wagon back up with Valerie and our sack of groceries, and headed out.

We were on Grand Avenue not far from Marie's Apparel when I was startled by a familiar figure in the distance. He was a tall man, broad-shouldered, wearing gray slacks, a blue cotton shirt, and a fishing hat. He was walking away from us, so I couldn't see his face, but it was the hat that caught my eye.

I stopped abruptly, my sneakers anchored to the sidewalk by my own uncertainty.

Tillie took a few more steps before she realized I wasn't keeping up. She stopped and looked back at me. "What's the matter, Roz?"

I didn't answer. The man had turned a corner and disappeared. Or, I told myself, maybe I was just seeing things and he hadn't really been there at all. I was hot and tired and hungry, and Mom said sometimes when you're not feeling quite right, your mind can play tricks on you. Even if the man was real, lots of men wore fishing hats, didn't they? The tan hemp kind with the one brown strip around the base and all the artificial lures fastened to it like Christmas tree ornaments.

"What is it, Roz?" Tillie asked again.

I shook my head. "Nothing."

After all, Daddy was hundreds of miles away in Minnesota, wasn't he?

CHAPTER 5

The next morning I awoke with a sore throat and a fever. Mom stood over my bed, frowning as she shook the thermometer down.

"I haven't found a doctor for the children yet," she said to Tillie, who was plumping up my pillow with her beefy fists.

"She doesn't need a doctor," Tillie said. "I'll take care of her."

"Maybe I should stay home, though, and —"

"Nonsense." Tillie slid an arm under my shoulders, lifted me high enough to slip the pillow back under my head, and lowered me down again. "You go on in to work and don't worry for a minute. I know how to care for a sick child."

In spite of the fever, a small chill ran up my spine. Visions of castor oil and mustard packs flashed through my head.

Tillie tapped my shoulder with one finger.

"I never put much stock in castor oil," she said.

"How did you know?" I whispered.

"We'll start with a cayenne and vinegar gargle and go from there."

"But I hate vinegar!"

I was talking to her back. She was headed for the door, already on her way to mix up the vile concoction.

I grabbed Mom's hand. "Don't go to work, Mom. Please don't leave me alone with *her*." I nodded toward the door through which Tillie had just disappeared.

Mom smiled. "You'll be fine, honey. Anyway, if I don't work, I don't get paid, and we need the money."

"But, Mom! I don't want Tillie taking care of me. She's so . . . well, you know. She's strange."

Mom looked thoughtful for a moment. "I know she seems a little eccentric at times, but really, what would I do without her? I'm beginning to think of her as a godsend."

"I don't want to gargle any cayenne and vinegar. Mom, please stay home. She's going to kill me with her poisons."

Mom laughed. "Oh, Roz, don't worry. A little vinegar isn't going to hurt you. And it will probably help. On my way home from work I'll stop by the drugstore and pick up some throat lozenges."

I pulled my hand away from Mom's and slid down under the covers. "You don't love me, do you?" I moaned.

Mom leaned over and kissed my forehead. "I love you very much, Roz. That's why I'm working and trying to provide for you." She straightened up. "Now, it's getting late, and I've got to go. You behave for Tillie, all right?"

As she left the room, I muttered, "Yeah, well, Tillie better behave for *me*."

When Tillie returned a few minutes later, she first tied one of Mom's silk scarves around my neck. "To keep the draughts off," she said. Then she marched me into the bathroom and handed me the cup of hot water laced with vinegar and cayenne pepper.

"I'll throw up," I threatened.

"Nonsense," she said. "Now gargle."

I glared at her before resigning myself and giving in. Holding my nose, I took a mouthful and gargled loudly. After spitting it out in the sink, I looked at Tillie and grimaced.

"See," she said a bit smugly, "you're still alive and in one piece. So keep going."

When the gargling was done, she tucked me back in to bed and spent the rest of the morning hovering over me like a mother hen. She fed me bowls of hot chicken broth and cold strawberry Jell-O and vanilla ice cream. From time to time she laid her heavy hand across my brow or poked the thermometer under my tongue to see whether the fever had broken. In between waiting on me, she fed and bathed Valerie and entertained her by making rag dolls out of dish towels.

In the early afternoon she came back to my room and announced, "There's nothing like warm sunshine to burn the cold germs out of a person." She told me to grab my pillow and follow her out to the porch. I was to lie on the porch swing while she and Valerie sat together on the folding chair.

"At least let me get dressed," I muttered as I tumbled out of bed.

"Don't bother. No one will see you."

"But —"

"Come on, Roz, while the sun's at her peak. Don't dillydally."

I snatched my pillow and reluctantly followed Tillie downstairs, wishing Wally were home to throw himself between me and this tyrant. How could she make me sit on the front porch in my baby doll pajamas, a silk kerchief tied around my neck like I was some sort of vaudeville dancer? As we passed by the living room, I grabbed a blanket from the couch to use both as a cushion and a cover to hide under.

I spread the blanket over the slats of the porch swing and settled myself on it, my head on the pillow, my knees drawn up to my chest so I fit on the two-seater bench. The sun was hot, but I used a corner of the blanket to cover myself anyway, just in case. Tillie was right, though; the lilac bushes blocked my view of the street and hid me from any passersby on the sidewalk.

Tillie sat on the folding chair and pulled Valerie into her lap. Valerie looked small but content; she leaned easily into the cradle of Tillie's shoulder and drank grape Kool-Aid drowsily from a small plastic cup.

"You know," Tillie said wistfully, "I always wanted a girl, but the good Lord didn't see fit to bless me with one. He gave me three boys instead. But that's all right. I'm not complaining. Johnny, Paul, and Lyle — they're three fine boys."

"Not Johnny," I reminded her. "He's awful. He put you in the old folks home."

Tillie laughed quietly. "No, even Johnny is a good man in his own way. I do get frustrated with him, I admit, but no, I'm proud of and thankful for all my sons. These walls . . ." She nodded her head toward the house behind us. "These walls know. They saw it all. All the years I spent raising my boys — it's all in there."

I was just about to ask her what she meant when she raised a hand and waved toward the street. "Hello, Leonard! About time you showed up. Where have you been the last week or more?"

Footsteps hurried up the walkway, and I gasped when a man leapt up to the porch, his shiny black shoes landing hard on the wooden boards. He lifted his mailman's cap off his balding head and nodded. "Afternoon, Mrs. Monroe. I've been gone on a little vacation. Took the family to Niagara Falls and on up into Canada. Just got back yesterday."

"Well that explains the young fool who's been delivering our mail. He's been leaving half the neighbors' bills here, as if I'm expected to pay them."

Leonard blinked several times at that, his eyelashes fluttering like butterfly wings behind his glasses. "I'm sorry about that, Mrs. Monroe," he said. "That's Bill Kardashian. He's new to the post office, and they had him filling in for me while I was gone. I'm sorry for the mix-ups, but he's just now learning the ropes."

"Well then, that's all right. You can be sure those bills found their way to the right houses, though I think the post office owes me some wages for the work I've done."

Leonard's eyes stopped blinking as they grew impossibly wide, each pupil becoming a dark island in a white sea. He decided to change the subject. "Well, Mrs. Monroe," he said, clearing his throat with a quick cough. "What are you doing here at the old homestead? You back for a visit?"

"Visiting? No, Leonard. I live here, remember?"

"But I thought —"

"Doesn't matter what you thought. What matters is what *is*. This is my house, and I intend to die here."

Leonard's jaw dropped, and from where I lay on the porch swing I could see the fillings in his upper teeth. A long moment passed before he finally said, "Well, all right. Then I ought to be leaving your mail here, same as always."

"Yes, sir. That's right. Same as always."

He momentarily rummaged around in the mailbag slung over his right shoulder and came up with several envelopes. "These are all addressed to a Janis Anthony. I don't believe I have anything for you today, Mrs. Monroe."

"That's all right, Leonard. You tried your best."

"But now, what do I do with Mrs. Anthony's mail?"

"You can leave that here too."

"She lives here with you, then?"

"That's right. She lives here with me. These are her daughters, Rosalind and Valerie."

Leonard nodded in my direction. I peeked at him over the rim of the blanket. "How do you do?" he asked.

I didn't respond. All I could think about was my frilly pajamas and the silk scarf and how Tillie had said no one would see me and how, not ten minutes out on the porch, a strange man was staring at me and asking questions.

"Well, okay," our mailman said, giving up on me and looking back at Tillie. "So any mail that comes for you or Mrs. Anthony, I leave it all here?"

"That's right, Leonard. Except if anything comes from *Mister* Anthony, send it right back to where it came from. I don't believe Mrs. Anthony would want it."

Leonard took off his cap and scratched the center of his bald spot. "Well now, I'm not sure I can do that, Mrs. Monroe. Tampering with the mail's a federal offense, you know."

"And failing to protect a lady is a moral

offense, Leonard, so take your pick."

Settling his cap back on his head, Leonard tucked the envelopes into the metal mailbox that hung beside the door. He stole another glance at Tillie, then began to back down the porch steps. "I'll see what I can do. Now, I'd best get back to the route. Nothing stops the mail, you know."

"Indeed," Tillie said, but by the time she spoke, Leonard was already gone. "He always was a coward, that one," she added. "Poor Leonard. It's pitiful."

"You think everything's pitiful, Tillie."

"No I don't," she said. "Not everything. Some things are downright beautiful."

"Yeah? Like what?"

"Well, like —"

"Yoo-hoo, Tillie!"

Now what? I thought.

"Yoo-hoo, yourself, Esther. Haven't seen you in a while."

"Well, I'll tell you what, Tillie. I've been out in Sausalito with Jenny for a week, taking care of my newborn twin granddaughters."

"Twin granddaughters, huh?"

"That's right. I'm a grandmother now, twice over!"

With that, the person the voice was attached to showed up on the porch. I recognized her as the next-door neighbor who had brought us a macaroni hot dish shortly after we moved in. She was short and plump with ruddy cheeks and a stiff graying haystack of hair at the top of her head.

"Good for you, Esther. Have these girls got any names?"

"Oh my, yes. Both of them named for me."

"Both of them?"

A nod of the head. "Iris Esther and Lily Esther."

"Well, of all things," Tillie said with a wave of her hand. "Sounds like Jenny's planted a garden instead of giving birth. Though I'm sure they're beautiful babies."

"Oh, they are. And I'm not just saying that because I'm their grandmother. Now, who's that on your lap? Isn't that Mrs. Anthony's little girl?"

"It sure is. She's Valerie and that one over there, she's Rosalind. You probably met them already, knowing you and your casseroles."

"Oh yes, in fact I *have* met them. I made my blue-ribbon recipe for them soon as they moved in — you know, the one that got me first place at the county fair —"

"Oh yes, that's a good one, Esther."

"And I brought it over to Mrs. Anthony warm from the oven. Fine woman, Mrs.

Anthony. I'm glad a nice family moved into your house."

"Me too, Esther. Roz, can you say hello to Mrs. Kinshaw?"

"Hello."

The woman nodded at me, then said to Tillie, "You back visiting? Or baby-sitting?"

"No, I'm back living here."

"You are?"

"Don't look so shocked, Esther. It's my house, isn't it?"

"Yes, but —"

"Ross and I built this place with our own hands."

"Of course I know that, but —"

"And I intend to die here."

"But —"

"Tillie," I interrupted.

"Yes, Roz?"

"I think you ought to take out an ad in the newspaper, tell the whole town at once. It would save you from having to repeat yourself."

"Now, there's a thought. I believe I'll look into that."

Esther Kinshaw stood there with her hands on her hips. "You mean you're back for good?"

"That's right." Tillie nodded.

"And the Anthonys . . . they're all living

here too?"

"Well sure. Why not? This house was built for a whole family."

"And Johnny let you move out of that nursing home?"

"Pshaw!" Tillie waved a hand. "He had no say. He can't keep an old woman from dying in her own home."

I moaned and said, "I'll call the newspaper for you, Tillie."

"Never mind that, Roz," Tillie said, "I'll do it myself. I've known the editor since the day he was born. Yup, little Winston Newberry, now the editor of the *Mills River Tribune*. Imagine. I used to change his diapers when his mother dropped him off at the church nursery. I'll never forget it — he had a birthmark on his backside the shape of the Eiffel Tower."

I pulled the blanket over my head, wishing I'd kept my mouth shut.

"You know," Mrs. Kinshaw said thoughtfully, "I heard it faded in later years."

"What's that, Esther?"

"The birthmark. Winston Newberry's birthmark. I heard it practically disappeared."

"Who told you that?"

Silence a moment, then, "I don't remember."

"Shame," Tillie said. "I thought it something of a mark of distinction. I used to show it off to all the workers in the nursery. It seemed like a sign he was destined for great things."

"Well, he did end up the editor of the *Mills River Tribune*. I guess that's something."

"Yes, I guess so." Tillie sighed. "But I wonder what he might have achieved had the birthmark not faded."

"Well, I — Oh look!" Mrs. Kinshaw said. "There's the Irelands. Aren't they adorable? Yoo-hoo, Rod and Marian!"

I sat up wondering what these adorable people looked like. I pictured leprechauns, the magical wee folk who sprang from Irish folklore. But the family I saw walking along in front of our house was a regular American family, a mother, a father, and a little red-haired girl about Valerie's age. The father was carrying the child on his shoulders, her little hands clasped firmly in his.

"Look who's back," Mrs. Kinshaw hollered. "Tillie has moved back in. We're all neighbors again!"

"Really?" the woman said. "But I thought —"

I moaned again, curled up into a ball on the swing, and pulled the blanket back over my head. I put my hands over my ears to block the chatter of voices, the questions, the exclamations, the laughter. I even started humming to myself. I was so tired of hearing Tillie say she'd come back to die in her own home and no one was going to stop her. If I heard her say that one more time, I was certain I'd kill her myself and let her be done with it.

After a few moments the porch quieted, and I peeked out from beneath the blanket. "Are they gone?" I asked.

"Lovely family, the Irelands."

I sat up and shrugged.

"That's exactly how it should be," Tillie went on.

"How what should be?"

"Families. Did you see the way Mr. Ireland loved on that little girl, how proud he was of her?"

"I was under the blanket, Tillie. I couldn't see anything."

"Yes, and that was really rather rude, Rosalind."

"Well, I never said I wanted to come out here. I don't feel good."

"Do you need another gargle?"

"No. I just need . . ."

"What, Roz?"

I thought of the little girl perched high on her father's shoulders and clenched my teeth. "You know, Tillie, I used to ride on my daddy's shoulders just like that."

"Did you now?"

"Yes, I did. And we used to go for walks, all up and down the streets of our neighborhood, sometimes all the way around Lake Calhoun and back home again. We'd take a bag of bread and feed the ducks and the fish and the geese."

"It sounds very nice."

"It *was* very nice. I don't care what you think. Daddy was a good man."

"I never said he wasn't."

"Yes you did. That's what you told the mailman."

"That's not what I told the mailman. I told him not to deliver any letters your father might send to your mother."

"That's the same thing."

"No it isn't."

I peered out over the lilac bush and toward the street. "Daddy was a hardworking man," I said.

"I don't doubt that." Tillie shifted her weight in the chair, settling a now slumbering Valerie in a more comfortable position on her lap.

"He worked construction, you know. He was a foreman. That's the boss."

"Uh-huh."

"Most days when he came home, he'd reach into his shirt pocket and pull out a Sugar Daddy for me, my favorite candy. He'd say, 'Here, Little Rose.' That's what he called me, his Little Rose. He'd say, 'Here, Little Rose, some sugar from your daddy, who loves you.' "

I pressed my lips together and looked at Tillie through narrowed eyes, daring her to deny my words, daring her to call me a liar. My daddy was every bit as good as Mr. Leprechaun from down the street, and I wouldn't have Tillie thinking otherwise. I wouldn't have her pitying me or my family. I watched as Tillie nodded slowly. She was stroking Valerie's cheek.

Finally she said, "It sounds like you have some good memories of your father."

"I do," I said. "I have plenty of good memories."

"Well then, you be sure to put those memories in a safe place and don't lose them. The time will come when you'll be glad you have something left of the man."

I didn't know what she meant and wasn't sure I wanted to know. All I wanted was to be as safe and as satisfied as the little redheaded girl appeared to be, up there on her daddy's shoulders.

"Lay yourself down now and take a nap,"

Tillie said quietly, "just like Valerie here. The sun and some sleep will do you a world of good. Uh-huh, nothing like sun and sleep to cure what ails you."

I was tired and did what I was told. As I settled my head on the pillow, I thought about Daddy. There were so many memories to pick through. I imagined myself a child gathering wild flowers in a field. The bad ones I plucked like weeds and tossed aside. The good ones I gathered together as though forming a bouquet, a keepsake of fragile images of the happy times with Daddy. I wanted to have at least that much of him. Once my bouquet was complete, I would tuck it away in a safe place, just as Tillie suggested, so that nothing and no one could take it away from me.

The warm sun was tempered by a soothing breeze, and soon I drifted off. I don't know how long I slept, and I don't think I dreamed. After a time I was awakened by Wally shaking my shoulder. "Roz, Tillie says you need to come in now."

I drew in a deep breath and stretched. "Your hand stinks," I said.

He lifted his fingers to his nose. "I washed," he said with a shrug. "Hard to get the smell of blood out."

76

"Blood? Yuck. I hate you working for the butcher."

"How come?"

"It's just . . . creepy."

Another shrug. "It's good practice."

"For what?"

"For 'Nam. For killing the Vietcong."

I sat up, shook my head. "I hope you're kidding, Wally. Or else you're turning really weird."

"You want us to win the war, don't you?"

I never even thought about the war. It had nothing at all to do with me, and it wasn't what I wanted to talk about. "Wally?"

"Yeah?"

"Do you think Daddy knows where we are?"

Wally sniffed in disgust. "Who cares about him?"

"But, I mean, do you think he can find us?"

"I don't know." Wally sat down on the swing beside me. "Probably. He's crazy but he's not stupid. I'm sure he'll figure out we went to live near Gramps."

"But do you think he'd ever come after us? You know, try to get us to go home?"

"Naw, I really don't think so. He's probably already found somebody else he can make miserable."

"But . . . what would you do if he did? I mean, what if he came around here and tried to talk Mom into going back to Minnesota?"

Wally looked out at the street, his head turning left and right like a beacon. And then he said easily, as though he were talking about swatting a fly, "If Alan Anthony ever came snooping around here looking for us, I'd kill him."

CHAPTER 6

"Wally is something of an angry young man, isn't he, dear?" Tillie asked.

Her words reached me from far away, and Mom's answer too seemed to float through the air a long time before finally coming to light in my mind. "He has good reason to be angry," Mom replied.

I'd been vaguely aware of their voices for some time, but I wasn't sure where they were, and as I struggled to rise up out of the depths of sleep, I wasn't even sure where *I* was. I thought at first I was still on the porch with Tillie, but when I opened my eyes I saw I wasn't on the porch at all but on the couch in the living room.

Oh yeah, I thought, *now I remember.* I had settled down with a book to read, but still listless from the fever of the day before, I drifted off to sleep. Today was Sunday, not Saturday, and Mom was on the porch swing with her mending basket, just beyond the open window. Tillie must have followed her out while I was asleep, and now they were talking about Wally, who wasn't home. He'd gone over to Grandpa's to cut the grass, as their gardener was on vacation. Even though Gramps was paying him, I still thought it was good of Wally to go on his day off from his butchering job.

"Pity," Tillie was saying. "He'd be such a nice boy if he just got rid of the chip on his shoulder."

"I'm not sure I'd call it a chip on his shoulder, Tillie," Mom said mildly. "He's been through a lot. It hasn't been easy for him."

"I suppose it has to do with his father. Not that it's any of my business."

Mom didn't respond for a long moment. I rubbed my eyes. I was fully awake now.

Finally Mom said, "Wally's father is dead. He was killed by a sniper in Korea while serving with a MASH unit."

"Merciful heavens," Tillie said quietly. "I'm sorry, Janis. I didn't know."

"Of course you didn't. How could you?"

"I . . . then . . . I . . ."

For the first time since she had come to live with us, Tillie was tongue-tied. I lay there enjoying it. I didn't think she ought to be saying bad things about Wally when he wasn't around to defend himself.

Mom, though, jumped to Tillie's rescue. "I remarried and had Roz and Valerie. Wally still carries his father's name; he's still a Sanderson. Alan didn't adopt him."

"Alan. So that's the man you ran away from."

I expected Mom's response to be angry, but she merely sounded resigned.

"Yes. That's why we're here," she said. "In your house," she added with a small laugh. Two weeks with Tillie and that's how Mom talked to her now, as though the house were still Tillie's, as though Gramps hadn't made the down payment fair and square, and as though Mom wasn't on her feet eight hours a day selling hats and gloves to pay the mortgage. I didn't know whether Mom was humoring Tillie or whether she decided that ownership *was* in fact a matter of the sweat, years, and love a person poured into a house. If the latter was true and could hold up in court, this house would be Tillie's long after she was dead.

"I'm sure you had good reason to leave," Tillie said.

"Our lives depended on it."

Another long silence followed Mom's statement. I lay there thinking about what she'd just said and wondering if it was true.

There were days with Daddy when we'd been afraid, but there were other days, good days, when we hadn't been afraid at all, but happy. Just the previous afternoon I'd begun to collect them, to make a keepsake bouquet of the memories, and hadn't even finished by the time I fell asleep. How could Mom say we had to leave Daddy because our lives depended on it?

"You did the right thing, Janis," Tillie said.

"Yes."

I imagined Mom nodding as her fingers worked the needle and thread.

"I suppose he drank?" Tillie asked.

"Oh yes." Mom sighed. "But it was more than that. It was like he was two people, and one of those people was crazy. One of them was dangerous. At first, it wasn't that way. The first couple of years were actually rather happy. But later . . ."

Mom's words drifted off, as though to leave the unspeakable unspoken.

"I'm sorry, dear," Tillie said, stitching up the frayed edges of the conversation. "A good woman like you deserves better than that. I know it took courage to leave the way you did. I'm glad you found the courage."

The chains holding the swing began to creak. Mom must have started swinging gently, pushing herself with the balls of her feet. "I wish I'd found the courage sooner," she said, her voice heavy with remorse. "I often ask myself why I stayed so long, for so many years. If I'd left sooner, it would have been far better for the children. Wally especially, I think."

"And for you too, no doubt," Tillie added. "But you know the old saying, it's never too late to turn around when you're headed down the wrong path."

"Hmm, yes. I suppose you're right. So I've turned around, and we're making a new life now. Maybe that's all that matters."

"Oh yes, that's all that matters. And you can stay right here in this house for as long as you like. I promise you'll be safe here."

"Thank you, Tillie."

"My pleasure, dear."

The porch swing went on creaking. Beyond the porch, from the direction of the blue spruce, came a tangle of birdsong, fitting background accompaniment to Tillie's promise of security.

"It *is* nice," Mom said, "not to be worried all the time, not to have to wonder who will come home, the good Alan or the bad Alan. No more lying awake nights in fear, no more terrible fights, no more riding in the car and wondering . . ."

There was a pause, followed by muffled sobs as Mom wept quietly. Then Tillie's voice drifted through the air in hushed and gentle tones. "Say no more, dear. It's all behind you now."

Just as Tillie instructed, Mom didn't say anything more, but I remembered. I remembered those times of riding in Daddy's car, the thought of which still made my mother cry. It had happened fairly often, especially toward the end, this wild game of Daddy's. His unpredictable desire to play came out of nowhere, and he didn't even have to be drinking.

The last time it happened, only a couple of months earlier, we were driving home late at night. We were on the long stretch of two-lane highway between the shores of Lake Minnetonka and our home in Minneapolis. The landscape offered little for miles, other than the dark-shrouded trees on either side of the road and the bright stars overhead. Our headlights cleared a path through the otherwise pitch-darkness of that little-traveled route.

Daddy was driving, of course, while Mom held Valerie on her lap in the front seat. Wally and I sat behind them on the vinyl bench seat of Dad's 1963 Chevy Impala. All was quiet save for the whirling of the tires over the asphalt. Exhausted from a long day in the sun, Wally and I laid our heads back against the seat and began to doze.

That's when it always started, when we were right there on the edge of sleep. It started with a slight acceleration, almost imperceptible at first, but growing greater until, jerked awake, I saw the trees whiz by at an impossible rate.

"Alan, please . . ." Mom said as she clutched Valerie tighter. "Please . . ."

Daddy's face was lighted up like he had front-row seats at a Minnesota Twins game. "Come on, Janis, it's fun. This road just begs for a game of chicken. Everybody ready? Anybody screams, I'm heading straight for the next tree."

I watched in horror as the needle on the speedometer climbed higher. I bit my lower lip to keep from crying out.

"This isn't funny, Alan," Mom said. "Please don't do this."

Wally sat up straight in the seat, his spine a ramrod, his hands curled into fists. "Stop it, Alan," he said, his jaw tight, teeth clenched.

"What's the matter, Wally? Chicken? Buck-buck, buck-buck!"

The needle climbed. Daddy laughed. He laughed so hard he cried.

"Alan." Mom was trying hard but failing to keep the panic out of her voice. "Alan, you're going to kill us. Please slow down."

"I promise not to run off the road unless somebody screams. Anyone screams, well . . ." He tugged at the wheel enough to send the car swerving onto the shoulder of the road. We bumped over the gravel for a few terrifying moments until Daddy pulled the car back into the lane.

By now, Valerie was awake and whimpering. Mom held a hand near Valerie's mouth, ready to stifle her cries. I had a firm two-handed hold on the armrest of the door, bracing myself for impact. Mom was at least secured by a lap belt but, without seat belts in the back, Wally and I were on our own. I imagined the car careening off the road and rolling over, Wally and I tossed about inside like a couple of rag dolls in a dryer.

I trembled. The Chevy trembled. I lifted fearful eyes to Wally. The muscles on the side of his face rippled, and his fists were on the back of the driver's seat, just behind Daddy's neck. "Slow down or I'll kill you, Alan," Wally said. "I swear I will."

Daddy laughed. "Yeah? And who's going to grab the wheel when I'm dead?"

Mom looked at Daddy, and I could see the tears running down her face. "These are your children, Alan," she pleaded. "Please don't hurt them."

At long last Daddy decelerated, letting the car slow down to the posted speed. He chuckled, shook his head, called us names I can't repeat. He took off his fisherman's hat, used the palm of one hand to wipe his eyes, tossed the hat back on the crown of his head.

And then he went on driving homeward through another dark Minnesota night.

And now, because I'd overheard Mom and Tillie's conversation, I had one more weed to try to uproot as I waded through that field of memories.

CHAPTER 7

Tillie and I were in the kitchen making spaghetti for supper when the doorbell rang and someone hollered through the screen door, "Mother!"

"That you, Johnny?"

"Can I come in?"

"Door's open."

Tillie stopped stirring the tomato sauce, wiped her hands on her apron, and smiled at her son as he walked into the kitchen. "Stay for supper, Johnny?"

John Monroe's round face was crimson; he was waving a newspaper in the air. "I didn't come for supper, Mother."

He glanced at me and nodded politely as he loosened his tie. The day was warm, and his full-length sleeves were rolled up past his elbows.

"What's the matter now, son?" Tillie turned to the sink and started filling a large pot with water.

"Have you seen today's paper?"

"Haven't had time to read it. What's Johnson gone and done now?"

"President Johnson has nothing to do with this, Mother. The question is, what have *you* gone and done now?"

"Oh dear, don't tell me I've landed on the obituary page again. You remember how your father nearly died that time he opened the paper and there was my picture among the deceased. My *picture,* no less."

"No, Mother, no. It's not that. It's *this.*" He pointed to a block of print surrounded by a black border on the bottom of the front page. "Is this some kind of joke?"

Tillie lifted the pot of water to the stove and turned on the burner. She glanced at the paper in her son's hand and nodded briefly. "Oh yes, that's my advertisement. Winston said he'd run it for me sometime this week. I had no idea he'd run it on the front page! Now, isn't that something?"

"You've run an ad in the paper telling everyone you've come back home?"

Tillie nodded. "Smart, huh? It was Roz's idea, actually. That way I don't have to keep repeating myself; you know, explaining why I'm here and not at St. Claire's. Now the whole town knows in one fell swoop."

Johnny Monroe turned his wide and by

now nearly maniacal eyes toward me. My breath caught in my throat, and I felt the color drain from my face as I took a step backward. I started to shake my head, to deny any part in this strange affair, but by the time I opened my mouth to speak, Johnny Monroe had already turned back to his mother.

"And you've invited the whole town to your welcome home party?"

"What?" Tillie was breaking up vermicelli noodles to be dropped into the water once it boiled. "What welcome home party?"

"It says here you're having a welcome home party, potluck, everyone invited. And it says it's today, Friday, September first, at six o'clock."

"Merciful heavens!" Tillie whirled around and grabbed the paper from Johnny's hand. She glanced up at the clock, then back down at the paper. "I never said anything to Winston about a welcome home party. Six o'clock? That's an hour from now!"

"So you're not throwing a party?"

"No. Well, yes, I guess I am. That Winston Newberry! What came over him, putting in something like that?"

"Mother!" The word exploded from Johnny Monroe's lips. Spittle flew everywhere. "Don't you know? He always said

90

he'd get you back."

Tillie looked up from the paper. "Get me back? For what?"

"For the birthmark, Mother. The birthmark you showed the whole town."

"Oh, nonsense, Johnny. I didn't show the whole town."

"Well, practically the whole town. Everyone and anyone who came through the church nursery saw the Eiffel Tower in red pigment on Winston Newberry's backside, thanks to you. Not only that, they kept on talking about it for years to come. He always said he'd get you back for that. This is only the latest —"

"Nonsense," Tillie said again. "I never heard him say any such thing."

"Listen, Mother, I went to school with him. I should know. How do you think you've ended up in the obits so many times?"

"Well, if that doesn't beat all." Tillie put a finger to her chin and frowned in thought. "We'd best get moving, then."

"And just what do you plan to do?"

"Have the party, of course. Don't just stand there with your mouth hanging open, Johnny. Go home and bring back all the folding tables and chairs you have. We're going to need them. Roz, once the water boils, throw the noodles in and keep an eye on the pot while I vacuum the house." She took her apron off and threw it on the counter. She moved to the front hall and hollered up the stairs, "Wally! Wal-*ly!*"

"What?"

"Come down here, will you? I'm sending you out for party supplies."

"For *what?*"

"Party supplies."

Wally's footsteps came thumping down the stairs. "Who's having a party?"

"We are."

"When?"

"Tonight."

"What the —"

"Now, Wally, I've asked you not to use that kind of language in my house."

"But what —"

"Here's the car keys —"

"I can take the car?"

"You'll have to. I'll make a list of what we need. You can pick it up at Jewel, and then on your way home stop by Marie's and pick up your mother. I'm going to need her help."

Esther Kinshaw from next door was the first one to arrive with a hamburger and hominy casserole in hand. She was followed by our neighbors on the other side, our neighbors across the street, neighbors we had met only in passing, neighbors we had never met at all, Fred the butcher, Hazel the cashier, Leonard the postman, and Winston Newberry, the editor and instigator of the whole affair. While everyone else came with a contribution of food for the potluck, Editor Newberry came with a camera slung around his neck and a tape recorder in hand. He was determined to get a story for the Sunday edition, he said, "and I'm going to handle this one myself."

"Is it true?" Tillie asked him when he first showed up.

"Is what true?" Winston Newberry said, one eyebrow raised.

"Is it true you did this because of the birthmark?"

The eyebrow dropped as Winston Newberry sniffed. "I have no idea what you're talking about, Mrs. Monroe." He snapped her picture, leaving her blinking wildly from the flash before moving on to the punch in the dining room.

I saw our car inching its way through the gauntlet of vehicles parked in front of the house. Wally turned into the drive, stopping midway to the detached garage in the backyard. Mom climbed out of the passenger side. Wally rolled on and parked while Mom stood in the middle of the driveway, looking dumbfounded, her feet refusing to carry her to the porch. I ran out to meet her.

"Roz, what's going on here?"

She didn't look happy. I tried to sound cheerful. "We're having a party."

"We are?"

"Well, Tillie is. Did you see the paper today?"

Mom shook her head dully.

"Oh, um, well there was an ad in the paper, right on the front page," I said.

"An ad about what?"

"Tillie's welcome home party."

"Her welcome home party?"

"Uh-huh."

"She didn't tell me she was having a party."

"She didn't know she was having it."

"She didn't? Then what —"

"She just found out an hour ago. Did Wally pick up the party supplies?"

"I don't know. I guess so. Roz, just who did she invite to this party?"

"The whole town."

"The whole town?"

"But don't worry, Mom. She doesn't think everyone's going to come."

94

At that moment Mom looked ready to collapse. I grabbed her hand and started pulling her toward the house. "It's going to be fun, Mom. You'll see."

Mom started forward, but her feet were reluctant to follow. Together we stumbled across the front yard and into the house, full now of warm bodies, loud chatter, and the aroma of dozens of homemade dishes. John Monroe had left and come back with folding tables that were scattered throughout the rooms downstairs. Women were busy arranging casseroles, salads, breads, and desserts on the tables, children scrambled underfoot, and two men were hanging a banner above the living room fireplace that read, "Welcome Home, Tillie!"

Mom faltered at the sight of the banner, but I pulled her down the hall to the kitchen, where Tillie was directing traffic. The kitchen was full of ladies heating dishes in the oven and stirring pitchers of lemonade and iced tea. Wally burst in through the kitchen door carrying two grocery bags and yelling, "Here's your paper goods and junk, Tillie."

"Just in time," she said. "We can't eat all this food without paper plates. Help me get everything unpacked, will you? Oh, Janis, you're home! Can you lend us a hand?"

Mom's eyes widened, and I felt sure I was going to lose her this time, but she mustered her strength and said, "Tillie, what on earth do you think you're doing?"

"Right now I'm just trying to feed the crowd."

"But . . . how could you —"

Tillie raised a hand. "You've got to believe me when I say I didn't plan this. Apparently I'm paying for past indiscretions. But I don't know, it's kind of nice, isn't it? All these people turning out to welcome me home."

"But, Tillie, I —"

It was at that moment that a fiddler and a banjo player marched down the hall and out the kitchen door, a snake of men, women, and children trailing them like a conga line. Out in the yard the two musicians met up with a bass player who was keeping time by pounding the grass with his foot. Spontaneous dancing broke out as the three men slid into some sort of hillbilly tune. Mom stepped to the window and stared, eyes wide, jaw unhinged.

By the time she turned around, Tillie had wandered off into the crowd. Mom looked from me to Wally to Valerie, who was watching the antics in the kitchen from her high chair. Squeezing her hands together and taking a deep breath, Mom said, "We will try to make the best of this."

Wally shook his head. "I told you it was a mistake to let her live here. We should have taken her right back to the old folks home."

Mom shut her eyes, slowly opened them. I thought for a moment she might agree, but she forced a smile and said, "Tillie's been a big help, and I need her. I'm sure this" — she swept the crowded room with her eyes — "won't happen again."

"Sure, Mom," Wally said, "just like you thought she'd never come back after that first time she showed up on the porch."

A woman none of us recognized handed Mom an apron and said, "As long as you're here, honey, you might as well make yourself useful."

Mom looked at the apron, shrugged, and put it on. "Wally and Roz, you two make yourselves useful too."

"Doing what?" Wally said.

"I don't know. Pass out some hors d'oeuvres or something. Roz, you take care of Valerie. And — Oh, Dad!"

I was surprised to see Grandpa striding down the hall. I ran to him and threw my arms around his waist. He kissed the top of my head, and together we walked the rest of the way to the kitchen. "Janis, honey," he said, "why didn't you tell me you were having a party? I'd have helped you out."

"Well, I didn't know. I —"

"You didn't know you were throwing a party?"

"No, I . . . well, never mind, Dad. Where's Marie?"

"She's still at the store. I was driving by and noticed all the cars parked on your street, so I thought I'd stop —"

"Yes. We seem to have attracted the whole town."

"Wow, honey, you've even hired a three-piece band. I didn't know you could throw a party like this. What's the occasion?"

"Gramps," I said, looking up at him, "did you see the paper today?"

He shook his head. "I haven't read it yet. Why?"

"Just wondering."

"Actually, Gramps," Wally said, "it's a party for Tillie."

"Tillie?"

"You know, the nutcase who lives with us."

"Wally!"

"Look, Mom, I just call them like I see them."

Gramps shook his head. "Wally, I've spoken with you before about disrespecting your elders."

"Yeah, well." Wally shrugged and smirked. "I've got to find some hors d'oeuvres to hand out to our guests."

He moved away, and Mom and Grandpa let him go. "Listen, Dad," Mom said, "as long as you're here, grab a plate and enjoy the food. I'd better get busy. I think it's going to be a long night."

Mom was right. It was a long night, with the party going on past midnight, our property invaded by a parade of mostly unfamiliar faces coming and going, eating and drinking, dancing and laughing and chattering. Tillie flitted about from guest to guest, the life of the party, queen for a day, the one being honored and cheered and welcomed back to the home that was no longer legally hers. Johnny Monroe stayed close by her side, toasting her again and again with a lift of a plastic cup filled with orange raspberry punch, explaining that yes, yes, the nursing home had been a temporary arrangement, only temporary, since who, after all, could separate Tillie Monroe from the house she had helped build with her own two hands?

I too moved around from room to room, eating, watching, listening, pulling Valerie along with me until she grew tired and began to whine. I eventually took her upstairs and put her to bed, then moved back down to the kitchen, where I found Mom in the middle of an assembly line of men washing dishes at the sink. One man handed dirty casserole dishes and pie tins and silverware to Mom, which she washed and handed off to two men on the other side of her who were drying the dishes and placing them in careful piles on the kitchen table.

Never having seen my mother surrounded by men, I watched in bewilderment. I wondered whether Mom was all right or whether I should fetch Grandpa so he could toss these strangers out on their ears.

"Mom?" I said.

She turned from the sink and beamed at me. "Yes, Roz?"

"Should I get Gramps?"

She looked puzzled. "Whatever for? Is there a problem?"

Apparently not. I felt myself frown.

As Mom turned back to the sink, she said something to the men, who erupted in laughter. I suddenly remembered Tillie's prediction: *"Someday your mother will marry again. She's young and pretty, and I can't imagine her living the rest of her life alone."*

I took a step backward, and then another, inching slowly away from this scene playing out at the kitchen sink. These men must have found Mom attractive, like she was a lady or something and not a mother, *my* mother. They might think they could date her, maybe even marry her.

I felt the urge to find Wally. "Mom?"

She turned to me again, looking a little less happy and a little more annoyed. "Yes, Roz?"

"Where's Wally?"

She surveyed the kitchen with her eyes, as though he was supposed to be there somewhere.

One of the men answered for her. "Last I saw, he was headed out back with the Delaney twins."

"The Delaney twins?" I echoed.

"Don't you know them?" The man looked at me from behind dark horn-rimmed glasses. His sleeves were rolled up, and he was swiping at a bread tin with one of our dish towels.

I shook my head. I was having trouble breathing.

"Luke and Lenny Delaney," he explained. "They live up the street."

"Oh."

"Yeah, the three of them were carrying some trash out back."

"Okay." I turned and ran out the kitchen

door and across the dark lawn toward the trash cans by the garage. A couple hours earlier the musicians had moved to the front yard to take advantage of the light of the streetlamps, leaving the backyard littered but empty of partiers.

I found Wally and the Delaney twins sitting on upturned cinderblocks between the garage and the neighbor's fence. They all three had small, tightly rolled cigarettes held to their lips. When they realized someone was among them in the dark, there was a shifting, a nervous dropping of hands, an uneasy silence.

Then, "Oh, it's you, Roz. What do you want?"

"What are you doing, Wally?"

"Nothing."

"Well, what's that funny smell?"

"Funny smell?"

"Yeah." I sniffed deeply. "Like . . . I don't know. Don't you smell it?"

The twins snickered. Wally said, "Maybe someone's burning leaves."

"Are you smoking?"

"What if I am?"

I didn't know what to say.

Wally said, "What'd you come out here for?"

"Listen, Wally, some men are helping

102

Mom wash the dishes."

Silence. Then the Delaney boys exploded into laughter.

"So?" Wally lifted the cigarette to his lips. I saw the end burn red as he inhaled.

Then it hit me. "You're smoking pot or something, aren't you?"

Wally exhaled, his head bobbing. "Maybe."

"You can't do that!"

More laughter from the twins. They were working on their own cigarettes again.

"Who says I can't?" Wally's voice was flat. I felt as though I weren't talking with my brother at all, but with someone I didn't know.

"I'm telling Mom," I threatened.

"No you're not."

"Says who?" I took a step backwards.

"Says Hamilton."

"Who's Hamilton?"

Wally tightened his lips around what I now understood to be a joint while he rummaged around in his shorts pocket. He pulled out a bill and waved it at me.

I didn't take it. "That's a bribe."

"That's right."

"I'm not taking it."

"You might want to reconsider. It's ten dollars."

"Where'd you get that kind of money?"

Wally shrugged. "I'm working, aren't I?"

The Delaney boys laughed again. I didn't know what they found so hilarious. One said, "You're going to give the kid ten dollars just to shut her up? You're crazy, Sanderson. Just tell her how it is."

Wally didn't say anything but went on holding the bill in my direction. Finally he muttered, "Go on. Buy yourself something pretty." The joint moved up and down as he spoke.

I stepped forward slowly and took the money.

"What a waste," the other Delaney boy said. "You know what you can get for ten bucks on the street?"

"Shut up, Delaney," Wally said. "It's my money, and I'll do what I want with it."

I looked at Wally, then at the twins. My stomach turned at the sickly sweet smell hanging over them. I looked back at Wally, hoping somehow to connect with him, but he was gazing up at the night sky like he was looking for a star to fly away to. Had he succeeded in flying off, he wouldn't have been any more lost to me than he was now. A stranger had taken over my brother's body; the Wally I knew had been pushed out, sent into exile, expelled from the world

I'd always known before tonight.

I turned and ran across the lawn and in through the kitchen door. Barely glancing at Mom and her helpers, I ran through the kitchen, down the hall, and up the stairs. I didn't stop running until I reached my bedroom. I flipped on the light and laid my hand on the jewelry box on my dresser. The box, a birthday gift from Daddy, was the keeper of my few treasures. When I lifted the padded pink lid, a tiny plastic ballerina inside popped up and started turning pirouettes to the tinny plucked tune of "You Are My Sunshine." How I loved that little ballerina in her pink plastic tutu, whirling and twirling till the music slowed to a stop and I had to turn the little knob on the bottom to wind it up again.

I sat on the edge of my bed, listening to the music, watching the ballerina go around and around. I picked up my treasures one by one and looked at them: a four-leaf clover pressed and ironed between two small squares of waxed paper; a whistle from a box of Cracker Jack; a string of plastic rosary beads from my best friend, June, in Minnesota; a 1923 silver dollar from Gramps; an envelope with my baby teeth (Mom said the tooth fairy gave them all back to her); and a fistful of candy wrappers. These, neatly folded, sticky-side in, were the wrappers from some of the Sugar Daddy lollipops my father had given me over the years.

That was Daddy for you. He'd be pulling candy out of his shirt pocket one minute and the next pulling threats out of some dark place in his mind. Sometimes I'd be sucking on a Sugar Daddy even as Daddy decided to race down another open road, intent on his game of chicken, intent on scaring us all to death even if we didn't hit a tree.

Dr. Jekyll and Mr. Hyde, Wally said. He was just like Jekyll and Hyde, and you were never sure which one would show up.

I sometimes wondered if Dr. Jekyll drank a potion to become the evil Mr. Hyde, wasn't there a potion we could give Daddy to make him always be the *good* Daddy? The kind and gentle Daddy? The Daddy who kissed me and gave me candy and said he loved me?

I tucked the ten dollars among my treasures and lowered the lid of the music box. I turned off the light and stepped to the window that overlooked the front yard.

What a strange, strange night it was. Wally was out back smoking pot, Mom was in the kitchen flirting with a circle of admirers,

106

and Tillie — merciful heavens! Tillie was with the crowd on the front lawn, dancing the Virginia reel with Grandpa! I could see them by the light of the streetlamp, the music from the three-piece band drifting up to me through the open windows. I gazed in curiosity at the sea of bobbing heads, clapping hands, dark figures milling about. Laughter hovered above it all, a cap on the night of Tillie's welcome home party.

I was just about to go down and join everyone when I glimpsed a figure standing on the rim of the streetlamp's circle of light. Leaning my palms against the windowsill, I peered harder and drew in a sharp breath. In another moment I was stumbling down the stairs and out the front door, pushing my way through the crowd and sweeping past the musicians still merrily sending up notes into the night. But by the time I reached the street, the man wearing what looked like a fishing hat was gone.

CHAPTER 8

With a high-pitched wailing of brakes, the school bus rolled to a stop at the corner of McDowell and Edgewood. The driver shifted into neutral, then moved his large hairy hand from the gearshift to the shiny silver knob that swung open the double doors. Seated right behind him, I had spent the trip from school alternately staring at the creases in the back of his neck and at that hardworking hand. I had no desire to see or be seen by the other kids on the bus. Not yet. It would take me a while to work up the courage to try to make new friends.

As soon as the doors opened, its two metal halves folding up like rubber-edged wings, I hurried down the steps and onto the sidewalk. Other kids got off, but I didn't pay them any attention. Instead, I clutched my books to my chest and moved hurriedly past the houses on McDowell Street until I reached ours, the now familiar white clapboard in the middle of the block.

The front door was unlocked, and I let myself in. The house was quiet. Mom was at work, and Wally was on his way to his job at Jewel, but I thought Tillie would be there to greet me.

I moved to the kitchen, dropped my books on the table, and looked around. "Tillie?"

No answer.

I peered out the window into the backyard. She wasn't hanging up laundry, carrying out the trash, or pushing the reel mower over the lawn — all of which I'd seen her do in recent days.

"Tillie?" I called again. Again, no answer.

I walked back down the hall and up the stairs to her room. And there she was, in her ancient padded rocking chair, some sheets of folded stationery on her lap.

Knocking on the open door, I said loudly, "Tillie?"

She jumped a foot and put a hand to her chest. The pages on her lap took flight and tumbled to the floor. She looked at me with startled eyes. "Merciful heavens, Roz!" she cried. "You just about scared the living daylights out of me."

"Sorry," I said. "I didn't know you were asleep."

"Well." She leaned over and gathered the

109

papers from the floor. "I guess I dozed off. What time is it?"

"I don't know. A little after three-thirty, I guess. I just got home from school."

"School! Oh, Roz, I meant to meet you when you got home, have a little snack ready. But I put Valerie down for her nap and came in here to read this letter from Lyle, and then I guess I just dozed off, like I said."

"That's okay, Tillie. I don't need a snack. Can I come in?"

"Well, sure, honey. Come on in and pull up that chair from the desk. We can visit for a while, if you'd like."

Though she'd lived with us for several weeks now, I hadn't yet looked around Tillie's room. At first it had been Valerie's room, but Mom moved Val into the master bedroom with her so Tillie could have her own place. The room was now furnished with items John Monroe and his wife had taken for their guest bedroom at the time they sold Tillie's house. When Tillie left the nursing home, she demanded everything back, including the huge brass bed she and her husband had shared for their entire married life. The bed, the chest of drawers, the desk and rocking chair, numerous paintings and framed photographs all came back, with Johnny complaining that if he'd known it was only going to come back he'd have left it all here in the first place. Her few items at the nursing home — a small end table, her wedding quilt, and other odds and ends — were also packed up and restored to their proper place on McDowell Street.

Everything in her room was old and quaint and frilly, like the lace curtains in the windows and the antimacassars on the arms of the rocking chair. Before we moved in, Gramps had furnished the house for us with contemporary furniture, so stepping into Tillie's room was like stepping back in time. I placed the desk chair across from Tillie and sat down while my eyes wandered around the room, taking it all in.

"Who's that?" I asked, pointing to a framed portrait on the wall.

"Why, that's Ross and me, shortly after we married."

"That's *you,* Tillie?"

She snorted out a small laugh. "Don't act so surprised, child. I was young once too, you know."

I *was* surprised, and she *had* been young once, and thin, and even pretty, with dark hair cascading past her ears in stylish waves, skin smooth and firm and wrapped snugly over cheekbone and jaw and down her long white neck. The photograph was black and white so it didn't capture the blue of her eyes, but it wasn't hard to imagine it, that blue, and the pink of her cheeks and the red of those lips that turned up in a small, close-lipped smile. The man beside her was handsome in a rugged way, with a cleft chin like Cary Grant's and dark hair combed straight back from his face. His eyes were dark and piercing, his smile sincere and filled with white marblelike teeth; he looked as though he sat on the edge of laughter, not because something was funny but simply because life was good.

"Ross went off to the First World War shortly after that picture was taken," Tillie said. "Thank God he came home again."

As though she didn't want to talk about the war, she waved toward a carnival glass dish on the table beside her. She lifted the lid and nodded toward the cream-colored candies inside. "Butter mint?" she asked.

"Sure," I said. I chose one of the mints and popped it into my mouth.

"How was the first day of school?"

I shrugged. "It was all right."

"Did you make any new friends?"

"Not yet."

"Well, friendships take time. I'm sure there are some nice little girls in your class."

I shrugged again and didn't say anything. Tillie took a mint for herself and placed the lid back on the dish. It settled into place with a small clinking sound.

Pocketing my mint in one cheek for a moment, I said, "Why do you have a baseball bat by your bed?"

"What? Oh, that. It belonged to Paul, my middle son. He was quite a good ball player. We thought at one time he might go professional."

"But he didn't?"

"No. He decided against it."

"So what does he do?"

"He went into real estate. He's made a good living for himself and his family."

"Well, how come he didn't come to your welcome home party?"

"He doesn't live in Mills River anymore. He moved to Florida years ago. Only Johnny lives here now, he and his wife, Elaine. My youngest son, Lyle, doesn't live here either." As she said that, she folded up the sheets of stationery in her lap and stuffed them into an envelope.

"Where's he live?"

"Bolivia."

"Bolivia?"

"That's right."

"Where's that?"

Tillie's right eyebrow shot up. "Don't you know?"

"If I knew I wouldn't ask you."

"Well, you've got a point. It's in South America."

"What's he doing there?"

"He teaches at a mission school. He teaches the children of missionaries."

"What for?"

"Well, they need to be educated too."

"I know, but I mean, what about his own children? Why would he want them to grow up down there?"

"He doesn't have any children. Doesn't have a wife either. He's never been married."

"Never?"

Tillie shook her head as she lifted the letter to her heart. "And now he's got another bout of malaria."

My eyes widened. "Is he going to die?"

"Oh no. But I hate to think of him sick like that, so far from home." She looked at me, gave a small apologetic laugh. "I guess I'll always be his mother."

"I'm sorry he's so far away."

"Me too. Another mint?"

She lifted the lid. I took one.

"Tillie?"

"Yes, Roz?"

"You got any grandchildren?"

"I've got two, a boy and a girl. They're Paul's children. They live in Florida, so I rarely see them. Pity," she said. Her eyes moved to the window, and she rocked a little bit, as though to soothe herself.

"Doesn't Johnny have kids?"

"No. They wanted children, but it turned out Elaine couldn't have any. I tried to talk them into adopting, but Elaine said it wouldn't be the same, having a child not really your own. I told her she'd love the child just the same, but . . ." Her words trailed off as she shook her head.

"Well," I said around the candy in my mouth, "at least you've got two grandkids."

"Yes, and I'm thankful for that."

For a moment, neither of us spoke. Tillie rocked quietly. I gazed at the candy dish, wishing for another piece.

Finally Tillie said, "I suppose one more won't spoil your supper."

She lifted the lid and offered me yet another butter mint.

"These are good," I said.

"They're my favorite." Tillie nodded. "I got this dish as a wedding gift, and it's been filled with butter mints ever since. Fifty years of butter mints."

"Did your husband like them too?"

"Oh my, yes. He'd eat a fistful at a time."
She smiled at the memory.

"Tillie?"

"Yes, Roz?"

"How long ago did he die?"

Tillie took a deep breath, let it out. "A little more than a year ago."

"You miss him?"

"More than I can say."

I don't know why, but her confession made me think of Daddy sitting on the front steps crying. I looked at Tillie. Her eyes were moist. "I'm sorry, Tillie," I said.

She nodded slightly, tried to smile. "You always know you're going to lose your loved ones in the end, but even so, you're never prepared for it. Not really."

The last bit of butter mint melted between my tongue and the roof of my mouth. I swallowed, savoring the taste. I didn't know what to say to Tillie; I'd never lost anyone other than my grandmother, who'd died when I was six.

Instead of finding something comforting to say, I asked, "He died in this house, didn't he?"

"Yes, he did." She nodded toward the wall. "Right there in the master bedroom. It was unexpected. He slipped away peacefully in his sleep."

I looked over my shoulder at Tillie's bed, splendid with its shiny brass frame and colorful wedding quilt. He must have died in that bed. "Tillie, do you believe in ghosts?"

"Goodness no. I believe in heaven."

I turned back to look at her. She was dabbing at her eyes with a tissue, which she stuffed back into her skirt pocket. I decided to get off the subject of her husband. I'd been wanting to talk with her about something else anyway.

"Tillie?"

"Yes?"

I pursed my lips. Finally I said, "Do you know anyone in Mills River who wears a fishing hat?"

"A fishing hat?"

"Yeah."

She frowned in thought. "Not that I can think of. Why do you ask?"

I wanted to give her an answer. I wanted to tell her I thought I'd seen Daddy twice, but I couldn't do it. If I let the words out of my mouth, I didn't know what kind of harm they would do, especially to Mom. Surely, I decided, I was seeing things. Or maybe there were plenty of men in Mills River who wore fishing hats like Daddy's. Why not? Daddy wasn't the only man in the world who liked to fish.

I shrugged. "I don't know," I said. "Forget it. It's nothing."

"You look worried," she said. "If something's bothering you, you can always tell me."

Valerie woke up from her nap then and began to cry. I was glad for the interruption.

"Well, there she blows," Tillie said. "Best get her up and start supper."

Tillie rose from the rocking chair and headed for the door. I followed, popping another butter mint into my mouth and momentarily swallowing my fears about Daddy.

CHAPTER 9

Late on a Saturday morning in mid-September, Tillie sent me into town to deliver some aspirin to Mom. She rolled a couple of tablets in a napkin, stuffed it into my shorts pocket, and sent me off with instructions to go straight to the store and not get sidetracked. As I walked the streets between our house and Marie's Apparel, I felt immensely important. Mom had a headache, and I was the one who was going to stop it. I was the chosen one, the *only* one who could accomplish a dangerous mission like this. The secret formula, the reliever of pain, had been entrusted to me, and I would brave anything to get it into the hands of my suffering mother: snow, sleet, hail, lightning, hordes of thieves, packs of wolves . . .

A car honked just as I was about to cross Grand Avenue, bringing me back to the serenity of downtown Mills River. I felt my shoulders hunch and my face turn red. The only dangerous thing about this town was my own imagination. If I was killed on the way to the store, it would be because I wasn't paying attention.

I waited for a break in traffic before crossing over to Marie's Apparel.

Mom was in the Accessories Department, ringing up a sale. When she saw me, she smiled and held up one finger to indicate she'd be with me in a minute. When the customer finally waddled off, carrying a package under each arm, I dug the aspirin out of my pocket and handed it to Mom.

"Thanks, Roz," she said. "I appreciate your coming down here."

"If you have a headache, Mom, maybe you should just go home and rest," I suggested.

She pulled a bottle of Coca-Cola from under the counter and took a swig of it to swallow the aspirin. "No," she said, shaking her head. "It's not that bad. The aspirin should help. How's everything at home?"

"Fine, I guess."

"You get your homework done?"

I nodded. "It's done. I didn't have much."

"Good. Well, run on back now. I'll be home around five-thirty."

"Mom?"

"Uh-huh?"

"Can I have some money for an ice cream cone?"

She thought a moment, then smiled. "All right. Consider it a reward for bringing me the aspirin." She dug a quarter out of her change purse and handed it to me.

"Thanks, Mom!"

I ran out of Marie's Apparel and into the drugstore next door, where they had a soda counter. I lingered happily over the selection of ice cream, trying to decide on a flavor.

"Make up your mind yet, little miss?" The man behind the counter, wearing a white apron and a white paper serving cap, smiled down at me. He waved a metal scoop over the barrels of ice cream displayed in the open freezer. "Plenty to choose from, but they're all good."

"I'll have a scoop of strawberry, please."

"In a cake cone?"

"Yeah."

"Good choice." He dug a ball of ice cream out of the barrel and plopped it on top of a cone. "Here you go, little miss."

I paid him, thanked him, and went outside to sit on the bench in front of the store. It was empty when I went in, but someone had sat down while I was inside making up my mind. The bench had plenty of room

121

for two, though, so I sat down, squeezing myself close to the armrest.

As I carved lines in the ice cream with my tongue, I studied my neighbor out of the corner of my eye. She was a girl about my own age, with creamy brown skin and black hair pulled back tightly into two stiff braids. She wore a white blouse, a red pleated skirt, and black patent leather shoes, the toes of which shone brightly, reflecting the noonday sun. Clutched in one hand was the stub of a number 2 pencil; she was using it to scribble furiously in a spiral-bound notebook. I listened to the scratching sound of lead against paper and wondered at the words being poured out in small neat rows across the page.

Finally she paused, lifted the pencil to her mouth, and captured the eraser in the snare of her teeth. She looked across the street, squinting in concentration. I couldn't help staring, even though Mom said it was impolite to stare. I'd been pulled in her direction by the strength of her desire to capture something and put it into words. She must have felt my gaze, because she released the pencil from her clenched jaw and turned to look at me. Her eyes were deep dark pools, at once serene and glowing with life. In the few seconds we sat staring at each other, she seemed to be gathering her thoughts from distant places and bringing her mind back to the bench in front of the drugstore on Grand Avenue.

I was trying to come up with an apology for staring, but before I could say anything at all, she whispered, "I know you."

I was hardly aware of the streams of melted ice cream dripping over the lip of the cone and down the rutted bank of my fingers. I had forgotten to grab a napkin from the canister on the counter inside.

"You're in Miss Fremont's class, right?" she asked.

I nodded. "Whose class are you in?"

"Mrs. Oberlin's."

"That's right. Now I remember. I've seen you at school."

"Yeah. You're new here."

"We moved here this summer. From Minnesota."

She lifted her chin in understanding. "What's your name?"

"Rosalind. But everyone calls me Roz."

"Roz what?"

"What do you mean, Roz what?"

"What's your last name?"

"Anthony."

"Anthony's your last name?"

"Uh-huh."

"Rosalind Anthony."

I nodded.

She smiled. "That's a good name."

"It is?"

"Sure. It flows like a poem."

"It does?"

"Uh-huh. Don't you hear it?"

I repeated my name in my head and tried to listen, but it didn't sound like a poem to me. It just sounded familiar and plain. "What's your name?" I asked.

"Mara Nightingale."

"Nightingale?"

"That's right."

"Like Florence Nightingale?"

She looked away, shaking her head. "No, not like that. Florence Nightingale was a white woman."

"So?"

"I'm colored."

"So?" I said again.

She gave me a sharp look before asking, "You ever been friends with a Negro?"

I pretended to think about that for a minute, though I knew right away what the answer was. Finally I shook my head.

"See?" she said, sounding triumphant.

"See what?"

"It matters that I'm colored."

"It doesn't matter to me."

She didn't respond. She seemed to be trying to gauge whether or not I was telling her the truth.

I asked, "You ever been friends with a white girl?"

She dropped her eyes then, but her face relaxed. She looked away, bit her lip, shook her head.

"Well then?"

"Well then, what?" she said.

"You want to be friends?"

She smiled again. "All right. I guess so." She glanced at my lap, back up at me. "You've got ice cream all over your shorts."

I looked at the tiny puddles of pink polka dots on my navy blue shorts. "You want some?" I asked, holding up the cone.

She shook her head. "No." Then she added, "Thanks."

"I better eat it fast." I licked the ice cream, the cone, and my hand in an attempt to clean up the mess.

Mara looked at the notebook in her lap, then closed it.

"What were you writing?" I asked.

"A poem."

"Can I hear it?"

An emphatic shake of her black braids. "It's not ready."

"Okay."

"But I'll read you another one, a poem I didn't write."

"All right," I said with a shrug.

Mara looked down at the yellow cover of the notebook, where she had written a poem in black ink. She paused just a moment before beginning to read in a clear, strong voice. " 'Hold fast to dreams, for if dreams die, life is a broken-winged bird that cannot fly.' " She looked at me, as though to make sure I had caught the image of that broken-winged bird. I nodded while wiping at my chin with the back of my free hand. She went on, something about life becoming a frozen field of some sort, but I'd stopped paying much attention to the poem, so captivated was I by the passion in Mara's voice and the look of intensity in her eye.

When she finished she sighed deeply and raised the notebook to her chest, as though to hold the words close to her heart. "That was nice," I said. "Who wrote it?"

"Langston Hughes."

"Never heard of him."

"No, I expect you wouldn't. He was a Negro poet. He died not long ago. Last spring. May 22, actually."

I cocked my head. "Did you know him or something?"

"No," she whispered sadly.

"Well, he wrote a nice poem," I said again.

"He wrote a lot of nice poems. Someday, I'm going to write poetry as good as his. I'm going to be a writer like him and like . . ."

When she didn't go on, I asked, "Like who?"

She shrugged. "No one." Her hand went to a locket the size of a dime that hung around her neck. She gave the locket a squeeze, then slipped it beneath her blouse.

"I've got to go now," she said. "Here come my mom and dad."

Approaching us from the direction of Woolworth's was a large man and a slender slip of a woman. The woman carried a shoe box under her arm. Both were dressed neatly, in formal church clothes, though as they came closer I could see their garments were worn and faded, the man's dress shirt frayed at the cuffs.

"You ready to go home, baby?" the man said. His face was dark and wrinkled like a prune, while his hair was a woolly white cap. He walked with a certain stiffness in his joints, as though, like the Tin Man, he needed oiling. *He's old,* I thought. Older than most of my friends' fathers back home. Certainly older than Daddy.

Mara jumped up from the bench, the

notebook held tight in her crossed arms. "I'm ready, Daddy."

"Sorry to take so long," the woman said. "Al wasn't in today, and only that young assistant of his was there. He's good at fixing shoes, but he's slower than molasses going up a hill in January. He gave me new heels, though. Take a look."

She opened the shoe box and lifted out one brown pump. Though the heel was new, the shoe itself looked as though it had walked a thousand miles. I wondered why she didn't just buy a new pair.

"Looks nice, Mama," Mara said.

The woman smiled and, looking pleased, tucked the shoe back into the box. I couldn't help but notice that she, like her husband, was older. Her hair was streaked with gray, and her hands were bony and gnarled. Fine lines sliced the skin at the corners of her eyes and dug tiny canals along her upper lip.

"Don't worry about taking a while, Mama," Mara said. "I've been talking to Roz. I know her from school."

"Oh?"

"Yeah. She and her family just moved here from Minnesota."

"Well." The woman smiled at me, a small uncertain smile. "Welcome, then," she said.

"I hope you like Mills River."

"Yes, ma'am," I said shyly. "I do."

The man nodded in my direction but didn't speak.

"Well, come on, Mara, let's get home and get some lunch." The woman put an arm around Mara's shoulder. "I don't know about you, but I'm starving."

As my new friend was being led away, she hollered back to me, "I'll see you in school, Roz."

I lifted a sticky hand in her direction and watched her go.

CHAPTER 10

Mara and I saw each other in school on Monday, but only from a distance. We didn't actually speak until Friday, when an air raid drill sent everyone scrambling for the halls to take cover. All over the school, hundreds of kids dropped to their knees, touched their heads to the wall, and clasped their hands over their necks, fingers locked. We all went along with it because we had to, though we doubted being rolled into a ball would protect us from a nuclear bomb, especially if we suffered a direct hit on Mills River Elementary.

Wally always claimed that a nuclear attack was a real possibility, seeing as how Russia was just itching to bomb America off the globe. Mom said they would do no such thing, since the Russians were every bit as civilized as we were. But whenever they argued about it, Wally brought up the Cuban Missile Crisis of 1962, which he remembered and I didn't. We might have all been blown sky-high right then, he'd say, and the Russian babushkas would have been dancing in the streets of Moscow.

I figured if there were no chance of our Cold War enemy bombing us, then the teachers wouldn't interrupt classes and make us line up in the hall like so many rows of sitting ducks. Surely they thought there was some merit to these drills. So whenever the air raid siren went off, I wondered whether all the old grandmothers in Moscow were putting on their dancing shoes.

That's what I was thinking about when the person in a fetal position next to me whispered my name. I peeked out from under my arm and saw one dark and roving eye peering out from under the arm of the person beside me.

"Mara! What are you doing here? You're supposed to be with your own class."

"When the siren went off, I ran down the hall to find you," she whispered.

"How come?"

"I had to ask you something."

"What?"

"Did you mean it?"

"Did I mean what?"

"Shh! Quiet please." It was Miss Fremont,

my homeroom teacher. Her heels tapped on the linoleum-tiled floor as she slowly paced the hall. Mara and I retreated like turtles into our shells.

After a moment, as the tapping of her heels grew distant, Mara said, "Well?"

"Well, what?"

"Did you mean it when you said you wanted to be friends?"

"Sure I meant it."

"All right, then. Can you meet me tomorrow on the bench outside the drugstore?"

"Well, yeah. What time?"

"Around noon."

"Okay."

A scrap of paper traveled the distance between her head and mine, propelled by Mara's index finger. "If you can't make it, call me. Here's my number."

I took the paper, clutched it in my fist. "Okay. But don't worry, I'll be there."

"If we don't get blown up first."

"We won't get blown up," I said, trying to convince myself as well as her.

"How do you know?" she asked.

Just then the all clear sounded, the wailing siren releasing us from our cramped positions and sending us back to our classrooms. I said good-bye to Mara, and we parted ways, having mercifully avoided the wrath of the Russians once more.

That night the doorbell rang promptly at six o'clock. Wally answered it. "Yeah?"

A well-dressed man stood on the porch, fedora in hand. He had a full-moon face, a sharply pointed nose and a swiftly receding chin. His dark hair, heavily greased, was parted on the side and combed flat against his head. Before he spoke, he pulled at the knot of his tie and thrust out his jaw. "I'm Tom Barrows," he finally announced.

Wally waited for more but was met with silence. I left the kitchen, where I was setting the table, and moved quietly out to the hall to get a better look.

"What do you want?" Wally finally asked.

The man tugged at his tie again, and a nervous fear flashed behind the lenses of his glasses. "I believe Mrs. Anthony is expecting me."

"She is?"

"Well, yes."

"For what?"

The man frowned, then sniffed. "We're having dinner and —"

Before the stranger could finish, my brother turned and hollered up the stairs. "Mom!"

"Yes, Wally?"

"Are you expecting someone?"

"Yes. Is he here?"

Wally looked at Tom Barrows, then back up the stairs. "I'm not sure."

"What do you mean, you're not sure? Is someone at the door or not?"

"Um, yeah. Some guy's here. Says he's looking for you."

"Well, invite him in, please, and tell him I'll be down in a minute."

Wally opened the door a little wider and waved toward the living room.

The man stepped inside, eyed me briefly, nodded at Wally. "Thank you," he said. Crab-like, he moved sideways into the living room, where he stopped just beyond the threshold. He seemed not to want to make himself at home.

Wally shut the door and crossed his arms. "You taking my mother out on a date or something?"

The fingers grew taut on the rim of the fedora. "We're having dinner and going to a movie."

"How do you know my mother?"

"I . . . well, I bought a hat from her."

Wally actually snorted. "You bought a hat from her?"

"Um, yes, but not for me, of course. For my mother. For her birthday. She liked it

134

very much."

Mom came down the stairs then, wearing one of her nicer dresses and smelling of perfume. "Hello, Tom," she said brightly.

"Hello, Janis," he said with a nod and a small, relieved smile. "You look lovely."

Wally took a step forward, as though to come between them. "Mom," he said, "you didn't ask me if you could go out tonight."

Mom looked startled. Then she gave a small laugh. "I'm sorry, Wally, but I didn't know I needed your permission."

"Yeah, well, I —"

"I'll be home after the movie, around eleven, I suppose. You don't need to wait up for me." A sweep of her eyes brought me into the conversation. "Now, the two of you mind Tillie and help her out with Valerie, will you?"

She retrieved her fall jacket from the closet, kissed the top of my head, and exited the house with a man neither of us had ever seen before, not even at Tillie's welcome home party.

Wally and I cornered Tillie in the kitchen. "Did you know Mom was going out to-night?" Wally demanded.

Tillie was kneading a batch of biscuit dough and didn't let Wally's question inter-rupt her work. "Of course. She put me in

135

charge of you kids."

"So why didn't she tell *us* she was going out?"

"I don't know, Wally." Tillie kneaded and shrugged. "Maybe she didn't want to have to fight with you about it."

"I wouldn't have fought with her about it. I would have just told her not to go."

"And why not?"

"Because the last thing we need around here is another man."

"Merciful heavens, Wally, she's not marrying him. She's just going to a movie with him."

"Yeah, and one thing leads to another, and next thing you know . . ." Wally slapped his hands together loudly. What that meant, I didn't know.

Tillie flattened the biscuit dough with her rolling pin. "Now, look, Wally. I know what you're thinking and I know what you're afraid of —"

"I'm not afraid of anything —"

"Not every man in the world is like your father."

Wally clamped his jaw shut and looked at Tillie. "He's not *my* father," he said.

"Be that as it may," Tillie countered, "your mother deserves some happiness. Wally, wait a minute. Where are you going?"

136

"Out." Wally flung open the kitchen door, slamming it shut behind him.

I looked at Tillie, who looked at me. She shrugged, picked up the cookie cutter, and cut circles in the dough. "He's going to have to let your mother live her own life," she said quietly.

"But, Tillie?"

"Yes, Roz?"

"Is he a nice man?"

"Mr. Barrows? I don't know him all that well, but he has a good reputation around town. He's county clerk, you know. Has been for years. Works over there in the courthouse in Wheaton."

"Oh yeah? Well, he looks kind of . . . I don't know. Boring, I guess."

"Maybe boring is exactly what your mother needs, after the last man she had."

She laughed lightly at that, but I didn't think it was funny. The last man in Mom's life was my father. Not Wally's father but mine.

I narrowed my eyes and wrinkled my nose. "But he's old and ugly, and anyway, isn't he married by now?"

Tillie nodded. "He was once. Some years back."

"So what happened?"

"The story I heard was that one of his

deputies left a pile of divorce filings on his desk. Tom looked through them and found his own, and that was how his wife let him know she was leaving him."

"She left him?"

"She did. Poor Tom didn't contest the divorce. He signed the papers, and even before the ink was dry, his wife ran off to Montana with the deputy county clerk."

"The one who left the papers on the desk?"

"One and the same."

I went back to setting the table. I couldn't help wondering whether Tom Barrows sat on his porch steps crying when his wife left him. It almost made me feel sorry for the guy, because I was sure he must be lonely, but I was just as sure I didn't want my mother to be the answer to his loneliness. One glance at him told me he'd never make her happy.

Tillie laid the biscuits on a baking sheet and slid them into the oven.

"Tillie?"

"Uh-huh?"

"You think Mom will really get married again someday?"

Shutting the oven door, Tillie turned to me and said, "Don't tell me you don't want your mother's happiness either. You're not like Wally, I hope."

"No, I . . ." I stopped, thought a moment, said quietly, "I *do* want Mom to be happy. That's the thing."

"Listen, Roz, a pretty young lady like your mother is going to get married again someday. I'd bet my bottom dollar on it. But like I said to Wally, going out on one date with Tom Barrows doesn't mean your mom is going to marry the man. Maybe she just wanted to get out of the house. Or maybe it was a movie she really wanted to see but she didn't want to spend the money on it herself. Who knows?" She smiled and shrugged. "There's no use trying to cross any bridges before you reach them."

I wasn't trying to cross any bridges. I just didn't want Mom walking down the aisle with Tom Barrows or any other man that wasn't Daddy. I wanted nothing to get in the way of the dream that had lately been taking shape in my mind, that of Daddy drinking the magic potion and becoming the good Dr. Jekyll permanently so he could come home again. He would come home, and we would all be a family like we were before — the way we were on the good days, when he acted like he loved us and we were happy.

I didn't realize until the night Tom Barrows showed up to run interference that what I wanted more than anything else in the world was Daddy.

CHAPTER 11

On Saturday morning I awoke to the aroma of bacon frying on the stove. Throwing on my bathrobe, vaguely aware I wasn't feeling well, I moved groggily downstairs to see whether Mom or Tillie was in the kitchen.

It was Mom, her apron tied around her waist over her long flannel nightgown. Valerie was in her high chair drinking orange juice. I stood in the hall for a moment studying Mom, looking for telltale signs of love and possible impending matrimony, but she looked the same as always — a little tired, pretty in spite of her rumpled hair, intent on the task at hand.

"Mom?"

Startled, she turned abruptly. "Oh, Roz! Good morning, honey. How's my sweetheart?"

How was I? Taking stock, I realized I was gritting my teeth against a sore throat and trying not to swallow. I didn't want to be sick. "I'm good," I said. "How was your . . . um, how was the movie?"

"Oh, I don't know. It was kind of ho-hum, really. Nothing you would have enjoyed."

"So you didn't have a good time?" I asked hopefully.

"Oh no. I didn't say that. It was all very nice, really."

That being the case, I didn't want to talk about it. I didn't want to know anything about this Tom Barrows fellow. Maybe if we didn't say his name, he'd go away.

"Are you working today?"

"Not today. It's my Saturday off."

"Where's Tillie?"

"She was in the shower when I came down. Listen, honey, while I'm making the scrambled eggs, would you mind pouring Valerie a bowl of Cheerios?"

I pulled Valerie's plastic bowl from the cupboard, poured cereal and milk into it, then set it on the tray in front of her. I picked up her little spoon from the tray and put it in her pudgy fist. "There you go, scooter pie," I said.

Mom stopped beating the eggs and looked at me over her shoulder.

I bit my lower lip sheepishly. "Sorry, Mom," I said. "It just came out." Scooter pie was what Daddy had always called

Valerie. Now that nickname brought Daddy into the house in a rush of bad memories.

Mom sighed heavily and shut her eyes a moment, as though waiting for the images to pass. When she drew in her next breath, she opened her eyes and tried to smile at me. Then she went back to beating the eggs — this time with a little more force, so that some of the goop splashed over the sides of the bowl and made yellow puddles on the counter.

I turned to Valerie and made a funny face. "Rozzy funny," she said with a laugh. I kissed her forehead and poured myself a cup of milk to drink. The cold felt good against my throat.

"Mom, can I go down to the drugstore today to get an ice cream cone?" I asked. "I'll use my own allowance money."

"I suppose that'll be all right. But I'd like to see you get some of your homework done first."

The morning dragged by as I worked and reworked long division problems. At my desk in my room, I could hear Mom and Wally downstairs arguing about Mom's date the night before.

"I'm just saying you could have asked me first," Wally said.

"What did you expect me to do, Wally?

Tell him I have to ask my *son's* permission to have dinner with him?"

"When we left Minnesota, you said it was just going to be the four of us from now on —"

"Well, I didn't mean I'd never —"

"And now, to start off, we've got some crazy old lady living with us —"

Tillie called from somewhere else in the house, "That's a fine way to talk about the person who's opened her home to you, young man."

"*We* own the house, Tillie, not you —"

"That's paperwork, Wally. All paperwork."

"Yeah, and money. Plenty of that."

"What's money compared to —"

"Yeah, I know, I know. Sweat equity. Stuff it, Tillie, I'm tired of hearing —"

Mom interrupted. "Wally, I won't have you talking to Tillie like that. You know we'd be in deep trouble without her."

"Well, if she came here to die, why doesn't she just go ahead and do it. What's she waiting for?"

"Wally!"

Tillie again. "I can't go until the Lord calls my name, and so far I don't hear Him calling."

"Wally, you apologize to Tillie this minute," Mom said.

"Nothing doing. I'm going to work. I'm already late."

The front door slammed. The house was quiet. I lifted my head and looked out the window, watching Wally pound down the sidewalk toward town.

"I'm sorry, Tillie," Mom said. "Honestly, sometimes I don't know what I'm going to do with that boy."

"Not to worry, Janis. If he thinks life will be better when I'm gone, he's just whistling Dixie. Just wait till it really happens. We'll see who's sorry then."

Mara was on the bench sipping a fountain drink by the time I got there. She squinted up at me against the sun. "I thought maybe you weren't coming," she said.

"My mom made me eat some lunch before I came."

"You want some ice cream?"

I shook my head, sat down on the bench. "Naw. I don't think so."

"You sick or something?"

"I don't know. I don't feel so good."

"What's the matter?"

I shrugged. "Just a sore throat."

"Maybe you shouldn't have come."

"I wanted to."

She looked at me a moment, put her lips

to the straw. Her cheeks caved in as she sipped. "Well, I'm glad you came. I've been wanting to talk to you."

"What about?"

"Well, I don't know. Anything. That's what friends do, right?"

I nodded. "Yeah. I guess so."

"So." She took another long sip while she looked out over the street. "How come you moved here all the way from Minnesota?"

I rolled my eyes toward the sky as I thought about how to answer. I thought for so long my new friend grew impatient. "Never mind," she said. "Forget I asked, if you don't want to tell me."

Drawing in a deep breath, I let it out quickly with the words, "Listen, Mara, I'll tell you why, but you have to swear never to tell anyone else."

Mara frowned, cocked her head at me. "All right. I swear."

For a moment our gazes met. Something told me I could trust the person behind those big brown eyes. I shifted my focus to the street and said quietly, "My parents split up. My grandpa lives here, so he helped us move down. Mom wanted to get away from Daddy."

Mara nodded as she went on sipping her drink. Finally she said, "What's so bad about it that you have to keep it a secret? Lots of kids' parents get divorced."

I shrugged, made a small taut line of my mouth.

Mara said, "There's more, isn't there?"

I nodded.

"I bet your daddy was a drunk."

Wide-eyed, I heard myself whisper, "How did you know?"

"Why else would a woman want to get away from a man?"

We didn't say anything for a long while. I listened as Mara slurped up the last drops of her soda. Then she said, "Did he ever beat her?"

I froze, every muscle in my body stiff as ice. How to answer? How to tell someone I hardly knew that my daddy had hit my mother more times than I could remember? It was a part of him that I wanted to forget, a part of him that I wanted to seal up behind a brick wall, so it couldn't escape and I wouldn't have to see it anymore. I swallowed the truth and shook my head. "No," I lied. "He never hit my mom."

"You were lucky then," she said. "Lots of men, once they get real drunk, they end up taking it out on their wife and kids."

"Yeah, well, not my daddy. He was always pretty good to us. He'd do a lot of fun stuff with me — you know, take me places, buy me things, stuff like that."

"Uh-huh." She sounded like she didn't quite believe me. "So your mama just got tired of the drinking."

"Yeah."

"He couldn't quit?"

I had to think a minute. "I don't think he ever tried."

"Not even when your mama left him? Sometimes a man will straighten up once his woman works up the courage to leave."

I shrugged. "If he's trying to quit, I don't know about it. We haven't been gone all that long, but we don't hear anything from Daddy."

"He doesn't have visiting rights?"

"I don't think so."

"Then you'll never see him again."

I wanted to tell Mara that I thought I *had* seen him, that I'd spotted someone in Mills River who wore a fishing hat just like his and maybe it *was* him, though I couldn't be sure. I said, "I don't know. I suppose I'll see him someday."

"Yeah," Mara said. "Maybe."

"Well, you're lucky. Your mom and dad are still together."

Mara's eyes grew small at that, and she lifted her hand to the locket that hung

148

around her neck. She didn't say anything.

"You got any brothers and sisters?" I asked.

"A whole slew of them," Mara said. She fingered the locket for a moment before tucking it under her shirt. "They're all a lot older than me. My mom and dad, they're grandparents already. They were grandparents before I was born."

I nodded. "I thought you might be a whoopsie."

"A whoopsie?" she echoed. "What's that?"

"That's what Daddy called a kid whose parents weren't trying to have any kids, but one came along anyway."

"A whoopsie," Mara said again, sounding out the word. "Yeah, your daddy's right. That's what I am."

"But that's nothing bad, you know."

"It isn't?"

"My mom says whoopsies must be destined for something special, because they come along even though nobody wants them. I mean, of course their parents want them after they're born, but . . . you know what I mean."

Mara nodded doubtfully. "I know I wasn't supposed to be here, but I'm here anyway. I hope your mom's right. I want to do something special."

"Like what?"

"Well, I want to be a college professor for one thing, and on top of that I want to be a writer, a great writer," she said. Her eyes took on a faraway look as she added quietly, "Like my daddy."

"Like your daddy?" I asked.

She snapped back to the present and turned to me warily. "Promise you won't —"

"Roz!"

Mara and I turned as one in the direction of the voice. Tillie was lumbering down the sidewalk, pulling the empty wagon behind her.

I lifted a hand, none too eagerly. "Hi, Tillie."

"Who's that?" Mara asked.

"Tillie. She lives with us and helps my mom with the housework and stuff."

"Like she's your maid or something?"

"Kind of. But don't tell her that. She thinks she owns our house."

"What?"

Tillie drew up alongside the bench and, stopped. "Your mom said you were here getting ice cream. I'm on my way to Jewel to pick up some groceries. Do you want to come along?"

I shook my head. "I don't think so."

150

She looked at Mara and back at me. Smiling, she asked, "Who's your friend?"

"Mara Nightingale," I said. "I know her from school."

"Nightingale," Tillie repeated. "Why, I know your folks. Willie and Hester, right?"

"Yes, ma'am." Mara nodded.

"Oh yes. Fine people, those two. We were on Mayor Hamilton's race relations committee some years back. We managed to get the roads paved for the Negro folks over in Crestmont. Got streetlights put in too. Folks in Mills River, well . . . I like to think we're ahead of our time."

"Yes, ma'am." Another nod.

"Though I predict the day's going to come when we won't see segregated neighborhoods the way we do now. Someday, whites and blacks will be neighbors, living side by side. Won't that be something?"

"Yes, ma'am. That'll be something."

"Is your mother still doing alterations down at Goodwin's?"

"Yes, ma'am. She's still there."

Tillie gave a satisfied nod. "She's one of the best seamstresses around. She did both my daughters-in-law's wedding gowns, you know."

"No, ma'am, I didn't know."

"You take after her? You like to sew?"

"No, ma'am. I'm no good with a needle."

"She's going to be a writer," I broke in. "She writes poetry and stuff. And, Mara, you don't have to say *ma'am* to Tillie. She's just Tillie."

Tillie didn't hear what I said to Mara because she was leaning over me, studying my face as though it were something indecipherable. "Merciful heavens, Roz!" she cried at last. "Your cheeks are all flushed. You not feeling well?"

By now I felt too lousy to try to hide it. I shook my head at Tillie and shrugged.

She laid a hand on my forehead. "You're burning with fever, child. I've got to get you home and into bed. Come on." She waved toward the wagon. "Hop in and I'll pull you."

"That's all right, Tillie," I said. "I can walk."

"Over my dead body. No child of mine is going to walk six blocks with a fever."

"But, Tillie —"

"In, young lady!"

I looked at Mara and made a face of feigned disgust. Secretly, I was glad to have Tillie pull me home.

"Soon as we get home, I'm calling Dr. Sawyer," Tillie said as I picked myself up off the bench. "He took care of all my boys.

I know I'm perfectly capable of nursing you back to health on my own, but let's call the doctor this time around, just to be on the safe side."

I settled in the wagon and, drawing my knees up to one cheekbone, made a pillow of my kneecaps.

"Hope I see you in school on Monday, Roz."

I lifted a hand toward Mara. I felt myself sinking fast.

"You give my regards to your folks, all right, Mara?" Tillie said amiably.

"Yes, ma'am, I will."

"Say, is your father still at Tinkerman's Garage?"

Mara didn't respond for a moment. Her eyes darted from me to Tillie and back again. Finally, very quietly, she said, "Yes, ma'am, he is."

"That's good to know. Mrs. Anthony's car could use some work and I need a good mechanic. I'll call Tinkerman's on Monday, see if Mr. Tinkerman can get Willie to look under the hood."

Mara lifted her chin in a small nod even as her eyes rolled toward me. Something unspoken passed between us, something sad and hurtful. When the wagon started up with a jerk, she looked away.

Our first real conversation as friends, and already she had lied to me about her daddy.

CHAPTER 12

Dr. Sawyer gave me a shot of penicillin and ordered three days of bed rest. Tillie played nursemaid, making chicken soup, bringing me aspirin, tracking my temperature. I read and worked on schoolwork and slept.

On Monday afternoon I awoke from a nap to find Tillie propped up on pillows on the other bed in my room, another pillow beneath the heels of her stocking feet, the newspaper spread open across her lap. But she wasn't reading. She was staring off into space with that glazed-over look in her eyes that I'd seen before. She could sit motionless like that for long stretches of time, gazing out the window or down at the floor, her eyes dull and more or less sightless, as though someone had pulled down the shades. Mom decided when Tillie got like that, she was napping with her eyes open. Wally complained that she'd gone catatonic on us. Once he said it loud enough for her to hear, and she snapped out of it long enough to say, "Keep it up and I'll show you catatonic, young man."

I pushed myself up on one elbow and asked quietly, "Tillie?"

No answer.

A little louder this time. "Tillie?"

She turned to me then, and it was almost as though I could see her coming back from far away. Once she was there, she said, "Yes, Roz?"

"What are you doing?"

"Oh." She smiled a small wistful smile. "Just remembering."

"Remembering what?"

Instead of answering my question, she said, "Do you realize how much of our lives we forget?"

She waited for an answer, but I didn't have one. I simply frowned and shook my head.

"Just think of it," she went on. "Every day has one thousand, four hundred and forty minutes. Did you know that?"

"No."

"That's a whole boatload of minutes."

"Yeah. I guess so."

"So if you multiply that by the number of days in a year, you get more than half a million. Every year you live more than half a million minutes, unless it's a leap year, and then you live one thousand, four hundred and forty minutes more. Like next year. Next year is a leap year, you know."

"Yeah? I didn't know that."

"Now, when you've lived for seventy years like I have, do you know how many minutes that is?"

She didn't go on. I fidgeted on the bed. "You don't want me to figure that out, do you, because I'm not that good at multiplying."

She smiled, shook her head. "No, you don't have to figure it out. Because by the end of the day — well, just by the end of the hour — it'll be a different number anyway. They're always going by, on and on and on, never stopping. So by the time you're my age, it's not just one boat you're talking about but a whole fleet. A whole fleet of minutes have sailed on by. And where do you suppose they all sail off to, Roz?"

By now my face was scrunched up into a tight ball of puzzlement. "I don't know, Tillie," I said.

"Well, I'll tell you, then."

"Okay."

"They sail right on over the horizon, and you never see them again, and most of them, you forget they ever were at all. Off they go, and" — she waved a hand — "they're as good as lost. You might as well never have lived them. *Unless,*" she said, looking intently at me now, "unless you make the effort to remember. If you go after them, you'll find some of them. A few, not many. But some."

"So is that what you do?"

Tillie nodded. "Oh yes. I ask God to help me remember the forgotten moments, and he always brings something good to mind."

"Like what?" I pushed my pillows up against the headboard and leaned back to listen.

"Well, like the time I was pinning up the laundry on the clothesline out back, and the neighbor next door — not Esther Kinshaw but a woman named Doris Haversham who used to live in the house on the other side — well, she had all her windows wide open, and she was playing a piece by Chopin on the piano. It was the most glorious thing. It was almost like being at Carnegie Hall, only better, because the open sky was my auditorium and I was the only one in the audience.

"And then there was the time — it was a winter night, and I was so cold but so exhausted from the babies I couldn't wake myself up enough to grab an extra blanket. But when Ross came to bed, he put a blanket over me, tucking it up under my chin. And then I was warm in body and soul both, because someone was taking care of me.

"And I remember the summer day when Johnny was little and he picked a fistful of dandelions for me from out in the yard. He was so proud when he gave them to me, I just had to put them in a vase and put them at the center of the dining room table. I couldn't bring myself to throw them away until they'd wilted beyond all recognition."

She was smiling as she spoke, and when she finished she went on smiling. I continued to be puzzled. "That's what you find when you go to this place of lost time?" I asked.

"Yes, lots of moments like those."

"What's so great about that stuff?"

"Oh, my dear!" Tillie said, her blue eyes wide. "Everything! That's the point. People look for greatness only in the extraordinary and completely overlook the wonder of the ordinary. That's why those moments are all forgotten, counted as nothing. It's a terrible loss."

She gathered up the pages of the newspaper and folded them. Then she sighed. "I don't expect you to understand, Roz. You're too young. You haven't lost enough time yet to care."

I thought about that for a moment. Then I said, "Maybe I understand a little, Tillie. It's like when you said I should remember the good things about Daddy and put all those memories in a safe place so I wouldn't forget them."

She shut her eyes, nodded, opened her eyes again. She smiled a warm, motherly smile at me. "I do believe you're on your way, Roz." She swung her feet over the side of the bed and wiggled them into the flats she wore around the house.

"Tillie?"

"Yes, child?"

"My daddy — do you think I'll ever see him again?"

She stood, smoothed out the bedcovers, then turned to gaze at me. "Probably. Someday. But we'll pray that by the time you see him again, he'll have changed. Until God gets that temper of his under control, I think it's best you stay away."

"But —"

"No telling what a man like that could do, even if he did treat you right sometimes."

"But, I think . . . Tillie, I think I might have seen . . ." I couldn't finish.

160

"What, Roz?"

I wanted to tell her, but something held me back. "I think I might have seen some gingersnaps in the cupboard," I said lamely. "Can I have some? I'm hungry."

"Not before supper, you don't. And no special favors just because you're sick."

"Okay, Tillie." I nodded and watched her as she left the room. When she was gone, I pushed back the covers and walked to the window. I looked out expectantly, half hoping to see Daddy out there on the sidewalk and half wondering whether Tillie was right, that there was no telling what Daddy might do should he find us here in Mills River.

CHAPTER 13

Two days later I stood in the doorway of Wally's room, dressed for school, my hair in pigtails. Wally, still in pajamas, lay stretched out on his bed, reading a book. He lowered the book an inch and stared at me over the top. "You back from the dead?" he asked.

"Very funny, Wally."

"Yeah? So what do you want?"

"Mom says to hurry up and get ready for school."

"Can't you see I'm busy?"

"Doing what?"

"Reading."

"You've already read that book a hundred times."

"Yeah. Kerouac had the right idea. A man should be on the road."

"You planning on taking a trip or something?"

Wally raised an eyebrow. "None of your business."

Just then Mom hollered up the stairs, "Roz, tell Wally if he doesn't come down for breakfast now, he'll miss the bus."

I glanced over my shoulder, then back at Wally. "Mom says —"

"Yeah, I heard." He closed *On the Road* and laid it on the bed.

"Well?" I asked.

Tucking his hands under his head, he stared up at the ceiling. "Where I'm going a person doesn't need school."

"Where are you going?"

"Like I said, Roz, that's none of your business."

Mom's voice came up the stairs again, "Wallace Franklin Sanderson! Don't make me come up there and get you!"

Wally sighed heavily, rolled off the bed, and pushed past me on his way to the bathroom. I stared after him, wondering if he'd be different somehow if Frank Sanderson hadn't been gunned down in Korea. But then, if Frank Sanderson hadn't died, I wouldn't be here and neither would Valerie. I didn't care to think about which of us Mom and Wally would rather have around. I was afraid of the answer.

Mara was waiting for me in front of the school, where the buses unloaded. She looked schoolgirl fresh in a white blouse and plaid skirt, a pair of Buster Browns on her feet. She wore a light brown cardigan against the morning chill, a color that matched exactly the creamy brown of her skin. Her dark hair was pulled back into a tight braid and held with clips. I thought she looked pretty and almost said so, until I remembered Saturday.

She strode up to me quickly, clutching her books in her arms. "You're finally back, Roz," she said. "You feeling better?"

"I'm all right." I diverted my eyes and kept on walking.

"Listen, about Saturday . . ." Her voice trailed off as she rushed to keep pace with me.

"What about it?" I had to speak loudly over the chatter of dozens of kids moving up the walkway toward the school.

"I wanted to explain."

"Explain what?"

"Listen, Roz, I know you think I lied. About my daddy, I mean."

"It doesn't matter."

"Yes it does. It matters. Won't you hold up just a minute so I can talk to you?"

We were inside the front hall now, where she would turn one way and I would turn another.

"We'll be late for homeroom," I said.

Her eyes narrowed. "So you just want to be mad at me?"

"I'm not mad at you."

"Yes you are."

"Your daddy is a mechanic who writes books on the side." I shrugged. "I get it."

We stood there a moment, an island in the stream of restless kids. Her face registered hurt, but I couldn't bring myself to back down.

She exhaled slowly, loosening her grip on her books. She fingered the locket she always wore around her neck, as though rubbing it gave her comfort. "Never mind, Roz," she said quietly. "You're right. It doesn't matter."

She turned and headed down the hall. I almost called after her, but even as I opened my mouth the morning bell rang. I rushed to class, my penny loafers adding to the tap-tap-tapping of a hundred footfalls against the polished floor. When I told Mara I wasn't mad at her, I had spoken the truth. I was mad, but not at her. At Wally, yes. At Daddy, yes. At the world. At life itself. But not at Mara. Why, then, had I treated her like that?

When I reached my homeroom, Miss Fremont greeted me kindly, her eyes shining behind her white cat-eye glasses. "Good morning, Roz. Welcome back. Are you feeling better?"

"Yes, thank you. I'm fine now."

A smile from Miss Fremont was a rare thing, but this morning she was all smiles. "I'm glad to hear that, Roz. I'm sure your whole family is glad you're feeling better too."

"Um, yeah. I guess so." The room had quieted, and I had a feeling all the other kids were curious about our teacher's sudden interest in my health. There'd been plenty of sick kids before me, but none of them had been welcomed back. It made me uncomfortable.

"Well," Miss Fremont said, "go ahead and hang up your sweater, then take your seat." She nodded at my desk and smiled again — strangely, I thought, as though she and I shared a secret.

I did as I was told, and as I moved about my tasks, my thoughts returned to Mara. Sliding into my seat, I promised myself I would somehow make things right. I would think of a way to apologize to her at recess. I would think about it all morning if I had to, so that Mara would know —

My train of thought jackknifed and crashed as soon as I opened the lid of my desk to put my books away. There, among the scattered papers, pencils, and erasers, were three Sugar Daddies, tied together with a pink ribbon.

Now I knew for sure.

Daddy had found us. He was here in Mills River.

CHAPTER 14

At recess I spotted Mara sitting under the red maple on the playground, scribbling something as usual in her spiral notebook. Rushing to her, I kneeled on the grass and exhibited in my open palm the evidence of my father's presence in town.

"Mara, look," I whispered.

She raised her eyes from the notebook slowly. She studied the Sugar Daddies a moment before lifting her gaze to my face. Her own face, her eyes, her words when she spoke revealed no emotion at all. Jutting her chin ever so slightly, she said, "No, thank you. I don't care for Sugar Daddies."

I shook my head. "No, Mara. You don't get it. I —"

"If you're trying to make up with me, you're wasting your time."

"Listen, I'm not mad at you."

"Well, you sure acted like it."

"But I'm not. You've got to believe me.

I'm sorry."

"Is it because I'm part Negro?"

I hesitated a moment. "What do you mean, part Negro?"

"Never mind. I should have known better than to think a white girl would want to be friends."

"But I do, Mara. I do want to be friends. Really. Please believe me."

By now I was fighting back tears. I locked onto Mara's gaze, and after a moment I could see her whole body give in and relax. "All right," she said, "I believe you. But what's with the candy?"

I'd been kneeling all this time. Now I collapsed on the grass and leaned in closer to her. "It means my daddy's here. Here in town. He knows where we are."

Her dark eyes narrowed, and she seemed to be struggling to understand what I'd just told her. "It does?" she asked doubtfully.

"Of course it does. Who else would leave something like this in my desk?"

"You think your daddy left those in your desk?"

"Well, yeah. It had to be him."

"You don't know that, Roz. It could have been anyone."

"Like who?"

She thought a moment. "I don't know.

169

Maybe you have some kind of secret admirer, some kid who's too scared to admit he likes you." Her eyes widened, and she smiled for the first time. "Just think, Roz, wouldn't that be romantic?"

I shook my head slowly back and forth. "No, Mara, no. You don't get it. I know it was Daddy. This is the candy he used to bring me when he came home from work. It's our special candy. So I know he's here."

She pinched her lips together so they disappeared into a small tight line. Then she said, "If that's true, what are you going to do?"

"I don't know." My voice trembled as I spoke.

"You better tell your mama."

"I can't."

"Why not?"

"I don't know. I just can't. I'm scared."

"You think he might hurt you?"

I drew back. "No. Daddy wouldn't hurt me."

"Well then?"

"I don't know. I don't know what to do."

"What do you think he wants?"

"I don't know."

"Why don't you ask him?"

"Ask him? How?"

"Well . . ." She frowned as she rubbed the

side of her head. "Why don't you write him a note and put it in your desk. Maybe he's planning on leaving you something else, and if he does, he'll find it."

I sat straight up. "Good idea!"

Mara ripped a page out of her notebook. "Here," she said. "Write it on this."

I took the paper and pencil she offered me and, using my thigh as a writing table, wrote slowly, *Dear Daddy.*

I looked up at Mara. "What else should I say?"

"Ask him what he wants."

After thinking about it a few minutes, I wrote, *Thank you for the Sugar Daddies. Why are you here? Your daughter, Rosalind Anthony.*

"What do you think he's going to say?" Mara asked.

"I don't know."

Mara lifted the candy from the grass, where I'd laid it. She fingered the ribbon and said, "It was kind of nice, you know. Giving you candy and all. Maybe he wants to make up and, you know, be a family again."

I was almost too afraid to hope. "Maybe." The word was small, barely a whisper.

Her gaze lingered on the Sugar Daddies as she said, "I think you're lucky."

"You do?"

She nodded, sighing wistfully. "Maybe your story will have a happy ending," she said, "the way it is in books. You know?"

I stared at her a moment, unsure of how to respond. I didn't have a clue what she meant, but I figured it was something a lover of books might say.

"Well," she said, "put the note in your desk and see what your daddy says."

"I will." I folded the note and held out my hand for the candy. She laid the three Sugar Daddies in my palm. "You can have one if you want," I offered.

She smiled sadly. "No, I really don't like them."

"All right." I stood to go, then remembered our earlier conversation in the hall. "What were you going to tell me about your daddy?"

She looked up at me, squinting against the afternoon sun. "Nothing important," she said.

"It's okay if it's not important. You can tell me anyway."

"Well, I'm not ashamed of Daddy being a mechanic, but sometimes I just pretend . . ."

"Pretend what?"

She lowered her eyes and closed the notebook she'd been writing in. I recognized it as the yellow spiral she'd had with her the first time we met on the bench outside the drugstore, the one with her favorite poem written on the cover. Something about holding fast to dreams so you don't become a broken-winged bird.

Mara hesitated a moment, then stood and wiped the grass and twigs off the back of her skirt. "Nothing," she said. "Come on, I'll go to your classroom with you while you put the note in your desk."

My new friend was something of a strange bird, I decided, but if she wanted to dream and pretend her daddy was something he wasn't, far be it from me to keep her from flying. Heaven knew, I had a few dreams of my own.

I held out my hand, and to my surprise, she took it. We walked across the playground toward the school, ignoring the stares of the other kids, both Negro and white. I was glad to have Mara as my friend, especially now, when I felt myself on the verge of a wonderful and life-changing adventure.

Chapter 15

"Are you feeling all right, Roz?" Mom moved across the kitchen and laid a hand on my forehead.

"I'm all right," I said.

"No sore throat?"

I shook my head while pretending to study the grammar book on the kitchen table in front of me.

"You just don't look right."

I didn't feel right. Nearly a week had passed, and Daddy hadn't picked up the note. He hadn't left more candy in my desk either. There was no sign of him, and I was beginning to wonder whether Mara had been right. Maybe someone else had left the Sugar Daddies. But I didn't want a secret admirer. I wanted Daddy.

Tillie paused in washing the dishes and looked at me over her shoulder. "Growing pains," she said.

"I don't know, Tillie," Mom said. "Maybe

Dr. Sawyer was right when he talked about getting her tonsils out."

"But I don't want to get my tonsils out, Mom!"

"You'll feel better all the way around if you do."

"But, Mom —"

"I'm not saying you *will* have your tonsils out, just that it's something to consider. I've only known you to mope around the house when you don't feel good, and I've seen a lot of moping these past few days."

"I'm fine, Mom. Really."

"Growing pains," Tillie said again. "I wouldn't worry about it too much, Janis. If she says she's fine, then I'm sure she's fine."

Mom gave me a long hard look before going back to drying the dishes. I turned my attention to the grammar book but couldn't concentrate. We had come to Mills River to get away from Daddy, and I knew I shouldn't want him to be there, but I couldn't help it. My mind was soaring to all sorts of dream places where my family was together again — only in a good way this time. My head was filled with visions of a good father, one who never drank or got angry or hit Mom, one who was always kind and loving.

"Roz," Mom said, "why don't you finish

up that homework and go on up to bed. You could probably use a good night's sleep."

I closed the book. "I can finish during homeroom tomorrow morning," I said.

"Good idea. Go on and brush your teeth. I'll be up to kiss you good-night in a minute."

"All right. Good night, Tillie."

"Good night, Roz. Sleep well."

I gathered all my books and papers and laid them on the small table in the front hall, ready to go in the morning. At the top of the stairs I peeked into Wally's room. He was at his desk by the window, drawing lines with a ruler on a sheet of graph paper. He sat with his back to me and couldn't see me watching him from the doorway.

"Wally?"

Startled, he turned his head. "Yeah?"

"What are you doing?"

"My mechanical drawing assignment. Why?"

I shrugged. "Just wondering."

He tapped the desk with the ruler a moment, then went back to work.

"Are you going to need that kind of thing where you're going?" I asked.

He laughed lightly. "It might come in handy." He drew a long line, the point of his pencil moving as slowly as a surgeon's scalpel. When he finished, he turned back around. "You need something?"

"No."

"You just feel like standing there staring at me?"

I pressed my lips together. He raised his brows. For a moment he looked like the Wally I used to know, when we were friends.

"Wally?"

"Yeah?"

"Can I ask you something?"

"Can I stop you?"

He smiled. I felt encouraged to go on. "There must have been something good about Daddy, wasn't there? I mean, I remember some good things . . ."

My words tapered off as the smile slid from his face. "Listen," he said quietly, "the best thing you can do is forget about Alan. Forget he's your father. Forget he ever existed."

My throat was tight. I didn't want to cry. "But, I mean, there was *something* good about him, wasn't there?"

Wally sat without speaking for what seemed like a long time. Finally he said, "Tell you what, Roz, if I can think of anything good about Alan, I'll let you know, all right? I promise. Now, I've got a lot of homework. You need to go away and let me finish."

I nodded. "All right." I took a step backward. "Good night, Wally. And thanks for thinking about it."

But he had already turned back to his homework and didn't respond.

CHAPTER 16

Mom gave me permission to go to the public library with Mara after school on Friday. Though we'd lived in Mills River since the summer, I hadn't yet been to the downtown library. Mara claimed she knew the place better than her own house; she had worked hard to memorize the exact location of all her favorite books, both fiction and nonfiction. When new books came into the library and old books were removed, shifting the shelf location of Mara's favorites, it left her feeling out of sorts. "I can't afford to buy all the books I want," she told me, "but I pretend the library copies are mine and I'm just letting other people use them."

The librarians all knew Mara by name, and when we arrived that Friday afternoon, the head librarian, a Mrs. Tisdale, presented Mara with two books that had the word *Withdrawn* stamped across the cover.

"I thought you might like these, Mara," Mrs. Tisdale said. She smiled as she slid them across the counter.

Mara picked them up and squealed quietly, fully aware that we had entered a sanctuary of near silence. "Thank you, Mrs. Tisdale!" she said, hugging the books to her chest.

"The library recently purchased new copies, so I saved these for you."

Both books were paperbacks, dog-eared from use. One was *The Adventures of Tom Sawyer* by Mark Twain, the other *Up From Slavery* by Booker T. Washington. The second book made me think about how, in some places not too long ago, Mara couldn't have even come into the library through the front door. She would have had to use the colored entrance, and once inside, she would have had to sit in separate rooms from the whites. Thoughts like that always hit me with a jolt. When I looked at Mara, I didn't see a Negro, I just saw Mara. Only at certain moments — like this one — did I remember that her skin was darker than mine.

"Are you here for anything in particular?" Mrs. Tisdale asked.

"We have to write a history paper on an invention. Any invention we want. I'm going to write about the printing press, and — oh yeah, this is my friend, Roz. She's new in town."

The pretty librarian looked at me, her polished lips turning up in a smile. "Well, nice to meet you. Welcome to Mills River."

"Thank you," I said shyly.

"Did Mara say your name is Ross?"

"No. It's Roz. Short for Rosalind."

"Oh yes, I see. Well, Roz, what invention are you going to write about?"

I shrugged. "I haven't decided yet."

"I'm going to show her where the nonfiction section is," Mara explained, "and let her look around."

Mrs. Tisdale nodded. "You may want to look for books on Thomas Edison. That'd be a place to start."

"All right," I said. "Thanks."

"Come on, Roz. Thanks again for the books, Mrs. Tisdale."

As I walked with Mara up the stairs to Young Adult Nonfiction, she whispered, "All the librarians know I'm going to be a great writer someday. I think they want to say they had a part in it, because they're always giving me books and stuff. I'm really lucky that way."

I nodded. She *was* lucky. I wished I had people giving me free stuff. And I wished I had a life goal. I wished I thought I was going to be great at *any*thing. But I didn't seem to have any particular talent, not like Mara and her writing.

"Here we are," she said as we came to a stop amid towering rows of books. "This is the right section, but let's look at the card catalog to see what they've got on the printing press for me and Thomas Edison for you."

An hour later she was seated at one of the tables, taking notes from several stacks of books that she'd piled around her. I was still wandering the aisles, trying in a slipshod fashion to decide what to write about. I figured everyone would pick an invention by Thomas Edison, and I wanted to do something different.

Absorbed in reading the spines of the books, I was only vaguely aware of the handful of people in the library. One teenaged girl strolled into Nonfiction, absently bumped into me, excused herself, moved on to another shelf. I scarcely glanced at her. Finally a book on Madame Curie caught my attention; I knew she had something to do with the invention of the X-ray machine. Rolling up on my toes, I had my fingers on the dust jacket when I was grabbed from behind. My mind needed a second to register that someone had me in his hold. In that second of dawning awareness my heart began to race, and I couldn't breathe. The stranger's hold was gentle, like a hug, with one hand around my waist and the other over my mouth. I instinctively tried to pull the hand away from my face so I could let go of the scream rising in my throat. But whoever held me was far stronger than I was. I sensed his face near mine. Wally? If this was a joke, it wasn't funny. I squirmed, trying to free myself, but his grasp only tightened.

"Roz, stand still. Don't scream. It's me. It's Daddy."

His breath tickled my ear, and I froze. The sound of his voice brought on a whole new rush of fear, while his words slithered like a bad dream right into my brain. I'd wanted Daddy, wanted to see him, wanted him to come back to us, but now that he was here, I wasn't so sure.

"Roz," he said again. "I'm going to let you go. But I want you to promise you won't scream. All right? Promise?"

I nodded, my wide eyes rolling and shifting rapidly as I tried to make sense of what was happening.

"Good. Good," he whispered. The pressure on my face was lifted. I realized I was holding my breath; my whole body trembled as I exhaled. Daddy's hands turned me around slowly.

And then I was looking into his face. He was kneeling now, both hands on my shoulders, his eyes roaming my face like he was drinking me in. "Oh, Little Rose. Little Rose," he said. "I've missed you."

I didn't know whether to run as fast as I could or throw my arms around him and hold on for dear life. I couldn't pull my gaze from that oh-so-familiar but forbidden face. I knew every inch of it, the lines beside his mouth, the small scar that nicked his right brow, the narrow bridge of his nose, those piercing brown eyes, soft as a doe's. They'd always perplexed me — those eyes — by speaking of tenderness. At that moment they were filled with tears.

"Daddy?" I lifted a hand to his cheek, as though I had to touch him to make sure he was real.

He smiled, nodded. "I'm here, Roz."

His skin was rough and warm. My palm tingled from his days' growth of whiskers even after I dropped my hand. "But how —"

He laid a finger to my lips. "No questions. Not now. We have so little time, but I wanted to see you."

I was still struggling to catch my breath. It was hard to speak. "You left the Sugar Daddies? In my desk?"

He nodded again.

Before either of us could say more, something caught my eye over his shoulder. At the far end of the aisle, the same teenaged girl who'd bumped into me earlier was pushing a cart of books and replacing them on the shelves. Daddy glanced over at her, then back at me.

"Roz, I've only got a minute, so I want you to listen carefully, all right?"

I met his eyes again. "All right."

He squeezed my shoulders tightly. "I can't live without you and your mom and Valerie. Ever since you went away, I've been dying inside, Roz. I want us to be together again, so . . ." He paused; he seemed to be looking for the right words. "I'm going to change, Roz. I'm going to make things right. But I need some time, so it's not going to happen overnight. Do you understand?"

I nodded, though I wasn't sure I did understand.

"I'm working on making us a better life, and I want you to know that. But meanwhile, I don't want you telling anyone you saw me. Don't tell your mother, don't tell

Wally, don't tell your friends. No one, you hear?"

I thought of Mara. "No one at all?"

"No one. Or it might ruin everything."

"But, Daddy —"

He looked back over his shoulder at the girl with the cart. "I've got to go now, Roz."

"Will I . . . Will I see you again?"

"Of course. And you can know that I'm always close by."

"But, Daddy —"

He kissed my forehead and stood. "I love you, Little Rose."

He looked at me a long while, waiting for me to respond. But I couldn't say anything. In another moment he was gone.

I stumbled weakly down the aisle and fell into a chair at the table where Mara had built her fortress of books. She paused in her writing and frowned at me. "You look like you've seen a ghost," she said.

I put my head down on the table and wept.

CHAPTER 17

The next morning I woke up sick again. This time I was diagnosed with strep throat, and this time Dr. Sawyer scheduled me for surgery in three weeks. On Friday, October 27, a few days before Halloween, I would have my tonsils removed.

No one thought about the fact that I wouldn't be able to go trick-or-treating. Not even me. All I could think about was Daddy, and when I would see him again, and whether or not he'd be able to put our Humpty-Dumpty family back together again.

In the first feverish forty-eight hours of my illness, my mind carried me back to the library and my few minutes there with Daddy. Over and over I felt his hands heavy on my shoulders, saw the look in his eyes, heard him say, "I love you, Little Rose." And in my fog, I answered, "Daddy, Daddy," until finally I awoke and saw my mother's face above me, her eyes wide with distress. Those eyes told me something awful was happening.

"What's the matter, Mom?" I asked fearfully, wondering whether I was sicker than she was letting on.

She tried to smile. "Nothing, sweetheart. Go back to sleep."

When she left, Tillie's face came into view. She too wore an odd expression. I swallowed hard in spite of the pain in my throat. "Tillie," I asked, "am I dying?"

She frowned at me. "Of course not, child."

"Then what's the matter with Mom?"

She hesitated before answering. Then she said, "You were crying for your daddy is all."

"I was?"

She nodded. "But never mind. A fever makes us do funny things. Your mother knows that."

I missed an entire week of school recovering from strep. Mara brought my homework by every day, but as much as I wanted to see her, Tillie wouldn't allow her past the front door. "We can't have that sweet little girl catching your germs and ending up sick herself," Tillie said.

Tillie worked tirelessly, nursing me back to health. She made sure I took my medicine on time; she fed me the usual homemade chicken soup and Jell-O; she plumped up my pillows and propped me up in bed so she could stick the thermometer under my tongue.

"You should have been a nurse, Tillie," I told her.

"I was," she said. "I had three boys, remember?"

My only outside visitor was Grandpa, who came by every day to read to me and help me pass the time.

"I have to have my tonsils out, Grandpa," I told him.

"So I heard. And do you know what that means?"

I shook my head.

"It means you'll get all the ice cream you want." He winked at me and smiled. I took his hand and pressed it against my cheek. How I loved Gramps. And how I wanted to tell him that Daddy was in town, right here in Mills River. I wanted to tell Gramps that I'd seen and talked with him, and that Daddy wanted me and Mom and Valerie back. Grandpa would know what to do.

"Gramps?"

"Yes, honey?"

But Daddy had said not to tell anyone, and surely that included Grandpa too. If I told, it would ruin everything.

"Grandpa, do you hate my father?" The words were a whisper.

A tiny muscle in Grandpa's jaw tightened. His brows moved lower over his eyes, and a deep line formed between them. "No, Roz," he said. "I don't hate him. I . . ." He paused and shook his head. "Listen, let's not talk about your father. You just need to rest."

"But, Gramps, there's something good about everyone, isn't there?"

Grandpa took a deep breath and let it out slowly. "Alan Anthony did one good thing," he said.

"What?"

"He gave me you." Grandpa leaned over and kissed my cheek. "I have to go home now. You close those pretty eyes and get some sleep."

In an odd sort of way, Grandpa's words comforted me. Maybe I could think of myself, and Valerie too, as something good Daddy had done. After Grandpa left, I slept, and it was a dreamless sleep. When I awoke, my fever had broken and I was on my way to getting better.

CHAPTER 18

"Of course, Hester. It's no trouble at all," Tillie said into the phone. "We'll be happy to have her stay as long as you need. Now, don't you worry about a thing."

When Tillie hung up the phone in the kitchen, I looked up from my bowl of oatmeal and caught her eye. "What was that about?" I asked.

"That was Hester Nightingale wanting to know if your little friend Mara could stay with us for a few days."

"Really?"

"Hester and Willie are going to Detroit to help out with their new grandbaby, and instead of staying with relatives here, Mara said she'd rather stay with you."

"Really! And it's all right?"

"Of course it is. You're all over the strep, and it'll be nice for you to have a friend here for a while. Willie and Hester will drop her off tomorrow afternoon on their way out of town. I figure she can sleep in your extra bed, can't she?"

"Sure she can!" I cried. "This is going to be fun!"

When the doorbell rang on Sunday afternoon, I flew down the stairs to get it. But by the time I reached the bottom step, Mom was already opening the door to Mara and her parents.

"Hello, Mrs. Nightingale, Mr. Nightingale. Won't you come in and have some coffee before you head out?"

Mr. Nightingale, carrying two suitcases, stepped sideways on his long legs into the front hall. He set down the suitcases and took off his fedora as Mrs. Nightingale and Mara stepped inside. "Thank you, Mrs. Anthony," he said, "but we've got a long drive ahead of us, so we best be on our way."

Mrs. Nightingale nodded and added, "But we're grateful, Mrs. Anthony, for your willingness to look after Mara while we're gone."

"Well, we're very happy to have her," Mom said.

Mara and I exchanged a smile as she pulled off her knit cap and unbuttoned her coat. "Hi, Roz," she said. "How are you feeling?"

"I'm better. But I have to have my tonsils out."

Mara grimaced and nodded. "I've had mine out —"

"There's nothing to it, honey," Mrs. Nightingale said, smiling at me. "Snip, snip, and they're gone."

It was the snip-snipping that worried me, but I tried to shrug nonchalantly. "I guess so," I said.

Tillie came out of the kitchen, wiping her hands on a dish towel. "Hello, Willie, Hester. Mara, honey, let me take your coat. Won't you all come in and have something to drink?"

Mr. Nightingale repeated his earlier regrets and thanked Tillie for the offer.

"Oh, by the way, Willie, since we're speaking of driving," Tillie went on, "the car's been running better than ever since you gave her that tune-up. You do work wonders, you know."

Mr. Nightingale smiled shyly. "That's fine, Mrs. Monroe. I'm glad to hear that. Any time you have problems, you bring the car to me."

"We will, certainly," Mom interjected.

Mrs. Nightingale pulled a piece of paper out of her pocketbook and handed it to Mom. "Here's the number where we'll be, just in case. Celia Greer, that's our daughter. We'll be staying with her."

Mom looked at the paper and nodded confidently. "I'm sure everything will be fine. You just go enjoy that new grandbaby of yours."

The Nightingales both smiled broadly at that, their white teeth shining in keen contrast to their dark skin. "We'll do that, Mrs. Anthony," Hester Nightingale said. "And thank you again for watching Mara." She leaned over and kissed Mara's cheek. "Now you be good, baby, and mind your manners."

"I will, Mama."

Her father laid his oversized hand on her head and patted her hair gently. His nails and palms were pink, though the skin on the back of his hand was tough and wrinkled as an elephant's. "Bye now, baby girl," he said quietly. "We'll be back in about a week."

"All right, Daddy." She hugged him around the waist, then picked up her suitcases and looked at me. "Where's your room?" she asked.

"Upstairs. Come on!"

I showed Mara the way and pointed to the bed that would be hers. She dropped the suitcases on it and sat beside them cross-legged. "I've been checking your desk at school every day while you've been gone," she said.

"You have?" I sat down on my own bed and cocked my head.

"Yeah. You know, to check on the note to your daddy. It's still there. He hasn't come."

"Oh." I looked past her to the window, not wanting to lie but afraid to tell her the truth, that I'd seen Daddy at the library. Now that I knew Daddy was in town, and now that I knew what he wanted, I'd get rid of the note in my desk in the morning. "Well —"

"Maybe whoever left those Sugar Daddies wasn't your daddy."

I couldn't bring myself to look at her. "Maybe."

"I'm sorry, Roz."

"It's all right."

"I know you were hoping . . ."

I shook my head. "It doesn't matter. What's in your suitcases?"

Mara looked at the suitcases wide-eyed. "I'll show you." She tapped on one of them, saying, "This is just clothes and stuff, but this one . . ." She finished by pulling the suitcase toward her and popping the two latches. She opened the lid and smiled at me, as though she were showing me a treasure.

"What's with all the books?" I asked.

"You haven't done your report on Marie Curie. I'm going to help you get it done, so I checked out every book in the library that says anything about her."

"All those books are about Madame Curie?"

"Well, not all of them. Some of them I'm just reading for fun. Like this one." She lifted one of the books so I could see the cover.

I squinted, as much in exasperation as in an effort to read from several feet away. *"Greatest American Poems of the Twentieth Century?* You read that kind of stuff for fun?"

"Sure! I love poetry. Besides, how am I going to be a great writer if I don't read important stuff?" She was beaming. I was frowning. She didn't seem to notice. "Do you want to start reading about Madame Curie?" she asked.

Schoolwork hadn't exactly been on my list of things to do when I learned Mara was coming over. But she'd gone to the trouble of getting the books I needed for my report, and anyway, I didn't want to disappoint her.

"Yeah, okay," I said with a shrug. "I guess I should get started on that paper."

I sure hadn't had any friends in Minneapolis like Mara Nightingale. She was like a grown-up living inside a little girl's skin. But I liked her, and so far she was my one and only friend in Mills River.

I took the book she offered and together we quietly read about the life and work of Madame Curie until finally, to my relief, Tillie called us down to supper.

That night, when I turned out the bedroom light at nine o'clock, Mara turned on a transistor radio she'd brought along with her.

"What are you doing?" I asked.

"Listening to a show. Will it bother you?"

"No, it's all right. What is it?"

"*The Literary Hour With William Remmick.* Though I don't know why they call it that, since it only lasts a half hour."

"I never heard of it."

"No, I didn't think you would have. It's coming out of Chicago."

"What's it about?"

"You know, books and stuff. Professor Remmick, he interviews authors and talks about their books. Stuff like that."

The radio was turned down low, nestled on the pillow close to Mara's ear. I heard the murmur of voices, first a man's voice, then a woman's. I couldn't quite make out the words, but I knew I wouldn't be interested anyway. I wondered why Mara wanted to listen to a show like that. I wondered even more why she'd rather listen to a grown-up talk show than talk with me. Mom had told us to go to sleep, but I'd have gladly lain awake whispering in the dark with Mara, and would have too, if it hadn't been for the radio putting a wedge between us.

I tried to keep the hurt out of my voice when I said, "Do you listen to this show every night?"

"No," she said. "Just Sundays and Wednesdays. That's when it's on."

"Oh, okay." I lay on my back in the dark, looking up at the ceiling. Laughter came from the radio, and Mara chuckled along with it. I felt like I'd been abandoned. "Well, I'm going to sleep now. Good night, Mara."

"Good night, Roz."

She probably thought I drifted off, but I didn't. Not quite, anyway. I might have been right on the edge of sleep, but after a time my dreams got snagged by the show's theme song rising up from Mara's pillow. Mara must have turned the volume up a notch, because I heard the man's voice say, "That's it for tonight, folks. We'll see you again on Wednesday, when we'll be interviewing best-selling author J. P. Westmoreland. Until then, this is William Remmick saying good-night and thank you for joining us. And good night to you, Beatrice. Sweet dreams."

And then Mara's soft voice drifted toward me as she whispered to that faraway man, "Good night, Daddy. I love you."

The radio clicked off, the room fell silent, and in another moment Mara's steady breathing told me she was asleep.

CHAPTER 19

In the morning, I didn't say anything to Mara about the man on the radio. But over the next three days, as we went to school, worked on homework, ate supper, helped Tillie with dishes, played with Valerie, and fell asleep side by side in the twin beds in my room, I regarded her with no small amount of suspicion. I had heard that crazy people could appear completely normal, and I wondered whether that was the case with Mara Nightingale. I thought maybe her dreams had carried her into a fantasyland and somehow imprisoned her there, though *imprisoned* may not be the right word. Maybe she wanted to stay in that place of make-believe, where some guy on the radio was her father. Maybe she was happier there than in the real world, since in the real world her daddy was a mechanic and not a professor of literature.

I couldn't wait for Wednesday night. I

wanted to see what Mara would do when the show came on again.

At nine o'clock I turned out the light. I heard the radio click on in the dark.

"Will it bother you?" she asked.

"No. It's all right. It won't keep me awake."

"Good night, then, Roz."

"Good night, Mara."

I didn't close my eyes. I pinched my earlobes against sleep as I listened to the low rumbling of Professor Remmick's voice. I heard Mara alternately sigh and softly laugh. After my eyes adjusted to the dark, I could make out the shape of her in the other bed. Her hand rested on the radio by her ear, and by the end of the half hour the little box was pressed against her cheek.

Then, as on Sunday night, the closing tune began to play, and this man named William Remmick signed off, saying, "That's it for tonight, folks. We'll see you again on Sunday, when my colleague Dr. Margaret Jamison will join us to talk about what's new in the *New York Times* Book Review. Until then, this is William Remmick saying good-night and thank you for joining us. And good night to you, Beatrice. Sweet dreams."

And then, as on Sunday night, Mara

whispered, "Good night, Daddy. I love you."

The radio clicked off. Mara placed it on the table between the beds, sighed, and rolled over. But this time I wasn't going to let it go.

I sat up and turned on the light. Mara, blinking, looked at me over her shoulder. For a long moment, neither of us spoke.

Then finally she said, "I thought you were asleep."

I narrowed my eyes. "Well, I wasn't."

She sat up and nodded. Her face was placid; her lips hinted at a smile. "Roz?"

I hesitated. My heart was pounding. She was scaring me, and I was ready to run, if need be. "Yeah?" I said.

"I want to read you something."

"Um, okay."

She had placed the radio on top of a paperback book. She reached for that book now, and when she opened it I saw it was the book of poetry she'd brought along, *Greatest American Poems of the Twentieth Century.*

She found her page, glanced up at me, and began to read. " 'Cross,' " she said, " 'by Langston Hughes.' " She looked at me again, uneasily now, and took a deep breath. In a quiet, almost faltering voice, she read, " 'My old man's a white old man, and my old mother's black.' " She stopped, shifted nervously, then sat up straighter and crossed her legs. She went on then, and though her voice went up in volume I didn't hear what she was saying. The first words of the poem were stuck in spin cycle in my head. A white old man? A black old mother? What was Mara trying to tell me? When she stopped once more she paused for so long I thought she was finished.

"Mara?" I said.

She didn't look at me, but raised one index finger to tell me to wait. She went on to read about the old man dying in a nice big house while the woman died in a shack, and finally, her voice dropping to a whisper, she concluded, " 'I wonder where I'm gonna die, being neither white nor black.' "

With that, she closed the book, pressed her lips together, and raised her eyes to mine. Those two dark eyes were filled with something I couldn't quite understand. Sadness? Shame? Longing?

I thought of the couple who had dropped Mara off at our house, the man and the woman in worn old coats, sadly outdated hats and shoes — and yet, on top of everything, a cloak of quiet dignity. Was she trying to tell me that this couple, Willie and Hester Nightingale, were not her father and

203

mother after all but some sort of adoptive parents?

"Mara?" I asked quietly, drawing my knees up to my chest in a kind of protective stance.

"Roz, I want to tell you something no one else knows. At least, not many people."

Why? I wanted to ask. Why me? I hugged my knees more tightly.

As though in answer to my unasked question, she said, "We're friends, aren't we?"

"Yeah."

"And I can trust you, right?"

I nodded.

She beckoned me over to her bed with a crook of her finger. Hesitantly, I unlocked my arms and willed my legs to carry me the short distance between the beds. When I arrived, claiming a spot on the quilt, she reached beneath the neck of her nightgown and pulled out the locket she always wore. Fingers trembling, she opened it and held it up for me to see.

Inside were two oval photographs, each one smaller than a dime. I leaned forward to get a better look. On the right side was a beautiful young Negro woman, hardly older than a teenager and looking hauntingly like Mara. The other was a white man, slightly older, fair-haired, serious and unsmiling, his eyes intelligent. Mara didn't say anything, as though the pictures themselves told the whole story. I gazed at them, waiting. Finally I looked to Mara in search of an answer.

"My mama and daddy," she whispered.

I gasped.

She nodded. She pinched the locket, and I heard it clasp. She tucked it back under her nightgown, where it rested against her heart.

"You mean, the Nightingales aren't your real parents?" I asked.

She shook her head. "They're my grandparents."

"Then who are . . ." I pointed to her chest, where the locket lay hidden.

"My mama's the one in Detroit who just had the baby, the one Mama and Daddy are visiting."

I was confused. "You mean your sister?"

"No. I have to tell people she's my sister, but she's not. She's my real mother. She had me when she was eighteen."

"Why didn't she keep you?"

"She couldn't marry my daddy."

"And he's . . ." Again, I pointed toward the locket.

She nodded, laying her hand over her chest. "He's the professor," she said. "William Remmick."

My eyes widened, and I knew my mouth hung open foolishly, but I couldn't help it. "The man on the radio really *is* your father?"

She nodded again, silently.

"But how do you know that?"

"My mama" — she tapped at her chest — "she told me. She gave me these pictures."

"But . . . but . . ." I was having trouble gathering my thoughts. "He calls you Beatrice. On the radio he says good-night to Beatrice."

"That's right. That's my real name."

"It is?"

"He told my mother, if I was a girl, to name me Beatrice after a character in one of Shakespeare's plays. He said Beatrice was strong and independent and intelligent, and that's what he wanted me to be. So he calls me Beatrice, but Mama gave me the middle name Mara, and that's what everyone calls me."

"But, how come? Why doesn't she just call you Beatrice too?"

"She thought Mara fit better. It's from the Bible, from the story of Ruth and Naomi. In the Old Testament, in Hebrew, Mara means bitter."

"But," I said, cocking my head, "you're not bitter."

"No, it's mama. She's the one who's bitter."

I thought a moment. "Because she couldn't marry your daddy?"

"Uh-huh."

"Because he's white and she's black?"

"Uh-huh."

"But it wasn't against the law, was it?"

"No. By that time it wasn't against the law. But his family didn't want it, and neither did mine. My grandma and grandpa threw a fit. They said they'd never allow their daughter to marry a white man."

"They did?" I thought of how Tillie said the Nightingales had worked with her on civil rights in Mills River. "What do your grandparents have against white people?" I asked.

"Nothing," Mara said. "Or not much, anyway. I mean, they let me stay with you when I asked them if I could, didn't they?"

"Well, sure. But so?"

"But marrying a white person, that's another thing. They didn't want their daughter marrying William Remmick. They said it was a sure recipe for disaster. You can't have whites and Negroes getting married and not expect them to have troubles every day for the rest of their lives. And the kids . . ." Mara looked away and shook her head.

"The kids aren't white, and they aren't Negro. Neither one. They don't belong anywhere at all. That's why my grandparents want me to pass for a full Negro. Anyway, I'd never pass for a full white, would I?"

She looked at me, waiting for an answer. I shook my head slowly. I watched as she laid her hand slowly over the hidden locket again.

"Your mom and daddy," I said, "did they love each other?"

To my surprise Mara's eyes glazed over. But her face turned stern; she seemed determined not to cry. "I believe they still do. At least a little bit, anyway."

"But your mom — she's married to someone else?"

Mara nodded. "To Raymond Greer. He's all right, I guess. They have three kids together."

"And your dad?"

"He's married too. He has two boys and a girl. But I only know that because he's mentioned them on the radio show."

"All those kids — they're your half brothers and sisters."

"Yeah."

"Do you know them?"

"I know Mama's girls, but I haven't met

208

the new little boy, Jeremiah. The one just born."

"You don't know your dad's children?"

"I don't know my dad, Roz. I never met him." Tears pooled in her eyes again. She brushed them away. "But someday I will. Someday, I'm going to meet him."

"You think he wants to meet you?"

"I know he does, Roz. I believe he's waiting for that day too."

"Well, why doesn't he come see you now? What's he waiting for?"

"It's not that easy. He can't just come here and claim me. He's got a wife and kids and an important job at a big-shot school. Not to mention that he's got a radio show and most of Chicago knows him."

I didn't know what to say.

After a moment Mara said wistfully, "I'm going to become a writer and a professor, just like him. I'm going to make him proud of me."

"Maybe he's already proud of you, Mara."

She didn't respond to that. She looked away, as though studying the shadows played out across the ceiling. "If he'll see me, the first thing I'll do is promise to never tell anyone. I'll swear to never tell anyone that I'm his daughter, just so long as I can see him sometimes. You know, talk to him . . . about poetry and things."

I understood the look in her eyes only too well. Mara wanted her father, wanted his companionship and his approval. And his love.

"Mara?"

"Yeah, Roz?" Those rich dark eyes flittered down from the ceiling and settled on my face.

"I have something I want to tell you too."

"All right."

"It's about my daddy."

Just then the door to my bedroom opened, and Mom stuck her head in. "What are you girls doing up?" she asked. "It's after ten. You were supposed to be asleep an hour ago."

"Oh, sorry, Mom," I said. "We were just talking."

"Well, it'll have to wait. Tomorrow's a school day. Turn out that light and go to sleep."

I hopped off Mara's bed and turned out the light. Sliding under the covers in my own bed, I said, "Good night, Mom."

"Good night, girls."

The door closed and Mom's footsteps moved down the hall. I waited another minute before whispering, "You got to promise not to tell anyone."

"Cross my heart and hope to die. As long as you don't tell anyone about my daddy."

"Cross my heart and hope to die," I repeated. Under the covers, I ran an index finger across my chest in an *X*. For a swift second I remembered Daddy's warning. But I pushed it aside. Mara could be trusted. And besides, if I didn't tell someone, I thought I might explode. I took a deep breath and said, "You remember when we went to the library, right?"

"Sure, I remember."

"Well, when we were there . . ."

Late into the night our whispers reached across the room, tying us together in a way that only the fatherless daughters of the world would understand.

CHAPTER 20

That night Mara and I made a deal. We swore we would pray for each other every day, asking God to give us our daddies back. We would pray faithfully until God answered, even if it took the rest of our lives. To seal the pact, which we decided to call our Daddy Deal, we stretched our arms across the gap between the beds and clasped pinkies, swearing aloud in unison, "I promise."

On Saturday night, the night before her grandparents were to pick her up, Mara met the greatest threat to the fulfillment of my dreams: Tom Barrows. He had been coming around regularly, taking Mom out to one place or another for the evening, and on those days he didn't come by, he made a general nuisance of himself by calling or sometimes even sending flowers. It was pretty clear to all of us what he wanted. Although he'd known Mom only a matter of weeks, he was determined to win her heart, dull and homely as he was, and make her his wife.

"Does your mom really like this guy?" Mara asked.

We were in the living room waiting for Tom Barrows to show up. Mom was upstairs getting dressed for the evening, but she'd had to work late at the store and was running behind. She asked Mara and me to greet Mr. Barrows when he arrived, ask him if he'd like something to drink, and generally keep him entertained while she finished getting ready. She didn't realize the mistake she'd made in asking us to do that. Neither did I, at first.

I shook my head in answer to Mara's question. "I don't think so. I mean, how could anyone like a guy like that?"

"Then why does she go out with him?"

"Well . . ." I paused a moment as I considered how to explain what I didn't understand myself. "I heard Mom and Tillie talking not too long ago."

"Yeah?"

"Tillie asked Mom if she thought she could ever love Tom Barrows."

"She did? She asked her straight out, just like that?"

"Yeah, she did."

"So what'd your mom say?"

Even as I thought about it, my brows came together in a frown. "She said she was too old for all that now."

"Too old for love?"

"I guess so. But Tillie said that was nonsense. She said Mom didn't know how young she still was."

"So what'd your mom say to that?"

"She said she didn't need love. She needed stability."

"What's that mean?"

"I don't know." I was sure it had something to do with Daddy, or with what Daddy hadn't been, but I couldn't put it into words. "Tillie told Mom stability was a good thing, but that she shouldn't accept stability without love. And Mom said . . ." I swallowed hard. It hurt to think of what Mom had said.

"What, Roz? What'd she say?"

"Mom said she didn't want to love anyone anymore. She said something like, 'God knows, if I could turn my heart to stone, I would. Life would be so much easier if I didn't have to feel anything.' "

Mara looked at me hard, and I could read the question in her eyes: *What exactly did your daddy do to your mama that she would talk like that?*

I looked away. I didn't want to think about it, much less talk about it. That was the past, and things were going to change. Daddy was going to change. He'd promised.

Mara whispered, "So do you think your mom will end up marrying this guy?"

With a heavy sigh I said, "I have to make sure she doesn't."

Mara nodded knowingly. We both looked out the living room window, expecting to see the dreaded object of our conversation coming up the walk at any moment.

"How come he's as old as he is and not married yet?" Mara asked.

"Tillie told me he was married once, but his wife left him."

"Oh yeah? Why'd she leave him?"

I shrugged. "How should I know?"

"Did they have any kids?"

"No. I don't think he likes kids very much."

"Oh!" Mara's eyes widened as she smiled at that.

The clock on the mantel chimed six times, and as usual, Mr. Barrows appeared right on time. "Shh." I put a finger to my lips. "Here he comes now."

In another moment my mother's suitor was at the door. I let him in and ushered him in to the living room.

"Mom's running behind," I explained, "because she had to work late at the store. She told me and Mara to keep you entertained until she's ready."

"Oh?" He reluctantly removed his hat and coat and draped them across the back of the easy chair by the window. Sitting down, he picked up the day-old paper from the footstool and snapped it open. "That won't be necessary. I'm perfectly —"

Mara jumped up from the couch and said, "Can we get you something to drink, Mr. Barrows? Some water, soda, hot tea?"

"Um, well —"

"This is my best friend, Mara Nightingale," I said with a wave of my hand. "I guess you haven't been here in a while, because you haven't met her yet, even though she's been with us all week."

Mr. Barrows turned his magnified gray eyes upon Mara and nodded. "How do you do?"

"Nice to meet you, sir," Mara said politely.

"As for something to drink, no thank you. I'm fine." He turned to the paper again. "I'll just —"

"Mrs. Anthony was kind enough to let me stay here while my mama and daddy went to Detroit to visit my sister and her new baby," Mara said. She sat back down, settling herself comfortably on the couch. She patted the cushion beside her, and I sat.

Without raising his chin Mr. Barrows peered at Mara over the rim of his glasses. "I see," he said. "Well, that was very nice."

"Yes, it was. And I'm obliged. Except for the fact that I could hardly sleep a wink all week."

Tom Barrows waited a fraction of a second before asking, "And why is that, Martha?"

"It's Mara. M-A-R-A. But that's okay. It's an unusual name, I know, and a lot of people don't get it at first. They call me Martha or Marla or Marta or even Dora, if you can imagine that. Dora doesn't even sound anything like Mara!"

"Uh-huh." The gray eyes dropped to the paper again.

"Like I said," Mara went on, "it's hard to sleep around here. I don't know how it is Roz doesn't wake up, what with all the noise." She interrupted herself with an enormous yawn, as though to prove her point.

"All the noise?" Tom Barrows asked. He turned a page of the newspaper and folded it in quarters.

Lowering her voice, Mara leaned forward and said, "It's Mrs. Anthony. I never heard anyone snore so bad. It's enough to make the whole house shake. Isn't it, Roz?"

She looked at me. Tongue-tied by her outright lie, I managed only to nod my head.

"It's enough to raise the dead," Mara concluded.

Tom Barrows stared at the two of us without saying a word. He cleared his throat before going back to the paper.

After a moment of silence Mara exclaimed, "And her cooking!"

The eyes behind the glasses reluctantly rolled up again.

"Please don't tell her I said so, Mr. Barrows, but I liked to die of starvation on the nights Mrs. Anthony cooked. Thank heavens Tillie was here to cook the other nights, or I'd be practically skin and bones. I mean, she's a nice lady and all, Mrs. Anthony, but she's a disaster in the kitchen."

Tom Barrows shifted his gaze to me. Receiving neither confirmation nor denial, he turned back to Mara once again.

"Mrs. Anthony is a wonderful cook, Martha," he said. "I've been here for dinner numerous times."

"Oh, but did you actually see her cook the meal, Mr. Barrows? Because it might just be that Tillie cooked it for her before you came."

Tom Barrows hesitated a moment before

saying, "Well, I'm sure it doesn't matter. One can always learn to cook. It isn't difficult to follow a recipe."

"Yeah, you got a point. I just hope Mrs. Anthony learns before all those kids come along."

"All those kids?"

"Yeah, you know. All those kids she wants. She told me it's her dream to have a dozen children. That Mrs. Anthony, she loves children, you know."

The now distressed eyes turned back to me, beseechingly. I merely shrugged.

"Well, she never mentioned any such thing to me, Martha," he said. "In fact, I was under the impression she was —" he paused a moment as Mara and I looked at him intently — "well, you know, finished with all that business."

I jumped as Mara laughed loudly just inches from my ear. "Finished?" she said. "Why, she's just getting started. She —"

"Who's just getting started with what?" Mom asked as she stepped into the living room.

Tom Barrows jumped up like a rocket from the chair and helped Mom on with her coat. "I'm glad you're here, Janis . . ."

"Sorry I'm late, Tom. I hope the girls were keeping you company."

He glanced helplessly at us. "Oh yes. Yes. Well, shall we go?"

In another moment, after Mom's parting instructions about minding Tillie and helping out with Valerie, they were on their way. Mara and I shut the door behind them and leaned against it heavily, exploding into laughter.

"I can't believe you said all those things, Mara!" I cried.

"The good news is," Mara said, "I think he believed me."

We clasped pinkies and sank to the floor, sighing happily.

CHAPTER 21

At school on Monday morning I found a note from Daddy in my desk.

Dear Roz,

There is a small café a few blocks from the library called Hot Diggity Dog. It's on Second Street, beside the Woolworth's. Meet me there today at 4:00 if you can.

I love you, Little Rose.

Dad

My breath left me, and my hands trembled as I smoothed the piece of paper on my desk with an open palm. My eyes darted around the room, wondering if anyone could possibly know, just by looking at me, that this morning was no ordinary morning, this piece of paper no ordinary piece of paper. None of the kids paid any attention to me as they hung up their jackets and got settled at their desks. But when my gaze fell upon Miss Fremont, I shivered. She was smiling at me knowingly, as though she shared my secret. She couldn't possibly know about Daddy, I told myself. I quickly dropped my eyes, folded up the note, and slipped it into the pocket of my skirt.

All morning I could hardly concentrate on what was happening in the classroom. When Miss Fremont called on me to answer a question, my mind was so far away I didn't hear. Normally when someone drifted off, Miss Fremont would rap on their desk with a ruler, but she didn't do that to me. Not today. She simply laid a hand on my shoulder and gave a gentle squeeze, calling me back from the places Daddy's note had taken me. I looked up at her questioningly, but again she only smiled.

Finally, in midafternoon, I was able to spill my secret to the one person who would understand. Recess was held outside in spite of the autumn chill, but Mara and I managed to find a small stretch of sun-baked bricks along an outer wall of the school. There, in our secluded spot, I pulled the note from my pocket and showed it to Mara.

She took it into her mittened hands and read it. I watched her eyes move slowly over the scribbled words, and when she lifted them to me, they were filled with doubt. "Are you going?" she asked.

"Of course I'm going. Why wouldn't I?"

Mara shrugged. "I don't know, Roz. I've been thinking . . ."

"About what?"

"About your dad. I mean, there must have been a good reason your mom left him."

I snatched the note out of her hand. "He's going to change. He promised."

"Yeah but . . ." She didn't finish. She looked away.

"We made a deal," I said.

"I know."

"We're going to get our daddies back, and nothing's going to stop us."

"I know, Roz. But my father, he —"

"He what?"

"He loved my mother."

"My father loves my mother too. He told me so."

She didn't say anything for a while. Then, "Just be careful, Roz."

Her words sent a ripple of fear through the pit of my stomach. "What do you mean?"

"Well, I don't know. Just . . . if he wants you to go somewhere with him, don't go. Just stay inside the restaurant, is all. You know, where people can see you."

I didn't like what she was saying, and I
didn't like feeling afraid. It made me angry.
"I thought you'd be happy for me, Mara."

"I am, Roz. Really I am." She tried to
smile, but the forced upturn of her mouth
didn't fool me for a minute.

She took off her mitten and held up her
pinkie. I hesitated a moment, then took off
my own mitten and clasped her finger with
mine. Still, not wanting to see the warning
there flashing like neon lights, I couldn't
bring myself to look her in the eye.

After the final bell Mara took the school
bus to the public library with me. Standing
outside on the sidewalk, she pointed me in
the right direction and told me to look for
the dancing hot dog. From the library I
walked on to the Hot Diggity Dog Café
alone, clutching my schoolbooks against my
chest as a shield against the cold wind. But
I shivered anyway — not just from the cold,
but from anxiety over seeing Daddy, and
from the fact that I was doing something I
wasn't supposed to do.

I'd lied to Tillie when I called home from
the office at school. "I need to go to the
library to do homework with Mara this
afternoon," I'd said.

"Why don't you girls come to the house

and do your homework here?" she suggested. "I've just pulled a fresh loaf of banana bread out of the oven."

"Thanks, Tillie, but we need to use some reference books that we can't bring home."

"Do you need me to talk to the secretary, give her permission for you to get off at the library?"

"No. Mom's already given permission for me to get off there anytime I want to. She said I just had to let you know when I'm doing it."

"What about Mara? Does her mother know where she is, or should I call Mrs. Nightingale and let her know?"

"No, her mother knows already. She's allowed to go to the library whenever she wants to."

"All right, then. Afterward, walk on over to Marie's, and you can get a ride home with your mother. It's too cold to be walking around very much out there."

The small trail of lies behind me and the unknown path ahead left me feeling sick. A small ache began to throb against my brow as I bent against the wind, and it seemed to beat in time to the echo of Mara's warning: *"Be careful, Roz. Be careful, Roz."*

I found the Hot Diggity Dog Café just as Mara said I would, with its brightly painted dancing hot dog winking down at me from the plate-glass window. He was a friendly little guy, his smile encouraging people to come on in and sit a while. But when I pulled open the heavy glass door, I found the place to be just another cheap diner, with barely enough room for a counter, stools on one side, and a row of booths on the other. No one was there except for a waitress wiping circles with a rag on the countertop. She glanced up at me, snapped her gum, looked back down.

I took a moment to catch my breath and revel in the warm air rising from a floor grate by the door. My heart beat wildly and my knees were weak, and for one brief moment I considered backing out the door and running, but curiosity pushed me forward. If Daddy was there, he'd be in the far corner booth drinking strong black coffee and smoking a Marlboro cigarette. How often I had seen him doing that very thing back home, sitting at our kitchen table in Minneapolis, nursing a steaming mug at the end of a long day, a cigarette reducing itself to ash between the thick and callused fingers of his right hand.

I moved forward, peering into every empty booth along the wall until finally, as I suspected, I found him in the last one. He sat there with his back to the door, hunched over the predicted cup of coffee, an ashtray on the table just beyond his right hand. It was full of cigarette butts, crisscrossed and crushed, like a pile of fallen soldiers after battle. One lighted cigarette lay in the crevice of the ashtray, wispy smoke rising as it gave up the ghost. Daddy must have gone through a whole pack just waiting for me to arrive.

I cleared my throat and tried to find my voice. "Daddy?"

He turned, and seeing me, his eyes filled first with joyful recognition followed by something like gratitude.

"You came, Roz," he said. I could smell the smoke on his breath and in his clothes. He only chain-smoked when he was nervous, and I wondered briefly if he was as afraid of seeing me as I was of seeing him. He might have been afraid, but he managed a smile as he waved toward the bench seat across the table. "Sit down, sweetheart. I ordered you a chocolate milk shake. I knew you'd like that."

I noticed then the tall beveled glass that sat there waiting, like Daddy, for someone who might not come. The head of whipped cream had melted and was sliding in tiny avalanches down the side, leaving white puddles on the table. The plump maraschino cherry floated in the milky swamp like a toppled boat. A paper straw leaned against the inner lip of the glass, looking shipwrecked itself.

"Thank you, Daddy," I said quietly.

"Well, go on, Roz. Have a seat and drink it."

I did as I was told, sliding into the booth and dropping my books on the seat beside me. I took off my mittens and unwrapped the scarf from around my neck. I unbuttoned my coat but left it on.

Pulling the milk shake toward me, I leaned forward and sucked on the straw while studying Daddy's face. "You grew a mustache since I saw you at the library," I said.

"Yeah." Daddy chuckled softly. "Like it?"

I shrugged. "I guess so. You look different."

"Uh-huh." The coffee cup shivered slightly in his hands as he raised it to his lips. When he'd settled the cup back in the saucer, he asked, "Listen, Roz, did you tell anyone I was here?"

I shook my head without letting go of the straw. I didn't want to lie out loud.

He took a deep breath while his index finger traveled the rim of the saucer. Suddenly he blurted, "I've missed you something terrible, Little Rose."

I lowered my eyes, pulled the shake closer to me.

"I want you back, honey," he went on. "You and Valerie and your mom. I can't live without you."

I let go of the straw then but didn't look up. "You knew we'd come here, didn't you?"

"Where else? Of course your grandfather would help your mother get away from me. But listen, I understand why he did. I really do." He reached across the table. I dropped my hand to my lap before he could catch it. "Roz, I know I drank too much. I know it. I know I did some things that . . ." He stopped, shook his head. "Like I told you, I'm making some changes. I'm not going to drink anymore."

I bit my lip, ventured a glance in his direction. His brown eyes pleaded with me. He reached into the left breast pocket of his flannel shirt and withdrew his pack of Marlboros. His fingers trembled slightly as he lifted yet another cigarette to his lips. An index finger went back into the pocket to fish out a lighter. He flicked the lighter once, twice, three times, but no flame appeared. He patted both shirt pockets as though in search of matches, then gave up and put both lighter and cigarette aside.

"Your mother," he said abruptly. "How is she?"

"She's fine."

"She's working," he said. It was a statement, not a question.

"Yeah. She's working at Grandma Marie's store. She's there right now."

He nodded, seemed to study his hands clutched together on the tabletop. "And Valerie? She doing okay?"

"She's fine, Daddy."

He let out his breath. "I can't tell you, Roz, how much I miss that baby girl. I bet she's grown just since I've seen her last, hasn't she?"

I wasn't sure she'd changed all that much, but I nodded anyway.

"I want to see her grow up, Roz. You and Valerie both. I want to see the two of you grow up."

I didn't say anything. A thick silence hung between us.

"Listen," Daddy said finally, "you want something to eat? A hot dog or something?"

"I'm not hungry."

"You know, they've got the best dogs in town here," he said, smiling briefly. "I should know. I eat here pretty often."

"You do?"

"Yeah. Here or . . . well, never mind."

"Daddy?"

He looked at me expectantly.

"Do you live here too now? I mean, in Mills River?"

He didn't answer my question. Instead, he looked around the café and said, "You know what this place reminds me of?"

I shook my head.

"No? You remember Sweet Pete's, don't you? That ice cream parlor up in Linden Hills where I used to take you and the boy for ice cream —"

"You mean Wally?"

"And you'd always get that hot fudge sundae with the peppermint ice cream. Remember that?"

"Yeah, I remember."

"Those were good times, weren't they? I mean, we had some good times together, didn't we?"

"Sure, Daddy." I liked the way he smiled at that, so I added, "And it was fun when you took us swimming at Lake Calhoun too."

"Yes, yes," he said, tapping the table with one finger. "You remember that, right? That sandy little beach on the north shore of the lake, not far from the boat rental place, remember?"

I shrugged. "Sure, Daddy, I remember all right."

"We had good times, didn't we, Little Rose?"

I nodded and he smiled again. He leaned closer to me and said, "Listen, how's school? Is the school any good here?"

I thought a moment before saying, "Well, yeah, it seems like an okay school to me. I'm doing good. Not so good in math, but good in everything else."

"That's my girl. And listen, you doing okay otherwise? I mean, you're all right, aren't you?"

I almost said yes until I remembered what was coming up. "I have to get my tonsils out."

"You do?"

"I've been having sore throats, and the doctor decided it was time for my tonsils to go."

"So when are you getting them out?"

"Friday."

"This Friday?"

I nodded. Daddy's eyes veered off toward the wall, and his lips moved slightly, as though he were calculating something. Then he said, "That's October the twenty-seventh."

"Yeah, I guess so. I'm kind of scared,

Daddy."

"Ah now, Roz. Don't worry." He reached for my hand again, which had sneaked out from under the table. I let him cover it with his own. "Listen, you might have had them out two weeks ago, on Friday the thirteenth. Then I wouldn't have been so sure. But the twenty-seventh, that's not a bad luck day, huh? So nothing to worry about."

Daddy had a system of bad luck and good luck days, the most obvious of which was Friday the thirteenth, which was definitely a bad luck day. I can remember him refusing to go to the job site, calling in sick rather than taking a chance of being hurt or even killed in a construction accident whenever the thirteenth fell on a Friday. But Daddy didn't stop there. He had a complicated and, to me, incomprehensible system of determining good and bad luck days, though Mom called it all nonsense and refused to pay attention to his calculations. Not long before Mom decided to leave him, Wally and I heard her say that with Alan Anthony, no day was a good day. They were all bad luck days, every single one.

"Besides," Daddy went on, "there's nothing to it. It's no worse than getting a tooth pulled."

"You don't have to go to the hospital to

get a tooth pulled," I argued.

"Listen, Roz, I wish I could be there for you, but don't worry. You'll be fine."

He squeezed my hand tight, and I found myself squeezing back. "Do you really think so, Daddy?"

He caught my gaze and held it. "Little Rose," he said gently, "do you think I'd lie to you?"

I hesitated just a moment before saying, "No, I guess not."

He smiled. "You'll be fine. And afterward you can meet me here, and I'll buy you another chocolate milk shake. How does that sound?"

"Good, I guess." I took a long, pensive sip of the shake before asking, "Daddy, do you really think we'll all be together again?"

He looked at me for a long moment, his face stony. Then nodding slowly, he said, "I'm going to make it work this time, Roz. I want you to believe that." He laced his fingers together and leaned forward over the table. "Listen, about the drinking, I know what it does to me. I know. And that's why I'm not drinking anymore. I swear to you, Roz, I haven't had a drink since you all left Minnesota and came down here."

"Really?" I asked, my voice thin.

"Really, Roz. Oh, I almost forgot." He

reached into the back pocket of his jeans and pulled out a folded piece of paper. He opened it and laid it on the table in front of me. "This is from the last AA meeting I went to. I brought it along just to show you I'm going. The group meets at a church in Wheaton, so I'm going over there as often as I can."

I pulled the paper closer and looked it over. Sure enough, it seemed to be an agenda for an Alcoholics Anonymous meeting, including the topic of discussion, the words to the Serenity Prayer, and a notice of upcoming events.

"If getting you back means no more drinking," Daddy went on, "so be it. I'm done with all that. You've got to believe me."

With the proof of his going to AA right there on the table between us, I gave him an agreeable nod. "I believe you, Daddy," I told him.

The door to the café opened, letting in a gust of cold air. We could feel the cold all the way at the back of the cafe. Daddy shivered as he glanced at the huge clock on the wall above the counter. "I'd better go, Roz," he said.

"Okay, Daddy."

"You have a way to get home?"

"I'm going to walk over to Marie's and

ride home with Mom."

Daddy slid out of the bench, dropping a five-dollar bill on the table as he stood. He lifted his jacket off the seat and put it on. Latching the zipper, he said, "I'll see you again soon, Roz. And listen, everything is going to be all right. I promise you that. But if you say anything to your mother, or to anyone at all, you'll ruin everything. I can trust you not to tell, can't I?"

A small lump rose in my throat. "I won't tell, Daddy."

"Promise?"

"I promise."

"That's my Little Rose."

He leaned over, cupped my face in his hands, and kissed my forehead. When he did, something — some small persistent rumbling in my mind — told me not to trust him. But something else, some far louder voice in my heart, told me that was silly, that of course I could accept my daddy's words as truth.

I looked up at Daddy and smiled. My father would be coming home, and all would be well.

Chapter 22

Tom Barrows stopped by the house the night before I was scheduled to get my tonsils out. He showed up without warning just as we were sitting down for dinner, so of course Mom invited him to join us.

"Tillie," Mom said as she bustled back to the kitchen, "let's move to the dining room table so there's room for everyone."

"All right, Janis," Tillie agreed. "I'll get the place mats out."

"But, Mom," I complained, "I just finished setting the kitchen table."

"Well, Roz, just get it *un*-set and take —"

"Never mind, Mom," Wally cut in. "He can sit at my place. I'll take a plate up to my room and eat there."

"Oh no, Wally. I won't have you doing that. You need to eat here with the rest of us."

"Yeah, well, no thanks." He gave Tom Barrows a grumpy look, served himself up a plate of pork chops and potatoes, and headed for the stairs.

"Wally!" Mom called.

"Let him go," Tillie said. "He'll poison the atmosphere if he stays, and then we'll all lose our appetites. These pork chops cost fifty-nine cents a pound, and I won't have them wasted."

Mom cast apologetic eyes at our visitor. "I'm sorry, Tom."

"It's all right, Janis. I was a teenaged boy myself once. I know how it is."

Tillie snorted out a laugh as she untied her apron and laid it over the back of her chair. "You were a teenager twenty years ago, Tom. Today's young men would make the worst of your lot look like a bunch of altar boys, hair all slicked down and shoes all spit-polished to a shine."

"What do you mean, Tillie?" Mom asked, looking stricken.

"You know exactly what I mean, Janis. Look at the world these kids are facing. What with the war and the hippies and all the drugs and this . . . this . . . this so-called sexual revolution," Tillie sputtered. " 'Make love, not war,' they say, when heaven knows they're far too young to be making either one —"

"Tillie," Mom interrupted, casting a

glance at me.

"Something's happening to this country, and it isn't good," Tillie went on, undeterred. "Something's happening, and it's happening fast."

The five of us were seated now, with warm serving dishes being passed from hand to hand. Tom Barrows spooned a mountain of mashed potatoes onto his plate with a swift flick of his wrist. "People have lost their civility," he said.

"Oh, they've lost a whole lot more than that," Tillie argued. "They've lost their faith, and that's the problem right there."

"Their faith in what?" Mom asked.

"Why, their faith in everything, Janis. *Every*thing. It's like an anchor's been cut, and the whole country's drifting, just drifting without any clear direction. It's as though no one knows where to go or even whether there *is* anywhere to go or if we're all just sailing along for no apparent reason. So our young men, who are supposed to be our up-and-coming leaders, mind you, they're all tuning themselves out like Timothy Leary and getting high on that marijuana tobacco and singing about some answer that's blowing in the wind. Blowing in the wind, my foot! The answer's plain as day, and it's blowing right over their long-haired heads."

To demonstrate, she drew an arc in the air from her chin to the back of her head.

"I'm not sure I'm following —"

"And everybody's angry, in case you haven't noticed," Tillie said, cutting Mom off. "The feminists are angry and the Negro folks are angry and the young folks are angry — with Wally a case in point — and the intellectuals are angry —"

"Tillie —"

"And the artists and the musicians are angry and the politicians are angry, especially the liberals, those fine folks who love all of humanity but can't stand individual people —"

"Well, surely, Tillie —"

"And meanwhile everyone's going around carrying peace signs and calling for peace and singing about peace and being angry about the fact that there's no peace to be had, while all the while they're mocking the very one, the only one, mind you, who can give them peace, and that's the Lord." By now Tillie was viciously buttering a piece of bread, and when she finished, she slammed the knife down on the table. "They mock Him by denying His very existence, but instead of feeling free, they just feel angry because suddenly life doesn't make sense anymore. They want to be rid of God, and they want life to have meaning anyway, and it just doesn't work and it makes them angry. And anger kills. I've lived long enough to know, and I can see it coming. Anger is going to be right at the heart of the demise of this country. America is going to fall, and when we do, we're not getting back up again." She paused and looked at each of us — Mom, wide-eyed and perplexed; Tom, blinking heavily behind his glasses; me, who didn't have a clue what she was carrying on about, though I wondered whether she wasn't a little bit angry herself.

Finally Tom Barrows gathered his wits about him and said, "I'm quite sure you're right about anger, Tillie. It can be very destructive, but —" he shot a worried look at Mom — "I don't think the country's in all that much danger of self-destruction, do you?"

"I certainly do, Tom," Tillie said. "Mark my words. America has one foot in the grave and the other on an oil-slicked roller skate, and it's too late to turn back now."

"Well —" Mom patted her lips with a napkin — "maybe there are more pleasant topics of conversation . . ." She looked around the table, as though frantically searching for one. Landing on me, she exclaimed, "Roz, you haven't eaten a bite of your supper!"

I looked down at my plate. She was right; instead of eating I'd been pushing mashed potatoes around with my fork. "I'm not hungry," I said.

"You're not? What's the matter?"

"She's probably nervous," Tillie noted.

"Nervous?" Mom cast a questioning glance at me. "What about?"

Had she forgotten, I wondered?

"Don't you remember?" Tillie echoed. "Poor child's getting her tonsils out tomorrow."

"Of course, I know," Mom said, "but . . . oh, Roz, is that what's bothering you?"

I winced and looked away.

"Well, listen, honey. Everybody gets their tonsils out sooner or later. There's nothing to it."

"That's right, Roz," Tom Barrows added, smiling at me as though we actually liked each other. "Don't worry for even a minute. Very few people die as a result of getting their tonsils out, you know."

The next moment was pandemonium. Mom's cry of "Tom!" collided with Tillie's howl of "Merciful heavens!" just as the fork fell out of my hand and landed with a clatter on the floor. I jumped from the table, ran to my room, and threw myself on my bed. I couldn't hold back the tears as I looked at the clock and considered what was coming. By this time tomorrow night, my surgery would be over, my tonsils would be out, and I might very well be dead. Now *there*, mind you, was something to be angry about.

CHAPTER 23

"Tillie?"

"Yes, child?"

I shifted my weight on the stretcher, trying to still the butterflies beating against the lining of my empty stomach. I hadn't slept well, wasn't allowed to eat breakfast, and was about to be wheeled into the unknown. I was certain the Grim Reaper was waiting for me in the operating room at Riverside Hospital, waiting to slash me right into the kingdom of unlucky statistics. I would be one of the few who died while getting her tonsils out. Too much anesthesia, a slip of the knife, an allergic reaction — the reasons were endless, the possibility of death just around the corner and moving closer by the minute.

"Tillie?"

"Yes, Roz. What is it?"

I found little comfort in the grip of her hand. It would be my last human contact before . . .

"You've been sedated, child. Just close your eyes and relax."

"But, Tillie?"

She sighed.

My mouth felt dry and hollow, a barren cave. I gritted my teeth and tried to work up some spit, then moistened my lips with the tip of my tongue. Finally I managed to ask, "How do you know if you're going to end up in heaven or . . . you know . . . the other place?"

Her hand came up and gently pushed my hair off my forehead. "Well now," she said with a smile, "as my dear mother always said, that all depends on who your father is."

"Who your father is?" The butterflies threw themselves against my stomach wall in one huge rebellion. I was certain I was going to be sick.

"Tillie," Mom said, suddenly there, "the nurse says they're ready to take her now."

"But —"

Tillie patted my shoulder. "I'm glad you asked, Roz, but we'll talk more about all that later."

Mom kissed my forehead. "I love you, Roz. I'll be here when you wake up."

And then I was being wheeled down a

long lifeless corridor by wordless people wearing white. I stifled a scream as the foot of the stretcher bumped up against a pair of double doors, pushing them open and letting me in to what I could only imagine was the gateway to death itself. If my getting into heaven depended on Daddy, I didn't have a chance. He had promised to change, to stop drinking, to be a good person, but he wasn't all those things yet — probably wasn't even close, and I was the one who was going to have to pay for it.

My mouth hung open in silent protest, and the room went blurry as my eyes glazed over, but at the same time a kind voice above me said, "There, there, don't cry. We're going to take very good care of you."

I recognized the nurse who had been with me from the beginning, her matronly face so serene I wanted to dive into that peacefulness and have it swallow me up. She dabbed at my eyes with the edge of the sheet and murmured soothing words, and that was the last thing I remember before I fell into a deep and dreamless sleep.

The canopy of black was pierced by soft, disembodied voices floating somewhere near my bed.

"How's she doing?" That was Grandpa.

I'd know his voice anywhere.

"She's fine. She came through the surgery like a trouper." Mom's hand came to rest on my shoulder. "They moved her out of recovery about a half hour ago. She's been slowly waking up for a while now."

"Good, good. Listen, don't worry about any medical expenses. Everything will be taken care of."

"But, Dad —"

"Don't argue with me, Janis. I know what Marie is paying you at the store, and I know the hospital bill might add up to be a pretty penny. You just leave that for your old man to settle, all right?"

A slight pause, then, "All right, Dad. Thanks. Honestly, I don't know where I'd be without you."

They were quiet a moment, and I felt Mom withdraw her hand from my shoulder. Then I heard gentle footfalls move across the room and out into the hall.

Groggily, I opened my eyes. The metallic taste of blood was on my tongue, and something large and painful filled my throat, threatening to gag me. I moaned, and when I did, the placid face — the last one I had seen before the surgery — appeared above me, speaking softly. "Are you waking up, Rosalind? That's a good girl. Here, I have some ice chips for you to suck on."

Something cold slipped through my parched lips, and my mouth welcomed the soothing chill. I savored the ice chip as it melted and mingled with my saliva, but when I swallowed I squirmed against the pain.

"That's right," the nurse said kindly. "I know your throat hurts and the uvula is swollen — that's what you're feeling at the back of your throat. But you'll feel better soon."

I managed to smile at her and offer a small nod of thanks. The surgery was over, my tonsils were out, and I was alive.

At home, Tillie fed me Jell-O, Popsicles, ice cream, and cold Cream of Wheat. She doled out my pain medication, kept me supplied with water and fruit juice, and checked me routinely for any symptoms of infection. She nursed me around the clock, even sleeping in the twin bed in my room in case I needed anything in the night.

Mom helped too, of course, but left much of the nursing up to Tillie while she went back to work. "I wish I could be here with you like a proper mother," she told me on Monday morning. "But as long as I have to work, I can't be here. So thank heavens for Tillie."

I nodded, reluctant still to speak. My throat felt better, but I had a ways to go before I was back to normal. I lay in bed wondering about how far I was falling behind in school and what Mara was doing and whether Daddy knew I was all right.

On Monday evening I was propped up on pillows reading when Mom came to my room and sat on the edge of the bed.

"How are you feeling?" she asked.

"Okay," I said, mouthing the word.

"Better?"

I nodded.

"Can I get you anything else to eat or drink?"

I shook my head no.

She smiled at me, but I didn't like the way she was squeezing her hands together in her lap. "Roz," she said, "I need to talk with you about something. It's about your father."

My eyes grew wide and my breath caught in my swollen throat. She knew! Mom knew Daddy was there in Mills River and that he had spoken to me! Closing my book and putting it aside, I slid down in the bed until my chin met the covers. I looked at Mom and waited.

A heavy frown weighed down her brow, and she seemed reluctant to speak. Finally she said, "Did you know you were calling for him when you were waking up in the hospital?"

I had no idea. I couldn't remember much at all about waking up after the surgery. Shaking my head, I pointed to my throat.

"Yes," Mom said, understanding. "You weren't exactly calling out, but you were mouthing the word, and it was clear what you were saying."

I shrugged, trying hard to look innocent.

"Listen, Roz, I know a person can't help what she says when she's coming out of anesthesia. And I'm not mad at you for asking for your father, but . . . well, I'm worried. I know our leaving him and coming here has been hard for you, but I did it because it needed to be done. I did it to keep you safe."

I went on staring at her and waiting.

"I want you to put that part of your life behind you," she said. "We're a different family now, and your father isn't part of it. But you have to believe me when I say it's better this way. I think, Roz . . . I think you know what I'm talking about, don't you?"

I hesitated before lifting my chin in a small nod.

Mom raised a hand and caressed my cheek with the back of her fingers. "Honey, I want you to be happy. Safe and happy, and that's why we're here. Do you think you can put the past behind you and we can all move forward together?"

She gave me a moment to think. But I wasn't thinking about her question; I was thinking about Dad's promise to change, to bring us all back together as a family. I couldn't tell Mom about that. . . . I didn't dare tell her. But one day she would see . . . she would see that Daddy could be part of the family and everything would be all right.

"Mom?" I whispered.

"Yes, honey?"

I moistened my lips to buy a few moments in which to work up my courage. Then I asked, "Did you ever love Daddy the way you loved Wally's father?"

Mom's eyes darted from mine, and her hands found each other again. She tightened her jaw and lifted her chin. "I suppose I did, once."

"Well . . ." I paused, wincing from the pain in my throat. "Could you love him again?"

The butterflies were back, beating against my stomach. In the next moment Mom would make or break my hope. All I hoped for was a father like she had in Grandpa, one who would love me and take care of me. That was all.

Slowly Mom shook her head. "Of course not, Roz. I could never —"

"But what if he changes? You know, stops drinking and all?"

She looked at me hard, making sure my eyes were locked onto hers. "Roz," she said, "that's what you have to understand. Your father will never change. Never. Do you hear me?"

I wanted to put my hands over my ears, to shake my head wildly, to cry out, "Yes he will! He promised!"

I turned my face away from Mom and shut my eyes.

"Roz, someday you'll understand, and you'll forgive me for leaving him."

She kissed my cheek, rose from the bed, and left me to ponder what I was sure I would never understand.

CHAPTER 24

Halloween night was cold but clear. In the early evening Mom bundled Valerie up, strapped a dime-store Cinderella mask over her face, and told Wally to keep an eye on her as she went around trick-or-treating. To everyone's surprise Wally didn't complain about taking a two-year-old up and down the streets of our neighborhood. My guess was that he wanted some of her candy at the end of the night. So did I, and I hoped she would share, as I wouldn't be getting any of my own.

Wrapped in a blanket on the couch in the living room, I watched my brother and little sister walk hand in hand down our driveway toward the street. I sucked on a Popsicle to soothe my sore throat, but even more painful was the wedge of self-pity caught in my chest. If only I'd gotten my tonsils out after Halloween, I could have been the one trick-or-treating with Valerie.

They turned left at the sidewalk, and in another moment they were gone. I was just on the edge of crying over the unfairness of it all when I saw Mara turn up the walkway to our house. Mom met her at the door and let her in.

"Hi, Mara," Mom said. "Where's your costume and goody bag? Aren't you out trick-or-treating?"

"Oh no, Mrs. Anthony. I'm not doing that this year. I've come over to be with Roz because I know she can't go out."

"How sweet of you. Come on in. She's resting on the couch."

When Mara stepped into the living room, her eyes shone, and she offered me a wide toothy smile. She looked like she had a secret she wanted to tell me before she burst.

"I can't believe you're here," I said.

She shrugged and sat down beside me. "Why not?"

"Don't you want to go out trick-or-treating?"

"Naw, not really."

Mom, who'd followed Mara into the room, asked, "Can I get you something to drink, Mara? A soda or something?"

"No thanks, Mrs. Anthony. I'm fine."

"All right — oh, there goes the doorbell.

The ghosts and goblins are starting to make the rounds." She gave a small laugh as she headed back to the door.

Mara drew her long legs up on the couch. By now I'd finished my Popsicle and laid the stick on a napkin on the coffee table. Pulling the blanket more tightly around me, I leaned toward her and said, "So what's up? You look like you just won a million dollars or something."

She glanced toward the hallway, then back at me. Quietly she said, "It's Daddy."

"Yeah? What about him?"

"On Sunday night's show, he signed off with a different message."

"He did?"

"Yeah. This time, instead of saying 'Sweet dreams' like he always does, he said 'Good night, Beatrice. May all your dreams come true.'"

She gave me a long knowing look, as though I should understand what this change meant. "Well . . ." I began, uncertain how to go on.

"May all your dreams come true," Mara repeated. "Don't you get it?"

"Not really."

She frowned at me then, like she was a teacher and I was a dimwitted student. "Think about it, Roz. What's my biggest

255

dream?"

"To be a writer?"

"I mean, besides that."

"To meet your father."

"Yup, that's it!" She nodded, finally looking satisfied.

I was still confused. "So?"

"Well, don't you get it, dummy? He wants to meet me too, and he's telling me now's the time."

"He is?"

Mara nodded once more. "My mama promised me —"

"Which mama?"

"My real mama."

"Your sister?"

"Yeah, my sister Celia, my real mother."

"All right."

"She promised me one day I'd meet my daddy. She said the last thing they did was make a pledge about it. They promised each other I'd meet him when the time was right."

"And you think now's the time?"

"Yeah, I do. Celia always told me that when I was old enough, I could meet him. Next month I'll be twelve. That's old enough."

"And you think he wants to meet you now? You think that's what he was trying to tell you?"

"I'm sure of it." Mara hugged her knees and looked dreamy. "I can feel it in my bones."

"So what are you going to do?"

"I'm going to ask Celia if she can arrange it."

"What if she says no?"

"She won't. I know she won't."

I leaned back against the couch cushions, trying to take it all in. I was happy for Mara, but at the same time the lump of self-pity in my chest grew larger. I envied Mara. We had only just made our Daddy Deal, and already fate seemed to be acting in her favor.

"When do you think you'll see him?" I asked.

"I don't know. Celia will have to make all the plans."

"Will she go with you?"

"No, she can't. Not with the new baby. And anyway —" she paused, dropping her gaze to her knees — "she said she didn't think she could ever see William Remmick again. Not because she's mad at him but because . . . well, you know, sometimes it's hard to forget."

I thought about that for a moment. Then I asked, "Because she still loves him?"

Mara nodded silently.

"What about her husband?"

"She says she loves him too, but it's not the same. So she can't ever see my daddy again."

I pressed my lips together and looked out the window at the darkening night. "I think that's the saddest thing I ever heard," I whispered.

"Me too."

"Why can't people just fall in love and be together?"

"I don't know," Mara said. "I hope I never know what it's like." She lifted a hand and held out her pinkie toward me. "Listen, Roz, promise me you'll pray every day that I can see my daddy soon. Not just soon, but I mean, before the end of the year."

I curled my pinkie around hers and squeezed. "I promise."

The doorbell rang again, and trick-or-treaters came and went while Mara and I talked together on the couch. Tillie came and brought us root beer floats and asked after the Nightingales and Willie and Hester's new little grandson — whom Tillie called Mara's nephew, though he was really her half brother. Mara took the confusion of her family life in stride and was able to remember who was what without a hitch. Though I envied Mara because she might get to meet her daddy, I was glad that the woman I called Mom was in fact my mother and not my grandmother, who, incidentally, was already dead. At least the people in my life were who they said they were, and that made everything far more simple.

After a time Mara said quietly, "Have you heard anything else from *your* daddy?"

I shook my head. "Nothing since Hot Diggity Dog."

"Does he know you had your tonsils out?"

"Yeah. He knows. I told him when I saw him at the café."

"I thought maybe he'd send you a get-well card or something."

I shrugged. "I don't know how he'd get it to me. I've been here at home ever since I got out of the hospital."

"Oh yeah. I guess he can't exactly show up at your house and give you a card."

"No," I said, shaking my head. "If he did that and Wally was home, Wally would kill him."

"Really? Wally would kill him?"

"That's what he said."

"He hates your daddy that much?"

"Yeah. Well, like I told you before, he's not Wally's father. He's Wally's stepfather. I bet Wally hated him even before he married Mom. Most kids hate their stepparents, you know, just because they're not their real parents."

Mara stared at me while loudly slurping the last of the root beer at the bottom of her glass. Then she said, "Aunt Josie came over the other day to visit with Mama —"

"Your grandma?"

She nodded. "And Aunt Josie started talking about some girl she works with and how she thinks the girl has found herself a sugar daddy." She stopped and frowned at me.

I waited. Then I said, "So?"

"I didn't know what she meant, so I asked her, and she said never mind, I wasn't meant to hear what she'd said. Later I called my cousin Bernadette, because she knows everything, and when I asked her what a sugar daddy was, she said she couldn't tell me because it was something ugly. I begged her to tell me, and she said all she was going to tell me was that it was something between old men and young girls, and if anyone ever wanted to be my sugar daddy, I should run."

A shiver ran through me. Whispering, I asked, "What do you think it means?"

She looked away and drew in a deep breath. "I don't know for sure, Roz, but I think a sugar daddy is someone who's only going to hurt you in the end."

She kept her gaze out the window, as though she didn't want to look at me. I paused only a moment before blurting, "You're talking about my daddy, aren't you? You think something bad's going to happen because of Daddy."

"I'm not saying that, Roz."

"Then what are you saying?"

Lips a taut line, she blinked several times. She seemed to be choosing her words carefully. "Just be careful."

I shut my eyes and leaned my head against the couch with an exaggerated sigh. "I know, Mara, I know. You told me that already, remember?"

"Yeah, but —"

"And then I met Daddy at the café, and everything was fine. Better than fine. Everything was good."

"I know, but —"

The doorbell rang again, interrupting Mara and ending our conversation. It was Willie Nightingale, here to pick her up. I peeked through half-closed lids when Mara said, "Hi, Daddy!"

"Time to get on home now, baby. School tomorrow." The huge man fidgeted in the hallway like a lumbering bear, hat in hand.

"All right, Daddy. I'm coming." She turned back to me, gave me her bright smile. "Bye, Roz."

I lifted one hand in farewell, and then she was gone. Heavy with fatigue and sadness both, I drifted off to sleep. Sometime later I was only vaguely aware of Wally and Valerie coming home, and of Tillie carrying a tired and cranky Cinderella upstairs to bed. I slept some more, snuggled in the blanket, one cheek pressed against the floral pattern of the couch. Next I knew, Mom was tugging gently at my hand, saying, "Come on, honey. Off to bed. It's getting late."

I groaned and slowly unfolded myself from the cushions. Mom put an arm around me to guide me up the stairs. We were halfway up when the doorbell rang.

"Can you believe it?" Mom said with a small click of her tongue. "Almost ten o'clock and the ghosts are still making the rounds."

"I'll get it, Mom." Wally's voice drifted up to us from somewhere. The front door opened, a gust of cold air rushed in, then Wally's voice again. "There's no one . . . oh, wait a minute. Someone left a paper bag with Roz's name on it."

"For heaven's sake . . ." Mom started, though her voice trailed off as Wally met us on the staircase and handed me the bag. I sat down on a step and opened it. My eyes widened at the treasure inside, every kind of candy imaginable, including at least a dozen Sugar Daddies and, on top of everything, a red silk rose.

"Who do you suppose left it?" Mom asked.

I looked up at her and lied. "Probably Mara. Who else?"

She didn't look convinced, but I could hardly tell her our final visitor was a ghost from her past, who seemed to me at that moment like the very best daddy in the world.

Chapter 25

Tillie sat alone in her room, laughing out loud and slapping the arm of her padded rocking chair with an open hand. I paused in her doorway and frowned at her. "Tillie?" I finally called.

She turned and, wiping tears from her eyes, said, "Oh, Roz, come on in. Have a seat. Butter mint?"

I moved across the room and took a mint from the candy dish. Then I pulled the desk chair over and sat down beside Tillie. "What's so funny?" I asked. Popping the mint into my mouth, I savored its sweetness and the fact that I could swallow without pain. Ten days after surgery, I was back to normal.

Tillie laid a hand across her chest, taking a moment to catch her breath. "I was thinking about Valerie, what she said just now when I was putting her to bed."

"Yeah? What'd she say?"

"Well, I'm teaching her to pray the 'Our Father,' but she hasn't quite mastered it yet. Instead of saying 'Our Father, who art in heaven,' do you know what she said?"

I shook my head. I didn't have a clue.

Tillie laughed again, a laugh so powerful I thought she might wake up not only Valerie but every other slumbering kid in the neighborhood too.

"She said —" more wiping of tears and amused sighs — "she said, 'Our Father, it's hot in heaven'!"

Another shriek followed, and I tried to join her, but I could only summon up a chuckle. Valerie's mistake didn't seem all that hilarious to me. By now Tillie was waving one hand in front of her face like a fan, as though the heat from Valerie's prayer were warming her.

"I told her, I said, 'Valerie, honey, you've got the wrong place.' "

I reached for another butter mint, pressed it against my tongue, looked at Tillie in quiet admiration. I liked the way she was so easily entertained.

She took one more deep breath, sighed heavily, then smiled at me. In the next moment, though, the smile disappeared as her eyebrows met over the bridge of her nose.

"Roz, you don't know the Lord's Prayer, do you?"

I shook my head and shrugged.

"No, I didn't think you would, since your mother doesn't take you to church. Pity."

"What's a pity, Tillie?" I mumbled around the mint.

"Why, that you don't go to church, and you don't know how to pray."

"But I know how to pray."

"You do?"

"Sure." Every day I prayed the same prayer: *Dear God, please give Mara and me our daddies back.* I had promised Mara I'd do it, and I was trying to keep my promise.

"I've asked your mother to come to church with me and to bring you kids along, but she'll have none of it."

"But we used to go —"

I stopped as a memory flashed across my mind. Mom, dressed for church, trying to get out the door; Dad, in a drunken rage at ten o'clock on a Sunday morning, yelling, swearing, fists flying . . .

I jumped up from the chair and walked to the window.

"What's the matter, Roz?" Tillie asked.

"Nothing." I pressed my forehead against the chilly glass, my breath forming a cloud on the windowpane. The night was dark and

266

starless, as though a curtain had been drawn across the world.

"I can tell you this much, Roz," Tillie said. "God answers prayer."

I turned around. "Yeah?"

"I've been praying Lyle would come home, and I got my answer today."

"Lyle?"

"My son. The one who lives in Bolivia."

I had to think a moment. Then, "Oh yeah. I remember. He has malaria."

"Not anymore, he doesn't. He's better now. But he's decided to come on back to Illinois and look for work here, sometime after the first of the year. Oh, I know, it was a selfish prayer." She paused a moment, rocking herself gently. "I should have been satisfied for him to stay in Bolivia if that's where God wanted him. But I had to ask anyway, just to see if I could have a little more time with him. Of course, I didn't tell Lyle I was praying for him to come home, but sure enough, he believes God's calling him to return to the States. He doesn't know why, but frankly, I don't care why. I'm concerned with the what, and the what is: I'll get to be near my son again. At least for a little while, before God calls *me* home. You know . . ." She lifted her eyes toward the ceiling and nodded. "I suspect he'll be calling me soon. Any day now, maybe. Though I hope it's after Lyle gets back."

"But . . . you can't go yet, Tillie."

"I can't?"

I shook my head. "Mom needs you."

"Ah." Tillie waved a hand. "Your mother will be all right. I won't go until she's taken care of."

"What do you mean, taken care of?"

"I don't know. Only God knows that."

"You think she's going to marry Tom Barrows, don't you?"

"Roz, honey, I don't know what God has in store for your mother. I'm afraid I'm not privy to his plans."

"Well, it wouldn't be God's decision anyway, it would be Mom's, and I hope she doesn't decide to marry him."

"Well now, that's not a very nice thing to hope for, if marrying Tom would make her happy."

I crossed my arms and turned back to the window.

"Tillie?"

"Yes, child?"

"If I pray for something, like you did, will God give it to me?"

"I don't know, Roz. He doesn't always give us what we think we want. Can you tell me what it is you're praying for?"

"No." My word sounded angry and abrupt, so I added, "I can't tell you, Tillie. Not yet."

"Fair enough. Is it a good thing, whatever it is?"

I turned around again. "Oh yes. It's a very good thing."

She nodded, satisfied. "Then maybe God will say yes."

"The way he said yes to Lyle coming back, right?"

"I suppose so. I — Oh, there goes the phone. I'd better get it." She pushed herself up from the chair, straightened her skirt, and headed for the door. "Your mother is trying to take a bubble bath and have a few minutes of peace and quiet. Heaven knows she deserves some little luxuries, the way she stands on her feet all day. . . ."

Tillie was still muttering to herself as she disappeared into the hall to pick up the extension there.

The cold night air entered as though by osmosis through the windowpane, and I shivered. Turning to go, I saw the baseball bat that Tillie kept beside her bed, a memento of her son Paul's athletic days. It looked strange and out of place in the midst of her lace curtains, her wedding quilt, her framed photographs, and all the rest of her frilly adornments, but since it was a family treasure of sorts, I decided it had as much right to be there as anything else.

I reached for it and grasped it with one hand while rubbing its long smooth neck with the other. I struck a batter's pose, bat resting on my right shoulder, knees bent, elbows out. I waited for the pitch, my right foot nervously pawing the ground, a missile of imaginary spit firing off my tongue and sailing over my left shoulder. Here it comes, a curve ball, and yet no ordinary leather ball. Instead, a memory — my father's angry face, angry words, angry fist — soaring through the air, coming at me with great speed. *Thwack!*

And there it goes, soaring through the sky beyond the outfield, disappearing somewhere in the far reaches of the stadium. And it's a home run, folks, a home run! Will you look at that! The organist up in the stands starts pounding the keys — da da da *dat* da *da!* — and the crowd goes wild.

But wait a minute, she's up at bat again. She's got her hawklike eyes on the pitcher, her primary opponent up there on the mound. He slaps the ball against his glove, draws back, leg up, releasing his ammunition at such a fierce rate it's almost too much for the human eye to see. But *she*

270

sees it. Oh yes, *she* sees the face of Tom Barrows hurling toward her like a great crashing meteor until . . . *Pow!* And it's out of the ball park, folks! This is amazing, unbelievable! Tom Barrows is out of the ball park, out of the picture. He'll never be seen again!

"What on earth are you doing, Roz?"

Tillie stood in the doorway, hands on hips.

I sheepishly lowered the bat and bit my lower lip. "Nothing."

The look on her face told me she didn't believe me, as though she herself had seen Tom Barrows cannonballing through the air and out of our lives.

"Well, it's getting late," she said. "Why don't you go on to bed."

I returned the bat to its place and slunk across the room. "All right, Tillie. Good night."

"Good night, Roz. Sleep tight."

I kept my head down so I wouldn't have to look her in the eye. She stepped aside to let me out the door.

"Oh, and Roz?"

I turned around, slowly lifted my gaze. "Yeah?"

"Nice fly ball."

I looked at her for a long while, trying unsuccessfully to read her expression.

Finally I simply muttered, "Thanks," and let it go at that.

CHAPTER 26

The Russians were at it again. When the air raid siren went off right in the middle of her lecture on the Louisiana Purchase, Miss Fremont looked annoyed. Most of us pressed our hands over our ears. I could see Miss Fremont's lips move, but I couldn't hear a word she said. But that was all right; we all knew the drill by now: single file out to the hall, kneel down side by side, crown of head against the wall, hands locked securely over neck. What a way to die — all rolled up in a neat little package like a baby in the womb.

Once we were in position, the siren was cut and an eerie silence descended over the school, broken only by an occasional cough, stifled giggles, and the sporadic tapping of the teachers' heels against the floor. And Mara's whispered word in my ear, "Roz!"

I jumped and rolled my eyes toward her voice. "Mara! How do you do that?"

"Do what?"

"How do you find me? You're supposed to be with your own class."

"But I have to tell you something. It's important."

"What?"

"I talked to Celia —"

"Your sister?"

"Yeah. I mean no. My mama. Last night I called her and told her I wanted to meet my daddy, and you'll never guess what she said."

"What?"

"She said she'd try to arrange it." She wiggled in excitement beside me.

"She did?"

"Yeah. She said maybe I could go up there for a day over Christmas vacation."

"Up to Chicago?"

"Uh-huh. She said I could take the train, and maybe Daddy could meet me at the station."

"Do you think he'll do it?"

"I don't know." She sucked in a deep breath. "I'm really scared. I hope he says yes."

"Well, he did say he wanted all your dreams to come true, right?"

"Yes. That's —"

"Shh! No talking." Miss Fremont's voice

reached us from somewhere down the hall. Mara and I exchanged a glance. The person on the other side of me, Jackson Riley, nudged me with the full side of his body and whispered, "Shut up!"

He pushed me into Mara, who pushed me back his way. I slammed up against him, and he poked me in the ribs with an elbow.

"*You* shut up," I said.

"You're the one talking with that nigger girl."

Now I was angry, and I started to say something I'd never said to anyone. "Jackson Riley, you can just go to —"

"I said quiet!" Miss Fremont's voice came crashing down from right above us. "Jackson Riley, Roz Anthony, do you want to end up in the principal's office?"

Jackson spoke first, responding in a muffled but distinctly fawning voice, "No, Miss Fremont."

From my own windpipe came a squeaky, "No, Miss Fremont."

"Then settle down and not another peep out of either of you."

My cheeks burned, and I clenched my jaw in frustration and embarrassment. I wasn't used to being reprimanded in front of the entire sixth-grade class. In fact, I wasn't used to being reprimanded at all. My first

time to get in trouble at Mills River Elementary and my name had to be called out in
tandem with that bully Jackson Riley. I felt
as though I'd just been handcuffed to a
common criminal.

If the Russians were going to drop the
bomb, let it be now.

"Sorry, Roz," Mara whispered.

I looked at her and gave one small nod,
but I didn't say anything.

The all clear came and the hall erupted
into chatter as everyone unfolded themselves and stood. I glared at Jackson, then
turned to Mara and said, "I'm sorry he
called you a . . . you know."

Mara shrugged. "It's all right. I'm used to
it."

"It's not all right —"

"I've got to go." She walked away beaming, the happy prospect of seeing her daddy
greater than the pain of prejudice.

I watched her until she'd disappeared into
the crowd. Then, eyes downcast, I fell into
line with my own class as we snaked our
way through the hall and back to our room.

It had been another practice drill; that was
all. The Russians hadn't yet decided to drop
the big one on us. For now we were safe,
and I realized that in spite of Miss Fremont's reprimand and my brief humiliation,

I was grateful to be alive. I wasn't ready to die. Not only because I was just eleven years old, but more importantly, I didn't know for sure where I would end up.

"*Tillie, how do you know you're going to heaven?*"

"*Well now, that all depends on who your father is.*"

Tillie's statement still sent shivers down my spine. I sure hoped Daddy would change like he said he would, because if Alan Anthony was my ticket to the afterlife, my prospects for reaching paradise looked pretty grim.

Chapter 27

On the second Saturday in November, we celebrated Wally's eighteenth birthday with a small family dinner at home. Mom told him he could throw a party and invite some friends from school, but he didn't want to. He said parties were for kids and he wasn't a kid anymore.

He would, though, he said, like to go to the roller rink with some of his friends after supper, if that was all right with Mom. I looked at him funny when he asked, but he didn't flinch. Mom believed his story about roller skating and said of course he could go, so long as he was home by midnight.

Tillie cooked up a big pot of chili, Mom made a double chocolate cake, and Grandpa and Marie came over and joined us.

"So my grandson's a man now," said Gramps, slapping Wally on the back.

"Yup," Wally said. "Looks that way." He accepted Grandpa's and Marie's coats and hung them up in the hall closet.

"Have you put any thought into colleges, Wally?" Grandpa asked.

"Nope."

"Well, what are you waiting for? Now's the time to be thinking about it. Education is the doorway to success, you know."

"Uh-huh."

"We have a number of fine schools right here in Illinois, my own alma mater, the University of Illinois, among them."

Wally shrugged.

"And listen, son" — Grandpa lowered his voice a notch — "if it's the price of tuition you're worried about, I'm prepared to help."

Marie looked stricken, as though she had just heard the clanging of a huge chunk of change falling out of their bank account. "And of course," she added with a tremulous smile, "there are always scholarships."

"Well, yes," Gramps said, rocking up on his toes, "but we may not have to resort to that kind of thing. There's so much paperwork involved —"

"You're just in time. Dinner's ready," Mom sang out, greeting Grandpa with a kiss on his cheek. She untied her apron and smoothed her skirt. "Everyone please be seated at the dining room table. Dad, we'll talk about colleges later, all right? Tonight's a night to celebrate."

It wasn't much of a celebration, as celebrations go. Wally was pensive and sullen. Marie was her usual self, a perfectly coifed model of propriety and as cold as the winter night. Mom seemed quietly troubled herself, maybe because her firstborn had grown up, and though he seemed largely directionless, he would no doubt be leaving home soon. Tillie and Grandpa were oblivious as they rattled on about newspaper headlines: NASA's Apollo 4 that had just been shot into orbit, the Soviet Union's Vostok missile that Brezhnev was threatening to shoot in our direction, the coast-to-coast protests against the seemingly endless war in Vietnam.

Only when they mentioned the war did Wally look up from his chili long enough to ask, "Do you think it'll last a while?"

"What's that, Wally?" Grandpa said.

"The war. Do you think it'll last a while?"

"It's lasted far too long already," Tillie interjected.

"But," Grandpa said, "it's going to take some time before we can untangle ourselves from the mess we've made over there."

Wally looked from Grandpa to Tillie and back. "So, you mean the war's not going to be over by the end of this year or anything, right?"

Grandpa shook his head. "I'm afraid not. Nor by the end of next year, nor maybe the year after that, unless McNamara outright refuses Westmoreland's repeated demands for more troops."

"Right, Archie," Tillie said with a snort. "That'll happen the day I start looking like Mae West in saloon-girl lingerie."

Wally must not have tried to picture Tillie as Mae West, because he gave a satisfied nod and went back to eating.

Later, while Mom served up the cake and ice cream, we gave Wally his birthday gifts. From Grandpa and Marie, there was a fifty-dollar savings bond. From Mom, a couple of new shirts and a Swiss Army knife. Tillie gave him a leather wallet that, as she explained, she bought for Ross, "but he died before he could use it, so it's still brand new." I'd scraped together enough money from my small allowance to buy him a box of chocolates and a cheap cardboard bookmark for the book he was always reading, the one by Jack Kerouac. The design on the bookmark was simply the word *PEACE* in purple against a paisley pattern of orange and green. I signed Valerie's name to my homemade card, since she was too young to buy Wally a gift herself.

When he had opened all the presents, he thanked us, tucked the box of chocolates under his arm, asked Mom for the car keys, and left us to finish the cake and ice cream without him.

I don't know exactly what time it was, but it must have been after midnight when Wally slipped into my room and sat down on the edge of my bed.

"Roz," he said, shaking my shoulder, "wake up a minute."

Groggily I opened my eyes. "What is it, Wally?" I asked. "What's the matter?"

"Nothing. I just wanted to give you something."

I groaned, sat up, and turned on the light. Wherever Wally had been, he was fresh from the chilly outdoors. He hadn't yet bothered to take off his jacket, and a layer of cold lingered about him like smoke. Along with the cold, he brought in an odor that was both nasty and familiar, and though I couldn't quite place it at first, it turned my stomach and set me on edge. Then I remembered. He smelled like Daddy after one of his binges.

"You've been drinking, haven't you, Wally?" I said.

"Yeah." Wally nodded and gave a small laugh.

"I think you're drunk."

"I hope so. I was trying my best."

"What'd you go and do that for?"

"It's my birthday, my *eighteenth* birthday. What'd you expect?"

"Does Mom know?"

Wally put a finger to his lips, shook his head, hiccoughed. "Mom's asleep."

"So was I before you woke me up."

"Ah Roz, don't be mad. Like I said, I've got something for you."

"Yeah? What is it?"

He unzipped his jacket and reached inside. "Here, kid," he said. With that, he placed a familiar dime-store paperback in my hand, worn and dog-eared from so many readings.

I stared at the book, trying to make sense of it all. "You're giving me your copy of *On the Road*?" I asked.

"Uh-huh."

"You want me to have your favorite book?"

He started to nod; this time it took him a second to lift his chin off his chest. "That's right."

"It's got the bookmark in it that I just gave you for your birthday. Don't you like the bookmark?"

"Oh sure. I like it. Yeah, peace. It's perfect. And the chocolates were great. We ate them all, the whole box."

"Who's *we*, Wally? I bet you were with those Delaney twins, weren't you?"

"Them, and a bunch of my other friends. We were having a good time. Oh yeah." He chuckled and his head started bobbing, as though he were listening to a tune I couldn't hear.

"Yeah, I bet." I felt my jaw tighten. I looked again at the book in my hand. "You sure you want me to have this?"

"Of course I'm sure."

"But why are you giving it to me?"

"Don't you know?"

I waited a moment. Then I shook my head and said, "Know what?"

Wally looked about the room as though he were searching for the words. Finally he found them. He drew in a deep breath and let them out slowly. "On his eighteenth birthday, a man's supposed to give his little sister his most prized possession."

My eyes narrowed. "He is? I never heard of that."

"Yeah. It's true." He laughed again. He sounded pleased with himself.

"So you're giving me your most prized possession?"

In the dim light I saw Wally's face become solemn. "Just take care of it for me, will you, Roz?"

I was unnerved by the shift in his mood. He looked as though something terrible was about to happen, but I couldn't imagine what. In my confusion I said simply, "Sure, Wally. I'll take care of it for you."

"Promise?"

I traced an *X* across my chest with one index finger. "Cross my heart, but why can't you just take care of it yourself?"

He put his finger to his lips again to shush me. "No questions, all right?"

I narrowed my eyes and thought a moment. I didn't like unanswered questions, but I finally relented. "All right," I said.

Wally smiled, nodded, and sighed in quick succession. "You know, Roz," he said, "you're really not such a bad kid."

"Well . . ." I felt myself frown. "Thanks, Wally."

He leaned toward me, and for one brief moment I was in his arms.

By the time I woke up the next morning, he was gone.

CHAPTER 28

Mom's screams brought Tillie and me running. "Merciful heavens!" Tillie called out as she pounded down the stairs. "What's the matter, Janis?"

"It's Wally," Mom cried. "It's Wally!"

But she couldn't get beyond those two words to tell us what was wrong with Wally. We found her in the kitchen, holding a piece of paper that had been ripped from a spiral notebook. With trembling fingers, she handed the paper to Tillie.

Tillie read it and afterwards slapped it with both hands against the spot above her heart. "That young fool!" she cried. "I can't believe he'd do this."

Bewildered and near tears, I looked from Mom to Tillie and back again. "What is it? Will somebody tell me what's going on?"

"Your brother has gone off to enlist in the army," Tillie explained. "That fool! He'll end up getting himself killed in Vietnam."

"Oh, Tillie!" Mom's eyes widened at the thought. Her tears spilled over and coursed down her pale cheeks.

"I'm sorry, Janis. I didn't mean that. He might not end up in 'Nam at all."

But it was too late. Mom sank to her knees, weeping as though Wally were already dead. Tillie bent over her and tried to console her while I ran upstairs to get Valerie, who had been awakened by Mom's screams and was now screaming herself.

By midmorning, our house resembled the scene of a wake. Grandpa came and called the police, and within minutes two cops arrived and read the note and listened to Mom's story, spilled out between sobs. To everyone's frustration, including the cops, they said they couldn't do anything because Wally was an adult and he had left voluntarily, but they stayed anyway at Tillie's invitation and drank cups of strong coffee and offered their speculations as to where Wally might be. Tom Barrows showed up and nervously paced the downstairs hall, looking as helpless and as useless as he was. Neighbors, alerted by the cop car in front of the house, came and went and came back again with casseroles and shoulder pats and well-intentioned words that did little to lessen Mom's grief. In a matter of a couple of hours the house was crawling with people, Mom floating blindly in the midst of them as though they weren't there at all.

"It's Frank all over again," she kept saying as she walked aimlessly from room to room, ringing her hands. "It's Frank all over again."

Once, when she and I came face-to-face in the living room, she looked at me with a haunted look and said, "Wally's father went to war, and he never came back. Did you know that, Roz? He never came back."

"I know, Mom," I said, giving in to the tears. "I've known that a long time now."

And on it went, Mom wandering and muttering, the cops drinking coffee, the neighbors mingling over food and murmuring among themselves — until Grandpa called a doctor who showed up with his black bag of tricks, including a sedative in a syringe. Mom protested only briefly, then complied, and after the shot was given Tillie walked Mom upstairs and put her to bed.

Grandpa stayed for a time, but everyone else left, and soon the house was quiet.

I snuggled next to Grandpa on the couch, and he put his arm around me and kissed my forehead. "What's going to happen to Wally?" I asked.

"I don't know, sweetheart," he said, shaking his head sadly. "But you can be sure he's not the first young man who's run off to war. They romanticize it, you see. They think it'll make them heroes, but . . . well . . . once they get there, they begin to see what it's all about."

He seemed to want to say more but didn't go on. "Were you ever in a war, Gramps?" I asked.

"Oh yes. I was in the Great War, over in Europe."

"And you came back, didn't you." It was a statement, not a question.

"Yes, I did. All in one piece."

"Then Wally will come back too."

Grandpa lifted his chin and offered me a tiny smile. "Of course he will. But in the meantime, he doesn't know how he's broken your mother's heart. We must be extra good to her, you and I, to help her get through this. Do you think you can do that, Roz?"

I nodded eagerly. I would be good to her, because I loved her and because I needed desperately to ease my guilt. I should have known Wally would leave; he had as good as told me more than once. If I had pieced together all the evidence — his favorite book, his talk of butchering the Vietcong, his talk of *leaving,* for crying out loud, that had seemed to me only so much foolish dreaming — but if I had pieced it all together I might have warned Mom, and she in turn might have somehow kept him from going.

But I hadn't spoken up, and now it was too late. Wally was gone, and we didn't know where he was or when he'd be coming back. Or whether he'd be coming back at all.

CHAPTER 29

A light snow drifted down from a steel gray sky, slowly and wistfully, as though reluctant to fall from the clouds. I looked up as I walked and followed the journey of first one flake and then another, watched them travel as single airborne beauties, only to get lost amid the slush and dirty snow of the streets and sidewalks. I understood their unwillingness to drop to earth. Why would they want to leave the sky only to fall on the dismal streets of Mills River? I wasn't all that keen on walking through these streets myself, except that I had somewhere important to go.

Daddy had left me another note, asking me to meet him at Hot Diggity Dog. I hadn't seen him in more than three weeks; since then I'd had my tonsils out and Wally had run away from home. I didn't want to tell him about Wally, but I figured he should know.

He was in the same booth as before, his mustache neatly trimmed but his hair a little longer. He smiled at me as I slid onto the bench across from him. Without a hello or any other greeting, he jumped right back into the conversation we'd been having weeks ago. "There, now see? I told you you'd be all right, didn't I?"

I nodded, trying to return his smile.

"So how are you feeling? Can you eat?"

"Yeah, I'm better now. My throat stopped hurting a long time ago."

I was hoping he'd hear my unspoken question of, *Where've you been, Daddy? What were you doing while I was recuperating from getting my tonsils out?*

He laced and unlaced his fingers on the tabletop. A half-empty coffee cup sat nearby. "Can I get you something to eat then? A hot dog or something?"

I thought a moment. "No, thanks. I don't think I need anything."

"Aw, come on. How about a shake? A chocolate shake would taste good, wouldn't it?"

I lifted my shoulders. "I guess so."

He waved a hand and called out my order to the waitress behind the counter. There were a couple of other people in one of the booths, but they were halfway through their

292

hamburgers and deep in conversation. With
nothing else to do, the waitress moved to
make my shake right away.

I looked back at Daddy. "Thanks for the
Halloween candy," I said.

"So you got it okay?"

"Yeah, I got it."

"I know how you favor those Sugar Daddies, so I wanted to get you a bunch of
those."

I nodded again. The waitress brought my
milk shake, plucked a straw out of her
apron, and set them both on the table in
front of me.

"Thanks, Darlene," Daddy said.

"Sure thing, Nelson," she responded with
a nod. "Can I warm up your coffee?"

Daddy stared at the cup by his right hand,
as though wondering where it came from
and how it got there. Then he said, "Sure,
why not?"

"And listen, you must be hungry. How
about something to eat? I could holler to
Joe to rustle up a couple of cows and make
'em cry."

Daddy looked at me. "You want a hamburger?" he asked.

I shook my head slowly.

"We'll pass on that, Darlene. Just the coffee."

"All right, Nels, honey. Be right back."

When she walked away, I leaned over the table toward Daddy. "Why'd she call you Nelson?"

"She thinks that's my name."

"Don't you want to tell her what your real name is?"

"Naw." He waved a hand. "It doesn't matter."

"Well, what does it mean to rustle up a couple of cows and make them cry?"

"It means to serve up a couple of hamburgers with onions."

"Oh." I leaned back against the padded bench and looked hard at Daddy. He was gazing intently after Darlene, watching as she moved behind the counter, where she pulled the coffee carafe from the burner. She was young and pretty, with wide blue eyes and heavily sprayed blond hair that turned up into a perfect flip at the ends. She moved with an ease and a confidence that told me she'd been doing her job for a long time, though she couldn't have been older than twenty-five. Probably not even that old.

She carried the coffee back to our table and filled Daddy's cup almost to the brim. As she poured, she indicated my presence with a quick roll of her eyes in my direction. "Your niece is real cute, Nelson. How old did you say she is?"

Daddy rubbed his cheek thoughtfully. "She's eleven," he said at length. "She'll be twelve in May" — he looked at me — "right, honey?"

I nodded. At least there was one accurate statement floating around the table.

"Well now, she's going to be a real heart-breaker one day. You'd best keep your eye on that one once the boys start coming around." Darlene's full red lips turned up in a smile, and she actually winked one blue eye at Daddy.

"That's what I aim to do, if I have any say in the matter," Daddy said.

"Sure I can't get you some cream for that coffee?"

"No thanks, Darlene."

"All right. You just holler if you need anything."

The front door opened and a trio of teenagers came in; Darlene turned her attention to them.

I looked at Daddy questioningly. "She thinks I'm your niece?"

He shrugged, took a sip of the hot coffee. "People get confused. It's hard to remember one customer from another."

"Oh." I finally unsheathed the straw and

stuck it in my milk shake.

"So listen, Roz," Daddy said, "how is everyone? How's your mother?"

I stopped sucking and swallowed hard. "Mom's not so good right now."

He looked up at me abruptly, his brow heavy with concern. "How come? What's the matter?"

"It's Wally," I blurted. "He ran away."

Daddy's eyes searched my face a long time, as though looking for evidence that I was lying. Finally he repeated what I'd just told him. "He ran away?"

"Yeah." The word came out a whisper.

"When?"

"Just a few days ago. He left a note saying he was going to join the army."

I waited for Daddy to say something. One corner of his mouth twitched, as if he wanted to smile but wouldn't let himself. "I'm sorry to hear that," he said, but his voice was lilting, and I didn't believe him.

He had never liked Wally; I knew that. And Wally had never liked him. But I thought Daddy would at least be worried for Mom's sake.

"Mom's pretty broken up about it," I said.

He lowered his eyes to the coffee cup. His hands cradled it for warmth. "I can imagine she is." He lifted the cup to his lips with both hands, blew ripples across the steamy surface, then sipped at it several times. When he lowered the cup back to the saucer, he said, "I wish there was something I could do to help, but . . ." He shrugged and shook his head.

"I know." I stirred my shake with the straw. "Mom doesn't know you're here. How could you help?"

"That's right." He seemed to wince, like the thought hurt him somehow. "Listen, Roz, I've got a job, I'm working —"

"Where?"

"That doesn't matter. There's plenty of call for construction workers around here. When I finish this job, I'll find another. Anyway, I'm saving money, putting it in the bank. I'm not spending it on booze. Not one red cent. And I'm going to AA, just like I said I would. I'm serious, Roz, I'm not going to drink anymore. One day, when I see your mother again, I'm going to be a new man, a changed man."

He stopped as abruptly as he'd started. When he finished his ramble, there was only one thing I wanted to know.

"When will you see Mom again?"

He shook his head and sipped his coffee loudly before answering. "When the time is right," he murmured. He lifted his eyes to me, and I saw a kind of desperation in them.

"How will you know when the time is right?"

"I'll just know."

I thought of Tom Barrows. I thought of how Mom didn't care if she loved him or not, how all she wanted was stability, whatever that meant for her. Probably a man who didn't drink, a man who wasn't angry, who brought home a paycheck, who worked so she didn't have to, who put money in the bank and still had money to spend. Tom Barrows was all those things, and maybe someday Daddy could be too if he worked at it the way he said he would. But if Daddy took too long, it would be too late. Tom Barrows would have already burrowed his way into our household, claiming Daddy's spot for himself.

"Daddy?"

"Yeah, Little Rose?"

But then I thought better of it. He didn't need to know about Tom Barrows. Not yet, anyway.

His eyes grew small as he asked, "What is it, Roz?"

"Nothing," I said. "Never mind."

"You sure?"

"Yeah."

"Hmm." He pulled a napkin out of the

shiny aluminum holder and started rubbing circles on the table where my milk shake had dripped. "So what are you doing for Thanksgiving?"

"We're going to Grandpa's, same as last year. Only this year I guess we don't have to travel so far."

"Uh-huh." The circles grew larger and larger.

On impulse I said, "I wish you could be with us this year."

He didn't look up. He crumpled the napkin into a little ball and tossed it aside. He didn't say anything.

"Maybe by next Thanksgiving?" I prodded.

He finally met my eyes. "For sure by next Thanksgiving." His voice aimed to reassure me, but the piercing indifference of his gaze chilled me to the bone.

CHAPTER 30

Our first letter from Wally arrived the day before Thanksgiving. He had hitchhiked back to Minnesota and was staying with friends while waiting to head out to basic training. He wouldn't tell us who his friends were, and we didn't recognize the return address, but at least we had a way of being in touch with him. Mom wrote him back the same day, and the next day when we went to Grandpa's house for Thanksgiving dinner, we had something to be thankful for. We knew where Wally was. His plans for joining the army hadn't changed, but at least we didn't feel so cut off from him.

With our plates piled high with turkey and all the trimmings, I looked around the table at my newly altered and seemingly shifting family. Mom and Valerie sat across from me, Tillie beside me, with Grandpa and Marie at either end of the table. Strange to think that we had been here the previous year, at this very table with Daddy and Wally, eating an identical meal. At that time Tillie must have been the rightful owner of the house on McDowell Street, where she would have been living alone. What a difference a year can make.

Tom Barrows didn't join us for Thanksgiving, which gave me one more reason to be thankful. Mom had invited him, but he'd had to drive his mother to Chicago. They were celebrating the holiday with one or the other of his siblings.

"Pass the cranberry sauce, please, Roz."

I snapped out of my thoughts and reached for the bowl. "Sure, Grandpa. Here you go."

"And while you're at it, the sweet potatoes."

"Here they come."

"Everything's delicious," Mom said to Marie.

Marie dabbed at her mouth with her napkin. "I'll pass your compliments on to Betty," she said. "She cooked the whole thing single-handedly."

I thought about Betty, their cook, and asked Marie where she was.

"Oh, well, she went home, of course," Marie replied. "To be with her own family."

"Did she have to cook a turkey for them too?"

"I'm sure I don't know, Roz. I don't meddle in her private affairs."

Tillie gestured at the food on the table and shook her head. "We have enough turkey here for her and her whole family and probably half of DuPage County to boot. Betty might as well have stayed and brought her own crew over here. Saved her from cooking another turkey if she'd done that."

Marie blinked rapidly several times. "She's our cook, Mrs. Monroe. She's hardly family."

"So you can't eat Thanksgiving dinner with someone who isn't family?"

"Well —" Marie started, but I interrupted.

"She already is, Tillie," I pointed out. "She's eating with you, and you're not family."

"Bite your tongue, Roz," Tillie said. "You don't have to be related by blood to be family."

"Uh-huh, yeah. You told me that a hundred times before."

"And I'll tell you a hundred times again, and one of these times you'll believe me."

"Well, whatever you are, Tillie," Mom said, "thank God you're with us."

Tillie nodded. "He's the one to thank, all right, and I'll be with you till he calls me home. Won't be long now, I suppose."

Marie gasped loudly, and the color drained from her face like someone had pulled a plug. "This is Thanksgiving, Mrs. Monroe," she said sharply. "Surely there are better things to talk about than death."

"Who's talking about death?" Tillie retorted. "Did I say something about death? All I said was someday God's going to call me home."

"Well yes, and that means —"

"And when that happens, I plan to shed this skin and finally fly. Does that sound like death to you?"

Marie sputtered, but Grandpa laughed outright. "Whatever you plan to do when you die, Tillie, my guess is you're going to outlive us all."

"Ah, no thank you, Archie," Tillie said. "No, I'll leave the living to the young folk. When the good Lord calls, I'm going straight up and straight on till morning." Her plump hand sailed over the table, and we all watched it fly upward. It stopped and hung suspended just beneath the chandelier for a minute before it finally drifted back down to her lap.

Everyone got quiet then and went back to eating.

I thought about Daddy, wondering where

he was and what he might be doing. I thought maybe he was eating a couple of weeping cows at the Hot Diggity Dog Café with a waitress who didn't even know his name, who called him Nelson instead of Alan and who called me his niece instead of his daughter. But then I realized the café was probably closed, this being a holiday, so I couldn't imagine what Daddy was doing while everyone else in Mills River was gathered with family, though I hoped he wasn't alone. I hoped he wasn't lonely. I wished I could call him and wish him a happy Thanksgiving, but I didn't know where he lived or how to get in touch with him. I couldn't call or send him a letter or travel to his house to see him. I was always waiting for a note in my desk telling me when to meet him next, and since our last meeting more than a week ago, I hadn't heard from him.

"What are you thinking so hard about, Roz?" Tillie asked.

I looked up, startled. "Nothing. Why?"

"You're frowning so, you look like the weight of the whole world is on your shoulders."

I shrugged my shoulders in response, as though to show Tillie they weren't weighted down by anything at all. "I don't know. I'm not thinking about anything. Really. Nothing. I'm just busy eating."

"Aha!" Tillie cried. " 'The lady doth protest too much!' "

"What?"

"Shakespeare!" Gramps chimed in. "She means, Roz, that if you really weren't thinking about anything, you wouldn't be trying so hard to convince us you weren't."

"What do you mean, Gramps?" By now I was really confused.

"But, Archie," Marie interrupted, "one's thoughts are a private affair. The child doesn't have to tell you what she was thinking."

Grandpa frowned and gave a small nod. "No, dear, you're right. Then again, I'm not the one who asked her."

"Asked me what?" I asked.

"What you were thinking. I believe that was Tillie. Wasn't it, Tillie?"

"I was wondering why she looked so pained, is all," Tillie said. "But of course she doesn't have to tell us. Though, if she told us what her question is, then maybe we could give her an answer."

Grandpa looked back to me. "Did you have a question, Roz?"

"I don't think so. I —"

"Archie, just leave the child alone and let

her eat."

"But, Marie, I —"

"First, we talk about death, and then we have to badger a child just to find out what kind of insipid —"

"Why don't I begin to clear the table," Mom cut in. She jumped up quickly and started gathering dirty dishes. "I'll put the coffee on so we can have it with dessert."

"I'll help you, Janis," Tillie volunteered.

"I'll help too," I said, pushing back my chair and standing up. "I'm ready for dessert."

With all the jumping up and the grabbing of dirty dishes and the rush to make coffee and get dessert, the discussion about what I was thinking was dropped and forgotten. Except by me. I told myself to be more careful in the future and not to think too hard about Daddy when there were grown-ups in the room. If they could ever penetrate my thoughts to learn that Daddy was in Mills River . . . Well, it was a good thing thoughts were a private affair and no one could read my mind.

CHAPTER 31

Mara and I sat cross-legged on my twin beds, with Valerie on the floor between us. Valerie made little cooing noises as she touched a plastic bottle to the puckered plastic lips of her doll. With the doll nestled in the crook of her arm, she rocked gently as she encouraged her baby to drink.

"What's your baby's name?" Mara asked.

Valerie paused and looked up. "Ginger," she said.

"That's a pretty name."

Valerie nodded and went back to rocking. Mom was making supper and had asked us to watch her. Tillie was on one of her rare visits to her son Johnny's house. Apparently discussions were underway between them as to how to help Tillie's missionary son get settled back in Mills River after the first of the year.

Tom Barrows was downstairs in the easy chair reading the paper. Mom had invited him to have supper with us, and he'd come to our house directly from work. I took his relaxed presence in the living room as a foreshadowing of things to come, and I didn't like it. But at the moment I was more interested in Mara than in Mom's questionable future as Mrs. Barrows.

"So come on and tell me what your mom — I mean, Celia — said already," I pleaded impatiently.

Mara took a deep breath and squeezed her hands together in front of her chest. I knew it was good news because her big brown eyes were shining.

"Mama got in touch with Daddy. She was able to reach him in his office at the university."

"Yeah?" I leaned forward expectantly.

"And he said he was willing to see me."

Squealing, we clapped and bounced on the beds. Valerie looked up at us with a frown. "Shh," she said, one small finger on her lips. "Ginger fell sleep."

We ignored her and went on squealing. "I can't believe it!" I cried.

"I can hardly believe it myself."

"How's it going to happen?"

"I'll take the train to Chicago, and he'll be there at the station to meet me."

"Really?"

She nodded happily. "That's what Mama said. Celia, I mean."

"And then what?"

"And then we'll go somewhere for lunch and just talk."

"What about his family? Will they know about it?"

Mara's rosy lips formed a taut line. "No. He'll have to lie to them about where he is."

"But that's . . ." I almost told her there were all sorts of lies involved whenever I saw my own daddy, but a glance at Valerie stopped me. Daddy was a secret that had to be kept even from my little sister. I changed tracks and asked, "Are you scared?"

Mara nodded again, slowly this time, her small chin moving up and down. "I'm real scared. What if he doesn't like me?"

"What if you don't like *him?*"

"Oh, I already know I like *him.* I listen to him twice a week, you know. I already know a lot of things about him, even what his voice sounds like. But he doesn't know anything about *me.*"

"He will soon. And he'll like you, Mara. He really will."

"Do you think so?"

"Oh yes. I'm sure he will."

Her eyes drifted toward the window. She

looked thoughtful. "Celia said it's the first time she's talked to him since I was born. In the beginning they wrote a few letters, but —" she paused and shrugged — "then they both got married and all."

"So how did she know how to find him?"

"Well, they've always known the day would come when he would meet me, so he's made sure Celia knows where he is."

"She must have been scared to call him, after all this time."

"Yeah." Another small nod. "She was scared, all right. She had to go to a phone booth to make the call, otherwise the long-distance number would show up on their phone bill. She was scared Raymond — that's her husband — would find out what she was doing. She was scared my daddy would say no. She was even scared she'd run out of dimes before they finished talking."

"But your daddy said yes, and she didn't run out of dimes."

"Uh-huh."

"So doesn't Raymond know about you?"

"Oh yeah, he knows. He knows I was born to Celia before those two got married. What he doesn't know is who my daddy is. That's what Celia doesn't want him to ever know."

"So you've got to keep it secret."

"That's right. One more secret I've got to remember to keep."

By now Valerie was stretched out on the floor, dozing with the doll in her arms. The plastic bottle lay on its side on the floor, having fallen from her grip. I gazed at her a moment, then back at Mara.

"So when are you going?"

"Sometime over Christmas vacation."

"Do your grandparents know?"

"Yeah, they know. They don't like it, but I'm going anyway." We were quiet a moment. Then Mara added, "Listen, Roz, I think this all happened because of the Daddy Deal. I really do. You've been praying for me to meet my daddy, praying every day, right?"

I nodded, though I felt a pinch of guilt for the days I had forgotten.

"And now it's coming true. I'm really going to meet him."

"I'm glad, Mara," I said, and I was. Glad that she was going to meet her daddy but envious at the same time.

As though she could sense my envy, she said, "So pretty soon maybe your daddy will decide it's time to come home."

"Yeah." I glanced again at Valerie to make sure she wasn't listening, but she was breathing that slow, rhythmic breath of

311

sleep. "But it's got to be soon, or Tom Barrows is going to marry Mom first, and then Daddy won't have a chance."

"Are they engaged or something? Your mom and Mr. Barrows, I mean?"

"No, I don't think so."

"So why do you think your mom's going to marry him?"

"I don't know. It's just that he's always over here, or they're always going out somewhere, or else they're on the phone with each other. It's like Mom actually likes him or something."

"Maybe she does."

"I don't think so. How could she?"

"Then why's she seeing him?"

"I don't know, Mara. I wish I did. No, what I really wish is that he'd just go away. I don't want him to propose to Mom before Daddy can come back."

"What about all the stuff I said? You know, like she can't cook and she snores real bad?"

"He didn't seem to care. He just kept on coming around."

Mara raised a hand to her chin and frowned in thought. Her eyes focused on first one thing and then another, finally coming to rest on Valerie.

"You say he doesn't like children, right?"

"I don't know whether he likes kids or

not, but he doesn't seem very interested."

"Well, if he marries your mom, that'll make him your dad, right?"

I laid a hand across my stomach. "Please, Mara, that's what I'm trying not to think about."

She snapped her fingers. "I've got an idea."

"What?"

She hopped off the bed and shook Valerie's shoulder.

"What are you doing?" I cried. "She's the worst grump in the world if you wake her up."

"That's what I'm banking on."

"I mean it, Mara. Don't wake her up. You know how she can scream."

Mara stopped shaking Valerie's shoulder and gave me a small, crooked smile. Before I could stop her, she pinched Valerie's thigh and started the child howling like a banshee.

I put my hands to my head in alarm. "Mara! What are you doing?"

"Trust me," she said.

"But —"

She wrestled the kicking, screaming Valerie into a tight strangle-hold, then picked her up and floundered till she found her balance. With Valerie's back to her chest, Mara looked like she had an extra pair of legs flailing in front of her. She gave a nod in my direction and said, "Follow me."

I followed her out of my room, through the hall, and down the stairs. From the kitchen I heard Mom's voice calling, "What on earth? Roz, can't you do something about Valerie?"

Ahead of me Mara said quietly, so Mom couldn't hear, "Yeah, we're taking care of everything."

She marched into the living room, where Tom Barrows sat, his balding hairline visible just above the rim of the newspaper. His stockinged feet were propped up on the footstool, and he was flexing his toes as though his feet were grateful to be loosed from the wingtip oxfords he always wore. He was the typical male, resting after a hard day's work, waiting for his supper, unalarmed by the screams of a toddler, since childcare, of course, was not his job. He didn't drop the paper to his lap until Mara was directly upon him, and even then his startled eyes behind the horn-rimmed glasses told me he didn't quite believe what was happening.

In the next moment he had a tantrum-throwing child in his lap. His arms flew out to his sides as though he didn't want to touch her, this creature that had suddenly

314

been thrust upon him from out of nowhere.

"What the —" he cried, throwing out an oath that would have bounced furiously around the room had the word been made of rubber.

"We can't quiet her down," Mara explained, speaking loudly over the screams, "so we thought you could try."

She didn't stay to see what he would do, but turned and beckoned me to follow. Halfway up the stairs we were rattled by the shriek of "Jannn*isss!*" that shot forth from Tom Barrows' throat and exploded in the living room.

Mara and I collapsed in my bedroom, doubled over with laughter. We would be in trouble for sure, but I didn't care. Small price to pay if it would help to rid our family of that nuisance known as Tom Barrows.

CHAPTER 32

"I hardly ever see you, Daddy."

"I'm sorry, Roz, but it's too dangerous."

"What do you mean, dangerous?"

"I mean, I can't risk being seen. If your mother finds out I'm here, everything will fall apart. She can't know until the right time."

"But when's the right time?"

He shook his head. "You've asked me that before, and my answer hasn't changed. I just don't know yet, honey."

We were back in our usual meeting place, the Hot Diggity Dog Café. Daddy had ordered me a banana split, and he was helping me eat it.

"Daddy?"

"Yeah, honey?"

"Christmas will be here soon."

The spoon stopped halfway to Daddy's mouth, and he looked as though he'd lost his appetite. "I know it will," he said.

"I don't guess we'll all be together on Christmas morning."

The spoon reached Daddy's mouth and came out empty. Daddy chewed slowly and thoughtfully before saying, "Now, you know that's just not possible, Roz."

"Wally won't be with us either."

"Are you sure? Even if he's in basic training by then, he should be allowed leave for the holidays."

I shook my head. "In his last letter he said he won't be home for a while, more than a year, probably. But he said not to worry about him. Mom worries all the time, though. Sometimes I see her crying, even though she pretends like she's not."

Daddy dug methodically at the ice cream, like he was looking for buried treasure. I waited, but he wouldn't look at me. Finally he said, "I'm sorry to hear that."

"I just want her to be happy, don't you, Daddy?"

He glanced at me, looked away. "Of course I want her to be happy. That's what I'm working toward."

I dipped my spoon in the dish, but my stomach reeled at the thought of another bite. It wasn't the ice cream making me feel sick; it was what I was about to say to Daddy. I licked my lips and took a deep breath. "I remember . . ."

He looked at me then, his forehead furrowed like a tilled field. "What, Roz?"

"Well, I remember . . . you know, sometimes Mom would cry because of you."

He tightened at that, like a current of electricity had just run through him. I thought for a second that he might blow up, and I lowered my head to shield myself from the explosion. But instead of getting angry, he flexed his neck and lifted his shoulders in an attempt to untie himself and relax. "I know, Roz," he said, "but it's not going to be that way anymore."

My heart beat wildly and my insides shook, but I forced myself to hold Daddy's gaze. "Do you promise?"

"Yes." He frowned and lifted a hand to the side of his face, his fingertips kneading circles over his temple. "I promise. Everything's going to be different this time. I — Roz, what's the matter?"

He must have heard me inhale sharply, and undoubtedly my face registered both shock and fear.

Daddy glanced back over his shoulder. "Roz, do you see someone you know?"

I could do little more than nod.

"Listen to me, Roz. Don't say anything. Just come over here and sit beside me." He pushed his jacket aside and patted the bench.

Too afraid to breathe, I followed Tom Barrows with my eyes, watching silently as he strode across the café toward our booth. I braced myself for what was about to happen, but instead of coming to the table and confronting Daddy, he stopped at the counter and removed his hat, gloves, and coat. He laid the coat across one of the stools and planted the gloves and fedora on top. With a hitch of his pants, he settled himself on the next stool over. He must have said something to Darlene, because she smiled and nodded and placed a cup of coffee in front of him.

With my gaze still firmly on Tom Barrows, I started to rise, but Daddy stretched a hand across the table to stop me. "Don't get up," he said quietly. "Go under the table. That's it."

I slid down under the table like I was inching my way under a limbo bar, scooted over the sticky linoleum floor, and popped up on the other side next to Daddy. He put his arm around me, and I nestled there between him and the wall, hidden to Tom Barrows and to anyone else who might happen into the Hot Diggity Dog Café.

I leaned my head into the hollow of Dad-

319

dy's shoulder, and he tightened his grip around me. He was strong and solid from years of construction work, but his embrace was just as I remembered: at once tough and tender. I took a long deep breath, savoring the moment. A warmth rose up from Daddy's skin; the opposing odors of sweat and soap collided and mingled in the fabric of his plaid flannel shirt. With my ear pressed heavily to his chest, I heard the faint echo of his heart, heard the air making its journey through his lungs, in and out, slowly and rhythmically. His life sounds were hypnotic, and in another moment I may have actually drifted off to sleep if Daddy hadn't interrupted.

"Roz, who is that guy?" he asked, his voice a whisper. "The one who just sat down."

I hesitated, not wanting to tell him. A teacher, I could say, or the man who lives next door. But then, if Daddy knew, if he realized his position in the family was in danger, maybe he'd come home sooner. Besides, I realized I couldn't get rid of Tom Barrows on my own. Mom had docked me two weeks' allowance for dropping Valerie in his lap — a bigger punishment than I'd expected. I could hardly afford to keep annoying the man in an effort to make him go away. So I said, "He's Mom's friend."

His breath stopped. His chest was still. I waited. Then he said simply, "Her friend?"

I nodded, my hair rubbing static against his shirt.

"You don't mean she's . . . seeing him?" As he spoke, his left hand — the one that had been resting on the table — began to work, opening, closing into a fist, opening again.

I immediately began to second-guess myself; maybe I should have lied. "Kind of, I guess."

"What do you mean, you guess?"

"I mean, they've gone to the movies a couple of times."

Daddy was quiet for several long minutes. I looked up and saw that he was looking intently at the profile of Mom's suitor, as though trying to memorize the man in detail. By now Tom Barrows had removed his suit jacket and was sitting there in a white dress shirt, the edge of a dark tie peeking out from beneath his collar. He held a coffee cup in one hand and a folded newspaper in the other.

"What's his name?" Daddy asked.

"Tom Barrows."

"What's he do?"

"What do you mean?"

"I mean, for a living. What's he do?"

I tried to remember. "I'm not sure. Tillie says he works for the county or something."

Another pause. Then, "Who's Tillie?"

Now I was really sorry. I never meant to tell him about Tillie. If he knew an old lady was living with us, he'd never want to come back. As I looked up at Daddy, our faces were only inches apart. I hadn't been this close to him for a long time. "Oh," I lied, "she's just someone who comes and helps Mom with Valerie."

"You mean like a nanny?"

"Yeah. Because, well, Mom has to work now, you know. So she can't be home all the time, even though she wishes she could."

Daddy looked back at Tom Barrows, then down at me. Something about his eyes had changed, though I couldn't say what.

When he didn't speak I said, "Daddy?"

"Yeah?"

"What if he sees me?"

"He won't."

"Are you sure?"

"I'm sure." He took a deep breath.

"Well, what if he stays here for a long time? I've got to go meet Mom pretty soon. If I don't show up, she'll go looking for me at the library."

Daddy's eyes narrowed, and his lips formed a small tense line. "Don't worry.

It'll be all right."

I wasn't so sure. I didn't say anything.

"But, honey?"

"Yeah?"

"We're going to have to be even more careful. You and your mom, you're not strangers in town anymore. People are starting to know you. I think, to play it safe, it might be a while before I can see you again."

"How long, Daddy?"

"I don't know."

"But you're coming back to us someday, and things are going to be better, right?"

He tried to smile. "You already asked me that, Roz. I wish you'd quit asking and just believe me."

A small ache rose up in my heart and sent shivers down my spine. Daddy must have felt it, because he held me a little tighter.

"Daddy," I pleaded quietly, "tell me what it's going to be like when we're all together again."

I wanted to hear visions of happy Christmas mornings and birthday parties and family vacations. I wanted to hear Daddy tell me that we'd all sit down together to eat supper at night, with him and Wally both there with us, and we'd all get along and talk and laugh, and afterward Mom would wash the dishes while Daddy helped me with homework and Valerie played with a puppy that Daddy had brought home for us. I wanted to know that he'd bring Mom flowers for no special reason, and he'd tell her she looked beautiful, and she *would* look beautiful because she wouldn't cry all the time anymore, and she'd never again have to cover the bruises on her cheeks with makeup or the black eyes with dark glasses. There would be none of that, none of that at all, because Daddy would be different, he'd be good, a real Daddy, one who loved us and took care of us and wanted the very best in life for us.

But when Daddy finally spoke, he said, "It's going to be good, Roz." That was all, and I had to do my dreaming without him.

CHAPTER 33

I sat on the edge of Valerie's bed, listening to her say her prayers with Tillie. "Our Fadder, it's hot in heaven . . ."

I bit my lower lip so as not to laugh. Tillie didn't miss a beat but quietly recited the prayer along with her, then pulled the covers up tight around her chin and kissed her cheek. "Good night, little one," she said.

"Night, Tillie. I love you."

"I love you too. Sweet dreams."

Tillie turned off the light on the bedside table, and a small nightlight took over, holding back the dark. I slipped off the bed and kissed my sister good-night. Her cheek was soft and smelled sweet and clean from her bubble bath.

"Night, Roz," she said sleepily.

"Good night, Valerie. See you in the morning."

Tillie and I treaded lightly out of the room and down the stairs. In the kitchen Tillie tied her apron back on and set about slicing apples for a pie she was making. I sat down at the table, resting my chin in the cup of my hands.

"What time did Mom say she'd be home?" I asked.

"She didn't," Tillie said, cutting an apple into halves. "It'll be late, since she and Tom have gone to Chicago to see the show. All she said was don't wait up."

I sniffed at the thought of her going all the way to Chicago with Tom Barrows on a Friday night. "How come she has to spend so much time with him?" I complained. "I wish she'd just stay home with us."

Tillie paused in her cutting and shook her head. "I don't have a good answer for you, Roz. Between you, me, and the lamppost, I don't think she ought to be seeing anyone."

"You don't? That's not what you said before. You said we should all just want her to be happy."

"Yes, I know," she said. "Frankly, though, I thought she and Tom might go out once, maybe twice, and that would be it. They don't really seem like a good match to me."

I raised my eyebrows, startled and happy to hear her say so. "They don't seem like a good match to me either, Tillie."

"So I thought the whole thing would just

kind of peter out on its own," she went on. "I sure never thought Tom would be coming around here so much. What I think your mother really needs is a chance to heal and get over your father. That's going to take some time, and I don't believe the real healing will begin until after the divorce is final. Heaven only knows when that will be, since they haven't even filed all the paperwork yet."

"The divorce?" I echoed. That was the first time I'd heard the word used in relation to Mom and Daddy.

"Well, sure. There's got to be a divorce, you know. That's what happens when husbands and wives end a marriage. But your grandfather has only just found your mother a lawyer. They're just getting started. Eventually they'll serve your father with the papers, and then there will be a lot of legal stuff to figure out. It might take some time before your mother's free to marry again."

"What does it mean that he'll get served with some papers?"

"Just that there are papers about the divorce that both your parents will have to sign to make it final."

"What if Daddy doesn't sign them?"

"He will. He may not want to at first, but he will eventually."

Not if they don't find him, I thought.

"Tillie?"

"Yes, Roz?" Tillie stirred sugar, cinnamon, and nutmeg in a bowl with a wooden spoon.

"We had another air raid drill in school today."

"Oh?" She added cornstarch and salt to the sugar mix, then sprinkled all of it over the apple slices. She may have thought I was changing the subject, but I wasn't.

"Every time we have an air raid drill, I think about what it would be like if the Russians dropped a bomb on us and killed us all."

"Merciful heavens!" Tillie said, turning to look at me sharply. "You shouldn't be worrying about something like that. I've half a mind to go to the school board and tell them to stop those silly drills. No one's going to drop any bombs on us."

"They aren't? Because we sure are practicing a lot for something that's not going to happen."

"Tell me, Roz, who's the principal out at your school now?"

"Mr. Waldrop."

"Wayne Waldrop?"

I gave a small shrug. "I think so."

"That figures," Tillie said with a satisfied nod. "That Wayne, he always did like the sound of a good siren. Fire truck sirens, police sirens, ambulance sirens. I bet you have a lot of fire drills at your school too, huh?"

"Yeah. It seems like it. Then we have to put our coats on and go stand outside in the cold."

Another nod. "Pay no attention to the drills, then. Wayne Waldrop was in the same grade as Lyle. I didn't know him so much, but I knew his mother well. Poor thing, she told me how Wayne was always getting into trouble for pulling the fire alarm at school. And he'd go down to the fire station too and ask the men if he could ride in the trucks with them and work the siren next time they had a call. Now that he can sound the alarm legitimately, it seems he's having a little bit too much fun with it."

"But even Wally's school — or the school he used to go to — they have air raid drills and fire drills too."

"Sure, you've got to have some. That's the law. But you don't have to worry about the Russians dropping the bomb. No one's going to be stupid enough to push the button that turns the Cold War into an all-out nuclear war. So you can just forget about that, Roz."

Tillie poured the apple mixture into the

pie pan, where the bottom crust waited. She added dabs of butter, draped the upper crust over the top, and cut slices in the dough to let the steam out while it baked. She popped the pie into the oven, took off her apron, and sat down at the table across from me.

"Listen, Roz, I know you're not little like Valerie, but you're still just a child. You should be thinking about good things, dreaming about the future. Remember what I told you about the moments, about how so many of them are lost?"

"Yeah, I remember."

"Life goes by so fast, Roz, and when you come to the end, you don't remember even half of it. You wonder where it's all gone. If I were your age, if I could start all over again, I'd spend far more time looking for what's good rather than dwelling on the bad. But then —" she sighed and leaned back in the chair — "I'm pretty much in the homestretch at this point. I guess that's why I cherish the good moments so much. Between now and heaven there aren't going to be too many more of them."

I leaned forward over the table and looked intently at Tillie. "But see, I'm afraid I'm not going to heaven like you are because . . . well, what if Mom gets the divorce and

330

Daddy never comes home?"

Tillie looked puzzled. "What does the divorce have to do with you going to heaven?"

"Well, remember, when I was having my tonsils out, you said it all depends on who your father is, and —"

But my last words were interrupted by Valerie crying out from a bad dream, calling for Mom, who wasn't yet home, so Tillie had to go and comfort her and rock her back to sleep. I took my question about heaven to bed with me and forgot to bring it up again with Tillie in the morning.

CHAPTER 34

Sometime in mid-December, Grandpa came over with a fragrant Douglas fir and a box of ornaments; Wally sent a small package postmarked Fort Dix, New Jersey; boxes started showing up from friends in Minnesota; and Tom Barrows gifted us by no longer coming around.

I was too busy to notice at first, with schoolwork, Christmas gifts, and Daddy's absence heavy on my mind. Not until Christmas was only five days away did I realize I hadn't seen Tom Barrows in more than a week. Mom hadn't spoken with him on the phone either. He simply wasn't there anymore, and I wondered why he had disappeared.

To get an answer I sidestepped Mom and went straight to Tillie. I found her in her room one afternoon, hemming a pair of pants for Valerie, who was napping on Tillie's bed beneath the wedding quilt. I pulled the desk chair close to Tillie and sat down.

Helping myself to the butter mints, I asked, "So what happened to Tom Barrows?"

She paused in her sewing and raised her brows. "What do you mean, what happened to him?"

"He hasn't come around lately, and I haven't seen Mom talking to him on the phone."

"Uh-huh. So your mother hasn't told you anything?"

I shook my head while savoring the mint. I liked the way it melted against the roof of my mouth.

"Well, Roz," Tillie said. She looked around the room and lowered her voice even though Mom was at work. "Apparently they decided to stop seeing so much of each other."

"They did!" I exclaimed, nearly jumping out of my seat. Tillie put a finger to her lips and nodded toward Valerie. Whispering now, I asked, "How come? Did you tell her to stop seeing him?"

"Me? Oh dear, no. I had my opinion about the whole thing, of course, but no, I didn't say a word."

"Then what happened?"

She looked pensive a moment as she

pulled at a knot in her thread. "I'm not really sure. It's one of those complicated grown-up things, I guess."

"But whose decision was it?"

"It was mutual, from what I understand. Though apparently Tom felt threatened."

"Threatened?"

"That's what your mother said."

"By what?"

"I don't know. Whatever men feel threatened by when they get involved in a relationship. Financial responsibilities, a lack of freedom, sudden fatherhood. It could be any number of things."

Sudden fatherhood? Suddenly the loss of two weeks' allowance seemed a paltry sum. Maybe dropping Valerie into Tom Barrows' lap *did* do the trick!

"Are they going to see each other at all anymore?" I asked.

"I couldn't tell you that. But whether they do or don't, it's up to them, and it's not our business."

I thought of Mom then, down at Marie's Apparel, going about the business of selling hats and gloves. Was she smiling at the customers and did that smile cover a broken heart, or was she secretly as relieved as I was to be rid of Tom Barrows?

"Tillie? Is Mom all right? I mean, is she

sad or anything?"

Tillie lifted her shoulders in a small shrug. "She doesn't seem sad to me. Your mother's a smart woman, Roz. I think she finally decided some things are more important than security."

Like love? I wondered. If only Mom would fall back in love with Daddy, everything would be perfect.

"Well," I said mildly, trying to curb my growing excitement, "I'm going to go finish my homework." I stood and dragged the chair back to the desk.

Tillie looked up at me. "Only two more days of school until Christmas vacation starts."

I nodded. "Are you going to be with us for Christmas?"

"Oh yes, I'll be here. On Christmas Eve I'll be going to church with Johnny and Elaine, but I always like to be in my own home on Christmas morning. It will be just us girls, you know. You, me, Valerie, and your mother. But we won't let that keep us from having a good time."

"Yeah. I guess."

No Wally. No Daddy. And thankfully, no Tom Barrows.

I took one step toward the door, and when I did an image flashed through my mind:

Tom Barrows sitting at the café counter drinking coffee and reading the paper while Daddy's fist opened and closed on the tabletop.

"Something the matter, Roz?"

Tillie's voice drew me back. She had stopped in midstitch and was staring at me with concern.

"Huh?"

"You look like something's bothering you," she said.

"Oh." I shook my head. "No. Nothing. Well, I've got a lot of homework."

Maybe Daddy had threatened Tom Barrows and maybe he hadn't. It didn't matter, so long as Tom was out of the picture. The way was clear now for Daddy to make his move. I hoped he'd do it soon.

An overcast sky left the streets of Mills River in an early twilight. The walk from the library to Marie's Apparel might have been hopelessly dismal had it not been for the colored lights that shone from store windows and from the branches of the trees lining the sidewalks. With Christmas right around the corner, I longed to feel the familiar excitement of the season, but I couldn't deny the sadness nudging at me as I trudged through the cold and the snow.

My heart tightened in my chest, and tears burned my eyes. That afternoon, school had let out for Christmas vacation and wouldn't start up again until January. My desk, the repository for Daddy's notes, was off limits to me now. I'd been hoping he would leave one more, asking me to meet him again at Hot Diggity Dog. I'd dreamed of his giving me a Christmas gift, something small and easy to conceal, but something that would let me know he loved me. The summons to meet him never came, though, and now it was too late. Maybe he could contact me some other way, but I couldn't imagine how.

Meanwhile, Mara would be going to Chicago in the morning to meet her father. I had just left her strolling through the aisles of the library's fiction section, looking for something to read on the train, something that would impress her father when he met her on the platform, the book tucked nonchalantly under her arm as though it belonged there. *Silas Marner*? I wondered. *David Copperfield*? Or why not go all out and choose *War and Peace*? It wouldn't be quite so heavy if she checked it out in paperback, though it would still be weighty enough, of course, to make a lasting impression on William Remmick, English professor and book lover.

Mara, with her bright eyes and nervous laughter, was the picture of giddiness. It was all arranged. Her grandparents would accompany her on the 9:05, which they would ride to the end of the line. Her father would meet them at the station and spend a few hours with Mara while her grandparents did some Christmas shopping in the city. Mara and her father would have lunch, talk about their lives and literature, exchange Christmas gifts — she had a small volume of Langston Hughes that she'd signed *With love from Beatrice* — and forge a lifelong bond that would keep them together even while they lived out their lives apart.

Clenching my jaw and clutching my books more tightly, I tried to push the thought of Mara and her daddy out of my mind. I was on my way to meet Mom at work so we could drive home together, but at the last minute I decided to turn down Second Street instead of sticking to the usual route. It would be a roundabout way to Marie's Apparel, but it would take me by the café. Maybe, just maybe, Daddy would be there, sipping hot coffee while warming his hands on the cup.

The plate-glass window of Hot Diggity Dog was rimmed with blinking colored lights. Someone had painted a Santa hat on the dancing hot dog and had written *Ho Ho Hot Dogs!* in a cartoon bubble near his head. He was surrounded by a storm of hand-cut paper snowflakes stuck to the window with Scotch Tape. Finding an open patch amid the blizzard, I pressed my forehead against the icy glass and lifted one gloved hand to the side of my face so I could peer inside. A few customers sat scattered here and there, but Daddy wasn't among them.

My breath steamed up the window, so I rubbed a circle with my glove to clear the fog. As I was doing that, Darlene came to the door and leaned out into the cold. "You looking for your uncle Nelson?" she asked.

I nodded dully.

"I haven't seen him around here for a while. Last I heard he'd got a temporary job in the city."

"Chicago?"

"Yeah. Didn't he tell you?"

I shook my head.

"Well," she went on, "it sounded like he'd be gone a couple of weeks. Three at the most. He should be back soon."

"Okay," I whispered. My throat was tight, and I knew that if I didn't go soon I'd break down crying in front of Darlene.

"Listen, honey," she said as she hugged herself and shivered, "it's freezing out here.

Why don't you come in for a nice cup of hot chocolate?"

But I didn't want to go inside. I didn't want to be in there without Daddy.

"It's all right," Darlene went on. "It'll be on me. Besides, your uncle Nelson is a generous tipper. I owe him one."

I looked up at the waitress, her cheeks now reddened by the cold, her teeth beginning to chatter. She was still talking, but my mind was whirling, and I couldn't make sense of the words. I wanted to ask her why she thought my father was my uncle Nelson, and what he told her when I wasn't around. I wanted to ask her what she really thought of him, beyond the fact that he was a generous tipper. Did she think he had it in him to be a good husband, a loving father, a man who didn't drink, didn't get angry, didn't lash out with his fists or threaten to drive his whole family off the road and into a tree? Did she think I could trust him when he told me he would change?

I wanted to ask her all these questions, but I didn't say a word. Because if she didn't even know his name was Alan and not Nelson, how could she be expected to know anything about him at all?

"Look, honey, you got to make up your mind because I need to shut the door. I'm letting all the cold air in."

I took one step backward, then turned and started to run.

"Well, all right, honey," Darlene called after me. "Maybe next time."

I didn't look back. There had to be a safe place ahead of me somewhere, if only I could run far enough to find it.

CHAPTER 35

Two days later when the doorbell rang in midmorning, I opened the door to find Mara standing on the front porch. She was wrapped up against the cold in a long woolen coat and knitted cap; only her eyes stared out from above the scarf circling her face. For a moment neither of us spoke as I stared into those unblinking eyes, those two dark pools of something bittersweet.

"Did you see him?" I asked.

She nodded. Tears rose up out of the depths of the pools.

I looked back over my shoulder to see whether Tillie had left the kitchen, but she hadn't. Mom had already gone to work. I motioned for Mara to come in, and I shut the door behind her. She slipped out of her boots first, then untangled herself from the massive coat. She pushed the hat and scarf into one sleeve, and tossing everything onto the couch in the living room, she followed me upstairs to my room.

We positioned ourselves on the beds, cross-legged. I waited. After a moment she lifted a hand to her locket and said, "He doesn't look like this anymore."

"What's he look like?"

"Older. His hair is turning gray."

"That's an old picture."

"Yeah. It was taken before I was born. It's more than twelve years old."

"People change a lot in that many years."

She nodded. "Yeah, they do."

I waited another minute. When she didn't go on, I said, "Well, what was he like?"

"He was like . . ." Her voice drifted off as she squeezed the locket. "He was like . . ."

"Yeah?"

"He was mostly like I imagined, I guess, except for looking older."

I could feel myself frowning. "That's good, isn't it?"

She pressed her lips together and squeezed her eyes shut. After taking a deep breath, she looked at me and said, "I was so scared, Roz. I've never been so scared."

I nodded. I understood.

"All the way up there on the train, I thought I was going to be sick," she went on. "I held on tight to *War and Peace* with both hands until the cover was all sweaty. I couldn't read. I couldn't do anything but look out the window and wonder what was going to happen. When we got to the station in Chicago, I felt all weak, and I didn't think I could even walk off the train. So I held on to Grandpa's arm real tight, and I think he knew how scared I was because he kept saying, 'It'll be all right, child. It'll be all right.' "

She took another deep breath and wet her lips with her tongue. "When we got off the train, the station was crowded with people everywhere. I kept looking around, but I didn't see anybody that looked familiar. Then finally Grandpa said, 'There he is now, Mara. See him?' I looked around and didn't see him, but I saw a man coming toward us, a tall white man wearing glasses and a hat that covered his hair. I didn't see anything about him that looked like the man in the photo.

"You know, it's funny, Roz, but I'd always pictured myself running into Daddy's arms and giving him the biggest hug he ever had in his life. But when I saw him and it was real, I couldn't do it. When he was still a little ways away, he took his hat off and kind of smoothed his hair down and then nodded at Grandpa like he recognized him. They knew each other from before, you know, back when Mama and he . . . well, you know.

"So he came up to us, and he shook hands with Grandpa and Grandma first before he even looked at me, and Grandpa had to tell him, 'Bill, this here's Mara.' And then he looked at me and held out his hand, and I shook it and I couldn't believe he was my daddy. I couldn't believe it, Roz. And he said, 'I'm glad to finally meet you, Beatrice,' and I just kind of mumbled something, and I could tell Grandpa and Grandma were looking at each other and wondering why he'd called me Beatrice when they'd just told him my name was Mara."

"But," I interrupted, "isn't Beatrice your first name?"

"Yeah, it is, and they know that, but no one ever calls me Beatrice. Except Daddy, when he says good-night to me on the radio. So I guess he couldn't see himself calling me anything else."

"So what happened after that?"

"Well, those three talked for a little while about the plans — you know, where everyone would be and when we'd meet up again. And then we left the station, and next thing I know Daddy and I were in his car driving out of the city. I asked him where we were going, and he said we were going up to Evanston for lunch, to a place he knew up there. I didn't ask him why we didn't stay in Chicago, because I knew. He couldn't be seen with me there. Everyone would say, 'Hey, isn't that William Remmick, the guy on the radio? So who's that little Negro girl with him?' And the next thing you know, word would get around and his wife would find out, and she'd ask him who I was and he'd have to lie about it, or he'd have to tell her the truth. Either way, he couldn't let it happen."

She paused. I nodded, urging her to go on.

"We didn't say too much at first," she said, looking far off beyond the walls of my room. "I think he might have been nervous, because he turned on the radio and kept changing the station. I put the book on the seat between us, and he said, 'You reading that?' and even though I hadn't started it, I said yeah, I was reading it. He said I was taking on a challenge, but he was glad I liked to read, and I said, 'When I grow up I'm going to be an English professor just like you and maybe even a writer.' For a minute I thought he looked kind of proud, like he was glad I wanted to be like him. But he didn't say anything. He just kind of nodded and fiddled with the radio, and then he lit a cigarette. I didn't even know he smoked."

As Mara spoke, I tried to picture her sitting in the car with her father, the two of them stiff and formal, the tall white professor fidgeting behind the wheel, the little dark-skinned girl sitting prim in the passenger seat. I imagined her hair pulled back and tied with ribbons, her winter coat buttoned up to her chin, her patent leather shoes polished to a shine. Her gloved hands would be in her lap, her laced fingers kneading each other nervously.

"He was smoking the cigarette," Mara went on, "and blowing the smoke out a little crack in the window, and he didn't say anything for a long time. Then he finally just said, 'You know, Beatrice, sometimes things just don't work out the way we hope they will.' He sounded real sad when he said it, and I thought maybe he was talking about our getting together, like maybe he hoped it would somehow be different or I would be different or something. But then he said, 'I want you to know up front that if it'd been up to me, I'd have married your mother. I didn't want to let either of you go.' And I said, 'Maybe you should have just married her then and kept us both,' and he looked even sadder and said, 'Sometimes

347

things get too complicated, more complicated than you can imagine.' I told him I didn't see why it was so complicated to just go ahead and marry the person you love, and he said maybe I would understand when I was older."

I was listening intently, my elbows on my knees, my chin in my hands. When she paused to take a breath, I said, "Grown-ups are always saying things like that, just so they don't have to explain."

Mara lifted her shoulders. She was still fingering the locket around her neck. "Yeah, well, all I know is he couldn't keep me and Mama because he's white and we're Negroes. I started thinking about it, and I started getting mad."

"But I thought you told me your family didn't want your mama to marry him either."

She nodded slowly and her eyes narrowed. "That's right," she said. "It's like black and white don't mix. But that's what I am, black and white both. So what does that say about me? I'm mixed!"

I didn't know what to say to that, so I didn't say anything.

After a moment she went on. "We'd been driving for a little while when I asked him, 'What should I call you?' because I didn't want to just jump in and start calling him Daddy, even though that's what I wanted to call him. And he said, like he was doing me a favor, 'Well, you can call me Bill, of course.' And I said, 'Call you *Bill?*' And he looked at me funny and said, 'Well sure. You don't want to call me Professor Remmick, do you?' and I said, 'No, I was hoping I could call you Daddy.' And then he looked real sad again, and he said, 'Bea, you have parents. They brought you to the train station,' and I said, 'They aren't my parents, they're my grandparents, and you know it,' and he said, 'Bea, listen to me, they're the ones raising you, so they're your mom and dad.'

"So then I just looked straight ahead for a long time, and he knew I was mad, because he lit up another cigarette and his fingers were trembling a little. Finally I said, 'You're sorry I came, aren't you?' And he said, 'No, I'm not. I've wanted to meet you since the day you were born. I've been waiting a long time for today.' And I said, 'Then how come you don't want to be my daddy?'"

She took a deep breath then and let it out slowly. She looked up at me and tried to smile, though her eyes glazed over as she fought back tears. She swallowed hard and jutted out her chin a little bit. "When I said that, he pulled the car right over to the side of the road, and he turned to me and said, 'Listen to me, Beatrice. I'm your birth father and I'm not denying that. You're here today because I wanted to meet you and you wanted to meet me. I'll always want to know what's going on in your life, and I will find a way to always know how you are and what's happening to you, but, Bea, that's not a daddy. I have three kids who call me Daddy, and I'm there for them and I take care of them and I scold them when they need it and I tell them every day I love them, but I can't do that for you. I wish I could. You've got to believe me when I say I wish I could. But I can't. And it's never going to happen. I'm really sorry, but that's just the way it is.'

"He sounded real mean when he said it, but the funny thing was, he was almost crying. I mean, his eyes were red and watery. But he didn't want to look like he was crying, so he started up the car and we pulled into the road again.

"I said, 'Do you think you could ever love me like you do your other kids?' and he said, 'Bea, I've always loved you. I want you to believe that.' I thought about it a little while and then I said, 'I guess I do, because you say good-night to me at the end of your show, and you don't say good-night to your other kids.' He said, 'No, that's just for you, because it's all I can give you. It's not enough, but it's all I have. And when the show goes off the air someday, I'll find another way to let you know I'm thinking about you.'

"I looked at him and I said, 'When you say good-night to me on the radio, who do your wife and kids think you're talking to?' He kind of smiled at that and said, 'To them, you're my Mrs. Calabash.' 'Your Mrs. *What?*' I asked. He told me about Jimmy Durante and how whenever he signed off on his radio program, he said 'Good night, Mrs. Calabash, wherever you are,' even though there probably wasn't any real Mrs. Calabash out there listening. So I thought, well, that figures, because to his family I'm not real, and I don't even exist.

"By that time we were almost to where we were going, and I was still thinking about what I should call him, and I said, 'I just don't think I can call you Bill.' He looked at me kind of funny, and he was smiling and he said, 'Well, how about you call me what your mother used to call me?' I asked him what that was, and he said, 'When she was mad at me, she'd call me knucklehead. Unless she was *really* mad at me. Then she'd

351

call me the worst mistake she ever made.' When he said that, I couldn't help it, I started laughing and then he started laughing, and we were both laughing, and after that, it was like everything was all right."

She said those last words with a kind of wonder. Mara looked toward the window with wistful eyes, as though she were seeing the previous day play itself out all over again. In the next moment the corners of her mouth hinted at a smile.

I myself felt as though I'd been left at a cliffhanger, and I was leaning forward on the bed, waiting for the next installment of the story. When Mara didn't go on, I insisted, "So *then* what happened?"

My words drew her back, and for a moment she looked annoyed. But then she smiled and shrugged her shoulders. "Then we ate lunch and talked about books and stuff."

"That's it?"

"Oh, and we gave each other Christmas gifts."

"Did he like the book?"

She nodded. "He said he'd always cherish it."

"So what did he give you?"

"This." She leaned back and dug around in the pocket of her jeans. She pulled out something silver and shiny and handed it to me across the gap between the beds. It was a charm bracelet bearing a single charm, round as a full moon and engraved on one side in an elegant script: *Sweet dreams, Beatrice.*

"It's real pretty," I said.

"Yeah." She smiled sadly.

"So are you ever going to see him again?"

"I think so. Someday. But probably not for a long time."

I studied the charm for a moment. "I'm sorry, Mara."

"It's all right."

"What are you going to do now?"

"About . . . William Remmick, you mean?"

"Yeah."

Mara nodded. "I'm writing it all down," she said.

"Like a book or something?"

"No." Her brow furrowed in thought. "I don't know why, but it's a play. That's how it came to me."

"A play?"

"Yeah. I wrote the first act on the train ride home. Because Daddy — William Remmick — said that's what a real poet does. She takes her sadness and turns it into something beautiful. He said almost all good literature springs from sorrow."

"It does?"

"Yeah. That's what he said, and I think he's right. He said if I'm serious about being a writer, that's what I need to learn to do."

I didn't understand, but then, I wasn't a writer. "Can I read the play when you're done?"

"Maybe someday." She took a long deep breath, and changed the subject. "Have you heard anything from your dad?" she asked quietly.

I shook my head no. "The waitress at the café said he's in Chicago."

"What for?"

"Work, I guess."

"Well, since he's up there, maybe he'll buy you a Christmas present from Marshall Field or someplace like that. They have much better stores there than they do here in Mills River."

"Yeah, maybe." I handed Mara the bracelet. "Hey, guess what."

"What?"

"Mom's not seeing Tom Barrows anymore. Or not so much, anyway."

For the first time that day, her face opened up in a genuine smile. "Yeah? What happened?"

"I don't know for sure. I guess —"

As I was speaking the doorbell rang, and in another moment Tillie called up the stairs, "Roz, is Mara up there with you?"

"Yeah," I called back. "She's up here."

"Well, tell her that her father's here looking for her."

I looked at Mara. "Your father's here."

"I heard." She giggled. "I'm not deaf."

"Do you have to go already?"

"Yeah. Daddy promised we'd go pick out our Christmas tree this morning."

"You don't have your tree yet?"

"No." Mara jumped from the bed and hollered toward the door, "Coming, Daddy!"

She stopped and turned, giving me the oddest look. Then she shrugged, smiled, called again, "I'll be right there, Daddy!" I watched her fly down the stairs and into the arms of the big dark teddy bear of a man waiting for her by the front door.

"Come on, baby," he said. "There's a tree out there with your name on it, and we've got to go find it before it ends up in the wrong house."

Mara turned back to me, smiled, and waved. Then she took her daddy's hand and disappeared out the door.

CHAPTER 36

Christmas came and went, followed by New Year's Eve, which passed with little fanfare. One day simply slipped into the next, and suddenly it was 1968, the year my brother would go off to war and the year my daddy would come home.

The atmosphere in the house was sullen as we slid into January. I often found Mom staring absently out the frosty windows, as though she were waiting for something that was likely never to come. She resembled Tillie in one of her spells, but instead of looking backward in time like Tillie did, I supposed Mom's mind was reluctantly reaching forward, wondering what would happen in the upcoming months, wondering whether Wally would die in the war the way his father had, his blood spilled out on foreign soil, in a place he was never meant to be. I imagined she saw all the barren days ahead — no son, no husband, her daughters grown and gone, leaving her to grow old and lonely in the house on McDowell Street.

Once, Tillie put her hand on Mom's shoulder and said, "He'll come home, dear. Try not to worry."

"Wally?"

"Yes. I feel sure of it."

"How can you be sure? We can't be sure of anything, can we?"

"Oh yes," Tillie countered, "there's much we can be sure of. Not everything, of course. But some things, yes."

What? I wanted to ask. *What can we be sure of?* But I was an eavesdropper and not a participant in the conversation, so I didn't ask.

Mom began to weep quietly. "It's the waiting, Tillie. It's the waiting to find out where he's going to end up, and once he's there, it'll be the waiting to find out whether he'll be coming back. It's all the waiting that I can't stand — the waiting and the not knowing."

"I understand, Janis," Tillie assured her. "I had three of my own go off to war, you know. Ross first, and later two of the boys. Different wars, of course. Only Lyle was spared, because he was too young."

"How did you bear it?" Mom asked, the

357

anguish in her voice as intense and bitter as the cold outside.

"I had to put them in the hands of the Lord, dear. I had to determine to accept his will, whether I liked it or not."

Mom shook her head slowly. "I don't have faith like that, Tillie. You know I don't. I'm not even sure God is there. If he is, I don't believe he has anything to do with what happens to us here."

"That's where you're wrong, Janis. He has everything to do with what happens to us here."

"Then . . . then . . ." Mom dried her eyes with one hand, lifted her chin. "Then he must be very cruel."

"Oh no, my dear," Tillie said gently. "His is the only real kindness in a cruel world. Without him, we would have no hope at all."

Mom turned from the window and looked at Tillie. "But, you see, I'm not sure I have any hope. If Wally dies . . . if Wally dies . . ."

Her voice trailed off, and she had no words for what she would do if Wally died. It was a threat she didn't yet know how to carry out.

"I will pray for Wally to come home," Tillie said, "just as I prayed for my own boys."

Mom nodded, but her face said Tillie's

prayers were, to her, little more than idle words.

There must have been *something* to Tillie's prayers, though, because not only did her husband and sons come home from war, but Lyle Monroe came home from Bolivia. She'd been praying he'd wrap up his missionary work there and come on back to Mills River, and sure enough, the second weekend in January, Johnny Monroe pulled up to our house in his Pontiac station wagon, his brother Lyle in the passenger seat beside him.

Tillie didn't even bother to put on a coat but stepped out into the furious cold in her blue cotton housedress. She stood at the edge of the porch, her hefty arms flung open wide and tears of joy streaming down her face.

"Welcome home, Lyle," she hollered as the car doors opened. Johnny exited the driver's side while a tall man in a dark overcoat emerged from the other. The tall man moved swiftly up the walkway and into Tillie's arms. With a joyful shout he lifted Tillie off her feet, her heavy shoes dangling several inches off the porch, her laughter ringing clear in the open air.

When he put her down, Tillie cupped the

man's face with her hands and said, "Let me look at you, son. How are you? Are you all right?"

The man nodded and laughed. His breath came out in little puffs of cloud. "I'm fine, Mother. Just fine. Jiminy, but it's good to be home."

"Come on in out of the cold, both of you boys," Tillie said, and in another moment they were in the front hallway, where Tillie, about to burst wide open with excitement and pride, introduced Mom and me to her son Lyle Monroe. A few more minutes and we were seated at the kitchen table drinking steaming cups of coffee and hot chocolate while Lyle talked about his journey back from Bolivia.

He was a friendly, cheerful man, with a dry wit and a quick laugh that sank into your bones like something warm and comforting. He must have taken after his father in appearance, because he didn't look at all like Tillie or Johnny. Where their faces were round, his was narrow; where they were short and plump, he was tall and lean. He had thick unruly hair and brown leathery skin that had no doubt been darkened by the South American sun. But the eyes . . . now those were his mother's. Blue and bright and flashing with a gaiety and a certain gentleness that I didn't often see.

About thirty minutes into the conversation, Lyle took Valerie onto his lap, where she settled easily. He patted her head and sighed. "Yes, sir, it's good to be here. That's not to say I didn't love Bolivia, because I did, loved every minute of my years there, but once I made up my mind to leave, I was ready to do it. I actually felt homesick for the first time ever, so I knew I'd made the right decision to come back. I'm not completely sure what God has planned for me here, but I'm ready to find out." He sighed again and looked around the room. "You know, there were days when I was sick with malaria that I thought I'd never see this old house again. It sure is good to be home."

Mom's eyes widened in alarm. If Wally were there, I knew he'd be jumping in right about then to make sure everyone understood this house belonged to Janis Anthony, and that while we had made room for one Monroe, we were hardly going to make room for another.

But Wally wasn't there, and Tillie was pouring Lyle yet another cup of coffee, and Lyle and Johnny were talking about the improvements Johnny had made to the house before he sold it, and I figured if Mom wasn't going to say something then

I'd better go ahead and do it. Because if Lyle Monroe planned on moving in like his mother had, there wouldn't be any room left at all for Daddy when he finally decided it was time to come back home.

"You don't plan to live here again, do you?" I blurted.

Lyle and Johnny fell silent, both looking as though I'd asked a question in a dead language. Lyle tapped one finger on the table and finally said, "You mean, live in this house?"

I nodded. "Yeah. Because we really don't have room for you here."

A smile spread across his face slowly, like molasses oozing over pancakes, and when the smile had reached as far as it could go, Lyle Monroe burst out laughing. "Of course I'm not going to live in this house with you," he said. He glanced at Mom, then looked back at me. "Why, that wouldn't even be proper. No, right now my bed is the couch in Johnny's living room, but I plan to move into Miss Charlotte's place temporarily, until I can find something more permanent."

"Miss Charlotte's place?" Mom asked. I noted the relief on her face, and congratulated myself on confronting this possible intruder when Wally wasn't there to do it.

Lyle Monroe nodded. "It's a boarding-house way up on the north side of town. Not many such houses left, but Miss Charlotte, she's a fixture around here. Like I say, I plan to take a room there for a little while, till I can get myself settled into a teaching job."

"I see," Mom said. "What do you teach, Mr. Monroe?"

"Elementary ed, which means I teach a little of everything — math, science, reading. That's what I was doing in Bolivia on the mission compound. Teaching the missionary kids."

"You like teaching, then?"

"Oh yes, Mrs. Anthony. I love it. I love the whole idea of influencing young lives, helping to shape young minds. When the kids grow up and get back to you years later and let you know that you made a difference in their lives . . . well, there's just not much that's better than that."

Mom nodded, took a sip of her coffee, gave me a small grateful smile. As long as Lyle Monroe didn't plan to live with us, Mom was happy. We were glad to have Tillie to help out around the house, but one Monroe under our roof was all that we could manage.

CHAPTER 37

As soon as Lyle Monroe got a room at Miss Charlotte's, Tillie decided to take him some warm clothes, fresh linens, and a lemon meringue pie. Mom gave Tillie the use of the car, and on a wintry mid-January evening she and I headed out to Cisco Avenue on the northern edge of Mills River.

"I've never been up this way," I mentioned. I peered out the window at the once elegant houses that now looked old and weary.

"No, I've never had reason to come up here much myself," Tillie said. "This used to be where the rich folks lived, but now it's more or less gone to seed. Most of these old houses have been divided up into apartments, and some of them have just plain been abandoned. See that one over there, how it's all boarded up?"

I nodded. "Too bad. It looks like it was a pretty place once."

"It was. Plenty of beautiful houses around here, once upon a time. The house where Lyle's living now belonged to Charlotte Ramsey's family for several generations. She was a Bigelow originally, and they were one of the oldest families in Mills River. The house became hers when she married Richard Ramsey, and that's where they lived till he went off to war and got himself shot down over Germany. He left poor Charlotte a childless widow."

"She never got married again?"

"No, she never did. But she wanted to keep that big old house of hers, so she turned it into a boardinghouse. Pretty smart of her in the long run, since there was a housing shortage after the war. Plenty of young newlyweds looking for a place to live, so her rooms were always full. Still are, far as I know, though she has the reputation of running a tight ship. No drinking, no bad language, and no mixing with the opposite sex if you happen not to be married. One infringement of the rules will get you kicked out fast as greased lightning."

"She sounds pretty strict."

"Strict but fair. I've known Charlotte a long time. She had the makings of a good mother, had she been so blessed. As it is, she's kind of a mother hen to all her boarders, no matter how old they might be."

A slivered moon had risen and a light snow was falling by the time we reached Cisco Avenue. I was captivated by the old gas lamps, now electric, that cast dim circles of light along the street. Snowflakes tumbled through each glowing circle, and I thought of dandelions casting off their pods in the wind.

"The snow looks pretty," I said, leaning closer to the passenger side window.

Tillie nodded as she parallel parked in front of a large brick house with a wraparound porch. "Well, here we are. This is Charlotte's place. Now listen, the north side isn't the safest part of town, Roz, so just keep your wits about you."

"Why'd you bring me here if it isn't safe?"

"Well, I don't mean that it isn't safe exactly. I just mean, if anything were ever to happen in Mills River, this is where it would happen. Though, of course, it's not going to happen. Then again, if it did happen and we got mugged or assaulted or something unthinkable like that, I suppose it would give Captain Strang something to do, since there's so little crime in this town. Think of the taxes we pay while our officers spend most of their time writing traffic tickets and rescuing cats out of trees. But then again, I like it that way. Don't you?"

Tillie looked at me and I looked at her, and after a long while I said, "Sometimes I think you're really strange, Tillie."

"And you're entitled to your opinion," she replied. "Now, help me by carrying the pie while I grab the bundles of clothes and linens."

Miss Charlotte herself answered Tillie's knock on the door. She was a tiny wisp of a woman, clothed in a dark dress, thick stockings, and black tie-up shoes. Her gray hair was pulled into a tight knot at the back of her head, and her steel gray eyes peered at us sharply from behind tiny oval-shaped lenses. When she recognized Tillie, she smiled. "Why, Tillie Monroe," she said amiably, opening the door wider so we could step into the foyer. "I've been expecting you to come by, now that your boy Lyle is here."

"I hope he's not giving you any trouble, Charlotte," Tillie said. She sounded stern, but I could tell she was trying to suppress a smile.

"Oh my, no!" Miss Charlotte exclaimed, hands thrown up in the air. "He's a good boy, that Lyle. Always has been. I imagine you're glad to have him back home again."

"You've got that right, Charlotte. Not that I was unhappy about him doing the Lord's work in Bolivia, of course —"

"Of course not, dear —"

"But I missed him —"

"I'm sure you did —"

"And I'm just as glad to have him back home."

Miss Charlotte nodded knowingly. "People belong at home, I always say. No use traipsing all over the globe. You'll never find any place as good as home."

With that, Tillie and Miss Charlotte both sighed happily. They spent the next several minutes talking pleasantries while I peered into the rooms on either side of the hall. On one side was a large formal parlor, where a middle-aged woman sat knitting in a wing chair beside an empty fireplace. Knitting needles clacking, she chattered away to a man who was hidden from view behind a fully opened newspaper. On the other side of the hall was a room of equal size, slightly less formal, in which four people sat at a folding table playing cards. The smoke from their cigarettes curled upward from the table and settled in a wispy haze over much of the room. Their occasional laughter, sudden and piercing, cut a swath through the otherwise quiet night.

My attention was snapped back to the hallway when Tillie, apparently remembering I was there, introduced me to Miss Charlotte. "This is Roz Anthony," she said. She pointed toward me with an elbow, since both hands were occupied with the linens and Lyle's clothes. "She and her family live with me now."

Miss Charlotte looked pleased. "How lovely!" she exclaimed. "I've hated to think of you all alone in that big old house since . . . well, since Ross left us, God rest his soul."

"Yes, Ross would be happy to know there's a family in the house again," Tillie remarked.

"That he would," Miss Charlotte agreed. "Well, it's very nice to meet you . . . I'm sorry, what was your name again?"

"Roz," I said. "Short for Rosalind."

"I see. Pretty name. And what's that you've got there? A pie, is it?"

"Lemon meringue," Tillie interjected. "Lyle's favorite. He hasn't had a taste of lemon pie since his last furlough two years ago. I baked it up special for him today."

"Lovely! Well, you'll want to go deposit that in the refrigerator right away, then, little lady," Miss Charlotte said.

"Where is it?" I asked timidly.

She raised an arm and pointed toward the back of the house. "Right down this hall, straight back. You may need to move a few things around in the refrigerator to make room."

"When you're finished with that, Roz," Tillie said, "meet me upstairs in Lyle's room."

"Which one is that?" I asked, suddenly feeling lost and overwhelmed in this big old house filled with strangers.

Miss Charlotte swung her arm around to the stairs. "Straight up, turn left, and it's the first room on the right."

Tillie nodded at me, my signal to go on to the kitchen. I almost asked her to come with me but decided against it. I moved uneasily from her side and down the hall. The slightly sloping hardwood floor squeaked beneath my feet. Off to the left two women sipped tea at a table in the dining room, a smattering of dirty dishes scattered nearby. On the right a door hung open to a dark walk-in pantry beneath the staircase; I scurried past, afraid of what might jump out at me.

Finally I stepped into the expansive kitchen at the back of the house, a tidy well-polished room with modern appliances, including a sunny yellow refrigerator on the far wall. On one side of the kitchen, beneath a window with frilly white curtains, was a small round table where a man sat eating, his back to me. I'd have to walk past him to get to the fridge. Lowering my gaze, I stepped gingerly across the room, trying to keep the soles of my shoes from slapping too sharply against the linoleum floor. I wanted to get in and get out without bothering the man eating his supper. With only a couple of steps to go, I heard someone softly call my name.

I stopped and slowly turned around. In the next moment I found myself staring into the eyes of the man at the table, the startled and puzzled eyes of Alan Anthony, my daddy.

The glass of water in his hand came crashing down against the tabletop. For a second I thought it might have shattered into a million pieces, but when he took his hand away, the glass was still intact. Daddy ran trembling fingers through his hair and swore quietly. "What are you doing here?" he asked.

"I-I . . ."

"Is your mother here?" He looked back over his shoulder in search of her.

I shook my head.

"Who are you here with?"

My tongue was thick with fear, my mouth

dry. "Just Tillie," I whispered.

"Who?"

"Tillie. The lady that helps take care of us."

He glanced again toward the entrance to the kitchen, then back at me. "Why are you here?"

I lifted the pie an inch or so, as though that explained everything. "I'm putting this in the fridge."

An oath from Daddy let me know I'd given him the wrong answer. He stood and grabbed my arm. I thought I might drop the pie, so I tightened my grip on the rim of the aluminum pan.

"Tell me what you're doing in this house," Daddy demanded.

His wild eyes terrified me. "I'm just . . . I'm just . . ." I started to cry. "You're hurting my arm!"

He glared at me, his breathing quick and shallow. Then, as though something passed over him, his eyes calmed and he loosened his grip. "I'm sorry, Roz. Here, give me the pie."

He took it to the refrigerator and moved around a few milk bottles and other containers to make a place for it. After shutting the door and giving me another long look, he sat back down and pulled me to him.

"Listen, Roz, stop crying, all right?" He wiped my eyes with the paper napkin, used and crumpled, beside his plate. Putting both hands on my shoulders, he said evenly, "I need you to tell me what you're doing here."

I took a deep breath, trying to steady myself. "I'm just . . . I'm just . . ."

"Just what, Roz?"

"Tillie and I just brought some stuff to her son. That's all."

"Her son?"

I nodded. "He lives here now. He just moved in yesterday."

Daddy's eyes narrowed slightly. "What's his name?"

"Mr. Monroe."

"What's his first name?"

"Lyle."

"Lyle Monroe," Daddy repeated. His eyes moved to the side as his thoughts pulled him away from me.

I waited for several long seconds before asking quietly, "Daddy, is this where you live?"

He came back to me then but didn't answer. Somebody stepped into the kitchen and Daddy stiffened. He picked up his fork and stabbed at a piece of meat on the plate in front of him.

"Good evening, Mr. Knutson," the man

said. He spoke with his back to us as he poured a cup of coffee from the percolator on the stove.

"Evening, Mr. Wainwright," Daddy said.

I looked at Daddy for direction; he was nodding toward the door, sending me away with his eyes. I took one step but stopped when Mr. Wainwright said, "You have a visitor tonight?"

Daddy chewed slowly, then took a long drink of water. "Naw," he said finally, pretending to laugh. "If you mean the kid — she belongs to someone else." To me, he said, "I'll make sure no one eats the pie you brought for Mr. Monroe."

My eyes darted from Daddy to Mr. Wainwright and back to Daddy again. "Thank you," I whispered.

Daddy nodded and went back to eating. Mr. Wainwright smiled at me as he stirred sugar into his coffee.

"Mr. Monroe," Mr. Wainwright said thoughtfully, the spoon scraping circles along the bottom of the cup. "He's the one who moved in yesterday, isn't he?"

He looked at me, waiting for an answer. He was a tall and incredibly round man, with a waist like a redwood tree. I nodded at him, saying nothing, fearing that if he caught me in a lie he could snuff me out like a tiny gnat pinched between his sausagelike fingers.

"Mr. Knutson there," he said with a smile toward Daddy, "he and I are getting to be the old-timers around here. Isn't that right, Nelson?"

"Yeah, I guess we are," Daddy agreed. He didn't look up from his food.

Mr. Wainwright laid the spoon in the sink and took a long sip of coffee. "Well, back to the game. I'm down ten dollars, but this next hand's mine. I can feel it."

"Yeah, well, good luck, then," Daddy said.

The stranger left. The other stranger who looked like my daddy stayed seated at the table, eating quietly.

"Daddy?"

"Go on, Roz, scoot," he said. "I'll talk with you later."

"But —"

"I said go on."

I didn't want to go; I wanted answers. But Daddy wouldn't look at me, let alone talk to me. I moved stiffly toward the hall, walking slowly, feeling unbearably heavy as I dragged all of my questions out of the kitchen with me.

Chapter 38

"I found out where my daddy's living."

The words were nearly lost to the din and clatter of the school cafeteria. Lately Mara's homeroom class and mine had been assigned to the same lunch period, so we always sat together. Mara stopped poking at her lima beans long enough to ask loudly, "What'd you say?"

I looked around and leaned in closer. "My dad . . . he's living at a boardinghouse owned by some old lady named Miss Charlotte."

Mara's eyes widened and her mouth followed suit. "How'd you find out?"

I told her how I'd seen Daddy there the previous night, adding that before I could go upstairs and find Tillie, I had to press my forehead against the cold glass of the front door window until my heart stopped beating crazily and I could breathe normally again.

"So," Mara said, "he acted like he was mad you found him?"

"Well, yeah," I said reluctantly. "I guess he was surprised to see me."

"He doesn't want you to know where he lives, does he?"

I tried to look nonchalant by shrugging my shoulders and taking a bite of fish stick before answering. "I don't know. I guess not."

"I bet he'll move now."

"Why should he move? I'm not going to tell anyone he's there."

"Yeah, but think about it, Roz. He doesn't want that guy, what's his name — Tillie's son — going to your house and blabbing about some guy named Alan Anthony living at the boardinghouse."

"He won't because Daddy's not using his real name. I think he's told everyone his name's Nelson Knutson."

"Nelson Knutson?"

I nodded.

"What kind of name is that? It sounds like something a magician would say . . . you know, like abracadabra."

"It does?"

"Yeah. You know, I'm waving my magic wand and . . . *Nelson Knutson!* . . . there's a rabbit in my hat!"

I narrowed my eyes and sneered at Mara. "Only you would think of something like that."

She smiled confidently.

"Listen, Mara," I went on, "up in Minnesota Knutson is kind of like Smith. I mean, practically everyone's named Knutson up there. We had a guy on our street named Nelson Knutson, but he died in a car wreck just before we moved."

Mara's smile faded. She looked at me a long time before saying, "This is giving me the creeps, Roz."

"What do you mean?"

"I don't know. I just don't like it."

"You don't like what?"

"This whole thing with your daddy, his coming down here and telling everybody he's someone he's not. Plus, he chooses the name of some dead guy. Doesn't that seem weird to you?"

I started to lift the milk carton to my lips, but my stomach was churning. I set it back down on the tray. "You know," I said, "I've been thinking about that. He doesn't want Mom to know he's in Mills River yet, so he has to use another name. That's all. It makes sense to me."

"Uh-huh." She looked unconvinced. "And has he really quit drinking?"

"He says he has."

"But do you know for sure?"

"How can I? I hardly ever see him. But when I do see him, he isn't drunk."

"Yeah, well, I guess not. He's not going to want you to see him drunk."

I looked up at the large institutional clock on the cafeteria wall, hanging there above the garbage cans where we dumped our uneaten food. The bell would ring soon, signaling the end of lunch and sending Mara and me our separate ways until mid-afternoon recess.

Sighing, I said, "Why do you have to think the worst? Can't you give my dad a chance?"

She chewed thoughtfully. Finally she said, "You know, Roz, I think you should tell your mom."

"Tell her what? That Daddy's here?"

She nodded. "Yeah. I think she needs to know."

"But Daddy said not to tell her."

"Maybe that's all the more reason *to* tell her."

"You don't think I can trust him, do you?"

She shrugged. "I don't know your daddy. All I know is your mom left him for a reason."

"But, Mara, what about the Daddy Deal? We promised we'd pray and ask for our daddies. You got yours, and now it's my turn to get mine."

She didn't answer for a while. She sipped her milk and pushed lima beans around her plate with her fork before saying, "Listen, Roz, I did and I didn't. I mean, William Remmick is my father, and I'm glad I finally got to meet him. But Grandpa is my daddy. I know that now."

I looked away, annoyed. Just because it didn't all work out exactly as Mara wanted and expected didn't mean it wasn't going to work out for me. "Yeah, well, my grandpa is *not* my daddy," I said, "and I'm not giving up."

She shrugged. "Suit yourself. But, Roz?"

"Yeah?"

"Just be careful, okay?"

The bell rang, and Mara gave me a fearful look before picking up her tray and heading for the garbage bins.

After school I found Tillie at the kitchen table, poring over a half dozen shoe boxes filled with photographs.

"What are you doing?" I asked.

She looked at me and smiled. "Johnny brought these over. He said I have to get these old photos organized and put into albums, or he's just going to toss them. He's right. It's time I put everything in order. I don't have much time left."

"You keep saying that, Tillie, but how do you know?"

"Honey, I'm seventy years old. That's all the years we're allotted in this world. Anything beyond that is borrowed time."

"But you could live to be eighty or even ninety. A lot of people do."

"Maybe. But I can't count on it. Anyway, when the call comes, I'm ready to go. I'm ready to see Jesus. And Ross too. In that order." She picked up a photograph and gazed at it lovingly. "That's Ross when he was just a young man. My, my." She clicked her tongue. "Wasn't he handsome?"

He wasn't as handsome as Daddy, I thought. But I simply nodded and said, "What was he like?"

She drew in a deep breath, and her eyes took on a kind of faraway look. "He was a wonderful man," she said quietly. "As fine a man as ever lived, I'd say. He was always kind to everyone."

"Didn't you ever fight and yell at each other, Tillie?"

"Me and Ross? We had our differences occasionally, but no, I can't say we fought very much. Now, I myself might have been a fighter if I'd married someone else, but Ross

— he was too mild-mannered for that sort of thing. He was a true gentleman."

"But . . ."

"What, Roz?"

"Did he ever lie to you?"

She arched her brows. "Gracious no. What makes you ask a thing like that?"

"I don't know. I mean, how do you know he never lied to you? Maybe he lied and you just didn't know it."

She laid the photo on the table and caressed it absently with her fingertips. "He was a man of his word. If he said he was going to do something, he did it. I can't remember ever catching him in a lie."

"So you could trust him?"

"Of course." She studied me a moment, then said, "Roz, why are you asking me this?"

"Well —" I pulled out a chair and sat down — "I'm just wondering how you can know if you can trust someone."

"Are you thinking of someone in particular?" When I nodded she said, "Have you known this person for a long time?" Another nod. "Well, has she ever lied to you in the past?"

"It's a he."

"Okay. So has he ever lied to you?"

I thought about that for a minute and

382

decided I could answer honestly, "I don't think so."

"There you go, then. That's a pretty good indication you can trust this person."

"Really?" There was excitement — or was it relief? — in my voice.

Tillie nodded, adding, "Of course, all of us are capable of lying from time to time, for whatever reason."

I chewed my lower lip in thought. "I wish it was impossible to lie," I said. "I wish people could only tell the truth."

"Now, that would be something, wouldn't it? That right there would take care of a whole boatload of problems in the world."

"Yeah, it sure would." If I knew Daddy was telling me the truth, I wouldn't have any problems at all.

"But don't count on that happening anytime soon," Tillie said with a laugh. "More people than you can imagine make their living by spinning tales. Like the charlatan who'll sell you colored water and promise it'll cure whatever ails you. Wolves in sheep's clothing, I call them. Those are the people you have to look out for."

"So how do you know if someone's a wolf in sheep's clothing?" I asked.

Tillie shrugged. "That's the problem, I guess. Sometimes you don't know, not until it's too late."

Too late for what? I wondered. But I didn't ask. I excused myself and went to my room, more confused than ever.

CHAPTER 39

I was reaching for *Huckleberry Finn* on a library shelf that was taller than I was when a familiar voice asked, "Can I give you a hand with that, little lady?"

I whirled around and looked up at my father's smiling face. "Daddy! How did you know I was here?"

He reached for the book and handed it to me. "I know you come here a couple times a week with your friend. I figured you'd show up again sooner or later."

Mara was in Nonfiction, searching for books on the Civil War for her social studies class. I nodded at Daddy and said, "That's Mara, you know. She loves books."

"I can see that. Bright little kid, isn't she."

"She's real smart. I wish I had her brains."

Daddy bent down to meet me eye to eye. "Now listen, Roz," he said. "You're every bit as smart as she is, and don't let anything make you think otherwise."

"How do you know I'm as smart as she is?"

"Because you're my daughter. I know how smart you are."

"But I don't get all As like Mara does."

"That doesn't matter. Grades aren't everything."

We gazed at each other a moment. I had a feeling he hadn't come here to talk about grades. Finally he said, "Mara doesn't know about me, does she?"

"No," I said. I was amazed at my own ability to look him in the eye and lie without flinching. Lying was easier than it used to be.

"That's good. Does anyone know I'm here?"

"If they do," I said, "it's not because I told them."

He smiled again and winked. "That's my girl. I told you you were smart. Because if anyone finds out, everything will be ruined."

I pursed my lips, searched his face for hints of what he meant. "What's *everything,* Daddy?"

"Well, you know, honey. I've already told you. I'm trying to put our life back together. I'm trying to put the family back together. You believe me, don't you?"

I was tired of not knowing what to believe.

I wanted to stop wavering and be settled and to live as though everything was going to be all right. At that moment I decided to throw in my lot with Daddy. "I believe you, Daddy," I told him.

"That's good, Roz. It won't be long now. There's a lucky day coming up, and I want to take advantage of it."

Sighing, I had to stop myself from rolling my eyes. Daddy and his lucky days. It had driven Mom crazy. We were always having to do or not do something, depending on whether or not it was a lucky day.

"What day's the lucky day, Daddy?" I asked, trying to sound agreeable.

"I can't tell you yet, but I'll tell you soon. Anyway, listen, I wanted to apologize for Wednesday night at the boardinghouse. You understand, don't you, that I really wasn't mad at you? I was just surprised, is all. I didn't expect to see you there, and it caught me off guard. And then when Mr. Wainwright came in, I had to act as though I didn't know you, but you understand why, don't you?"

When I nodded, he put both hands on my shoulders and held my gaze. "Listen, honey, I'm working real hard to make everything right again. I mean it. And someday I'm going to be proud to tell people I'm your father, but I just can't do it yet. But soon. You'll see. And Roz, I missed Christmas, and I'm sorry about that, but I was up in Chicago working, and I couldn't get away. But I have something for you." He moved one hand off my shoulder and reached into his shirt pocket. I watched expectantly, wondering what it was. "Hold out your hand," he said.

I did, and he dropped something silver and shiny into it. I laid *Huckleberry Finn* on a shelf to free up my other hand, then picked up the necklace by the chain and watched the heart-shaped pendant swing like a pendulum. "It's beautiful, Daddy," I whispered.

"It means I love you."

My chest felt tight, and I thought I might cry. "I love you too, Daddy."

He opened his arms and I fell into them. Then my arms were around his neck, and he was kissing my cheek and caressing my hair and telling me how much he loved me. And then the tears came, because I felt as though I finally had everything I ever wanted. Daddy wasn't a wolf in sheep's clothing. He was a good man, and he loved me.

When I pulled back and he saw my tears, he asked gently, "What's this?" He held my face in his hands and wiped at my cheeks with both thumbs. "Why are you crying, Roz?"

I shrugged. "I'm just happy, Daddy."

He took a deep breath and smiled. "I'm glad, honey. And pretty soon we're going to be happy together, and nothing's going to separate us again. Okay?"

"Okay."

"Do you want to put the necklace on?"

I nodded. I unlatched the chain and handed it to Daddy. He put it around my neck and fastened it again. "A pretty necklace for a pretty girl."

I reached for the heart and held it tight in my hand. "Thank you, Daddy. It's the best Christmas gift ever."

"You're welcome, honey. But listen, it'd be best if your mother doesn't see it, all right?"

"All right."

"Because then you'd have to explain . . ."

"I know, Daddy. I won't let her see it."

He gave a satisfied nod. He looked over my shoulder, then back at me. "Listen, sweetheart, I've got to go. The more time I spend with you, the more I'm pushing my luck." He stood and stretched his legs. I picked up *Huckleberry Finn*. "You going to read that?" he asked.

"Yeah. I have to do a book report on it."

"Uh-huh." He was stalling for time, and I knew it. I had the feeling there was something left unsaid. Finally he asked, "Say, Roz, that guy, Tom Barrows. Your mother still seeing him?"

"Naw. They broke up a little while back."

"Uh-huh." His mouth twitched as he tried unsuccessfully to suppress a smile. "She's not seeing anyone else, is she? What about this Monroe fellow who just moved in?"

"What about him?"

"Tell me again who he is."

"He's just Tillie's son. And Tillie's our . . . well, she helps Mom around the house with cooking and cleaning and stuff. And she takes care of Valerie."

"So where does Tillie live?"

I paused a moment. "I don't know. Over on Sayles Street, I think."

"So how come her son isn't living with her?"

I shrugged. "I don't know, Daddy. He's a grown-up. Would you want to live with your mother?"

He looked amused and chuckled softly. "You've got a point there, Roz. All right, well . . . so your mother isn't seeing anyone?"

"No, she's not seeing anyone, and I'm

glad about it too."

"Yeah, that's good. It would just complicate things."

I looked down at my necklace and gave it a small pat before tucking it under my blouse. I couldn't wait to show Mara my gift from Daddy. Smiling, I lifted my head to look up at Daddy, but even as my chin was rising, I remembered something that happened not once but many times: Daddy, crazy jealous, accusing Mom of flirting with someone or other; Mom denying it, her voice trembling, her one arm rising to shield her face.

When my eyes met Daddy's, though, it wasn't the Daddy of the memory I saw. I found myself looking into eyes that held compassion and a certain hopefulness. Everything was changing. Everything was going to be all right.

The memory faded. "Daddy?"

"Yes, honey?"

"You love Mom, right?"

He took a deep breath, let it out. "Oh, darling," he said quietly, "more than life itself."

And then he kissed the top of my head and disappeared.

CHAPTER 40

I soon began to wonder. Not about Daddy, but about Lyle Monroe. He started hopping on the city bus and coming over for supper two or three times a week, supposedly to see Tillie, but more often than not he ended up talking long hours with Mom. The two of them drank coffee in the living room while Tillie and I washed the dishes and put Valerie to bed.

I didn't like it. Not one bit. I figured I was going to have to put Mara to work again, playing it up about the snoring and the cooking and maybe even dropping Valerie into Lyle Monroe's lap. But I couldn't deny the fact that, after Lyle began coming around, Mom started looking happy. And for the first time in a long time, she looked rested. Even younger, somehow. And then there was that undeniable sparkle in her eye the night Lyle surprised her with a sketch pad and a collection of charcoal pencils.

You'd think he'd handed her the keys to a mansion, a Rolls Royce, and a prosperous future, the way she carried on about those art supplies.

"I don't know what to say," she exclaimed repeatedly, her hands on her cheeks, her eyes wide, till Lyle finally hushed her by saying, "You don't have to say anything at all. You just have to sketch."

Until that night I didn't have a clue that my mother liked to draw. I didn't know she had any interest in art at all, as I'd never seen her so much as doodle while talking on the telephone. But in just a short time that sketch pad was filled with amazingly good drawings — flowerpots, fruit bowls, land and seascapes, portraits of Valerie and me.

Eventually I cornered Lyle Monroe in the living room and asked, "How did you know my mom likes to draw?"

"I asked her," he said simply. He was sitting in the easy chair listening to classical music on the radio, but he turned the volume down so we could talk.

"Why did you ask her?"

"Because I wanted to know about her. I wanted to know what she likes."

"How come?"

He cocked his head. "That's how you get

to know a person, I suppose. You find out what they like, what interests them." He smiled, waved a finger briefly to the notes drifting from the radio.

"You like music?" I asked.

"I appreciate certain composers, though I'm not a musician myself. But your mother, she's a wonderful artist, don't you think?"

I nodded. "But I've never seen her draw before. I didn't even know she could."

"Yes, well, that's what happens. You get married, have children, and little by little some of these things fall by the wayside."

"You mean she stopped drawing because of me?"

"Well, not because of you per se. But . . . I'm not sure that came out right. You see, once a person becomes a parent, the child becomes the most important thing in the world, more important than hobbies or . . . you know, other interests. A parent is glad to give her time over to her children."

"How do you know? You don't have kids, do you?"

He sighed behind his smile. "No, I don't. But I've talked with plenty of parents over the years. I know what's important to them."

I thought of Daddy, wondering whether I was important to him. I decided I was. The necklace was tucked safely away in my jewelry box, along with my Sugar Daddy wrappers. I looked at it every morning and every night.

"Mr. Monroe?"

"Yes, Roz?"

"Do you know a guy who lives where you live called Nelson Knutson?"

"Nelson . . . sure, I've met him. Why?"

"I was just wondering. Do you like him?"

He looked thoughtful a moment. "I don't know much about him, but he seems like a nice enough fellow. How do you know him?"

"Oh, I've seen him at the library a couple of times. You know, that big library downtown. He's helped me find some books." It wasn't a lie. At least not completely.

Nevertheless, Lyle Monroe didn't look happy. He leaned forward, made a V of his index fingers, and tapped at his mouth a moment. Then — sounding like the schoolteacher that he was — he said, "You shouldn't be talking to strangers, Roz. Especially men. You know that, don't you?"

"But . . ."

"If you need help finding a book, ask a librarian. That's what they're there for."

"But you said yourself he's a nice guy."

"Yes, but not everyone is, so just be careful in the future." The two lines between his brows ran deep as he gave me a look of concern.

"Don't worry, Mr. Monroe," I assured him. "I'll be careful. But I was lucky this time, right, to meet somebody nice like Mr. Knutson? I mean, he wouldn't hurt me, would he?"

Lyle Monroe gazed at me sternly another moment before sniffing out a small laugh. "No, Roz, I'm sure Mr. Knutson wouldn't hurt you. But I'm glad to hear you say you'll be careful. Now —" he lifted his chin and breathed deeply — "something smells good, doesn't it? What do you say we go see what the ladies have cooked up for supper?"

CHAPTER 41

Sitting on my bed, leaning back against the headboard, I held Wally's book in my hands, the one he gave me the night he ran away. I wished he were there now, sitting at his desk in the next room, his finger scrolling over the pages of *On the Road* as though he were carefully studying every line.

I wanted Wally back, but I didn't want him to be the Wally he was right before he went away. No, I had to go back farther, back several years, back to the days before . . .

But that was the hard part. I shut my eyes and squeezed the book tightly with both hands. I wanted to go all the way back to my earliest memories, when life was quieter and Wally and I were friends. But I couldn't rewind the years without seeing the bad parts too. I couldn't look backward without bumping up against that one event in particular, the thing that happened when Wally finally got big enough to fight back.

Valerie was about a year old. A series of colds and ear infections had kept her crying day and night for weeks. We were tired, all of us, a weariness made worse by the humid heat of the summer evening. All the windows in the house were thrown open and fans blew relentlessly in nearly every room, but nothing gave us much relief from the heat. Between the weather and Valerie's cries, we were all on edge.

Mom went to Valerie's day crib, the one set up in the den just off the kitchen. Before she could reach into the crib, Daddy was there, yelling, grabbing Mom's wrists, telling her to leave Valerie alone, to let her cry it out so she would sleep from exhaustion. Mom pulled away and they began to argue, hurling harsh and ugly words at each other. I crouched in the kitchen watching, clutching my doll, fighting back tears. I was afraid for Mom, afraid of what Daddy might do. Usually I didn't see the fights, only the aftermath: Mom's black eye, her bloodied lip.

Daddy raised a fist and I screamed, my own fist pressed hard against my mouth. Turning to flee, I unlocked my knees and started to rise, but even before I was fully upright, I heard Wally's bare feet slapping against the kitchen floor. He sprinted past me and into the den, head-butting Daddy in the gut like a linebacker making a tackle. He knocked Daddy off his feet and dove on top of him. Pinning him down, Wally began slamming his fists into Daddy's face over and over again. Finally Daddy was able to throw Wally off, but the fight went on, the two of them swinging and punching until they were both dripping huge drops of sweat and blood. Mom screamed and pleaded with them to stop, but they ignored her, leaping at each other like wild animals, prompted by a rage so thick it hung in the air. I put my hands over my ears, but I couldn't drown out the sounds: Valerie's wails, Mom's cries, the smack of flesh against flesh, the crash of bodies against furniture.

I cried and prayed to God, asking him to save my brother, as I was sure Daddy would kill him. Wally was tall, but he wasn't muscular like Daddy. When Daddy pushed Wally up against the wall, both hands around his throat, Mom reached for the phone. Her hands shook so hard she could scarcely dial zero for the operator. Even before the call went through, the front door flew open, and Uncle Joe was there, pulling Daddy off Wally and wrestling him to the floor. Daddy was big, but Uncle Joe was bigger, and he managed to hold Daddy down till his anger subsided.

"That boy tried to kill me," Daddy said amid a hail of oaths. He wiped at his bloodied nose with the back of his hand.

"Looked to me like you were killing him," Uncle Joe said, "and let me tell you something, little brother, that ain't right. It ain't right."

That was the night Wally became permanently angry. I suppose that was the night too that Mom began to think of leaving. Daddy disappeared for a couple of days after that, and when he came back, his arms loaded with gifts, he begged for another chance, even from Wally, who refused to forgive him.

We stayed with Daddy for one more year, and then we left.

"What are you doing, Roz?"

I looked up and saw Mom standing in the doorway. She was smiling.

"I was just thinking about Wally," I said.

"Oh?" She stepped across the room and sat beside me on the bed.

"I miss him."

She nodded, her smile fading. "I do too."

We were quiet a moment. Then Mom asked, "What were you thinking about?"

I looked toward the window and drew back one corner of my mouth. "I was thinking about how he used to fight with Daddy."

When I turned back, her expression turned grave, and I saw the sadness in her eyes. "That's not a very pleasant thing to think about, Roz. Why don't you think about something else?"

But I didn't want to let it go. I still had so many questions. "Is that why we moved away from Daddy?" I asked.

"That's part of it. A big part of it, yes."

"Because they didn't get along very well."

Mom sniffed at that, looking almost amused. "No, not very well, I'm afraid."

"When Wally comes back from being a soldier, will he live with us again?"

"Well, I don't know." Mom cocked her head. "He'll probably get a job and start living on his own. He's all grown up now, you know."

I nodded. If Wally didn't live with us, Daddy would have less reason to get angry.

"Mom?"

"Yes, honey?"

"Did Daddy love me?"

Mom hesitated only a moment before saying, "Of course he did, Roz."

"You know, he never got mad at me the

way he got mad at Wally. He was good to me."

Mom sat up a little straighter and looked at me a long time. "Roz," she said finally, "we've talked about all this before. I know you have some fond memories of your father, but that's all in the past. You need to leave that behind you and move on. Your father isn't with us, but we're still a family, just the way we are."

"But . . ."

"But what?"

"It doesn't feel like a real family without a father. You know, without Daddy. Are you sure we can't ask him to come back?"

"Yes, Roz. I'm very sure."

I thought then about my conversation with Mara, how she'd said, *"I think you should tell your mom."*

"Tell her what?" I'd asked. *"That Daddy's here?"*

"Yeah. I think she needs to know."

"But Daddy said not to tell her."

"Maybe that's all the more reason to tell her."

I wanted to tell her. I was aching to tell her. *Daddy's here! He's here in Mills River. He's promised to change. He's promised to stop drinking and to make us a family again.*

But when I looked at Mom's eyes, the words fell apart, like ash rubbed between a thumb and a finger. I was afraid. Afraid of her reaction. Afraid of ruining Daddy's plans. Afraid of ruining my own dreams.

And then she said something I didn't expect. "I wasn't sure I wanted to tell you this, Roz, but your father has moved to California."

For a moment I was left speechless as I tried to make sense of it all. Finally I managed to whisper, "He has?"

Mom nodded.

"How do you know?"

"Uncle Joe told me. In fact, your father left Minneapolis shortly after we did. He told Joe he wanted to start over, that he might as well look for work where it's warmer. He was tired of the winters, tired of working outdoors for months in the snow and cold. Anyway, it seems he's accepted the fact that he's not a part of this family anymore. You need to accept that fact too."

"But . . ."

"But what, Roz?"

That's a lie! I wanted to say. *Daddy's not in California. He's here. I've seen him!*

I shook off the urge to tell. I looked at Mom, and with heart thumping, I asked, "Can I have a stamp?"

"Sure. Are you going to write to Wally?"

"Not tonight. I think I'll write to Uncle Joe."

"Uncle Joe?"

I shrugged. "Yeah. I mean, since you mentioned him I realize I haven't written him since we got here."

Mom found her smile again. "Well, that'd be nice. I'm sure he and Aunt Linda would appreciate hearing from you."

Why hadn't I thought of Uncle Joe before? I'd write and tell him everything that had happened since we got there. How Daddy had followed us down and how he was calling himself Nelson Knutson and how he wanted to be with Mom and me and Valerie again. Uncle Joe would know what to do. After all, he was Daddy's brother. If he thought I should tell Mom that Daddy was in Mills River, then I'd do it.

When Mom left to get the stamp, I found some paper and started writing.

CHAPTER 42

Some days later, at five o'clock in the morning, I was startled out of sleep by the ringing of the telephone and by Tillie's cry of "Merciful heavens!" that followed soon after. Slipping out of bed, I tiptoed to the door of my room and stood there listening as Tillie talked into the extension in the hall. Mom appeared in her doorway too, hugging herself against both the cold in the house and the fear brought on by an early morning phone call from who knew where.

Tillie's face was pale and her hair, let loose from its bun, hung in wispy gray waves all the way down to the shoulders of her white cotton gown. In her rush she hadn't bothered to throw on her robe, though she'd wiggled her feet into the blue fuzzy slippers that always waited for her beside the bed.

Mom and I exchanged worried glances as she talked, unable to pick up any clues about to whom she was talking and what they were talking about. She didn't say much other than "Uh-huh" and "All right," until finally she said, "Tell him I'll be there as soon as I can," and hung up.

She looked at Mom and then at me to make sure she had our attention. We were way beyond giving her our attention and aching to know what was happening.

"That was a nurse down at Riverside Hospital," Tillie said. "They're just about to wheel Lyle into surgery. His appendix is inflamed and about ready to burst."

I heard Mom gasp. "Oh, Tillie," she whispered, lifting a hand to her mouth. To my surprise, her eyes glazed over with tears, as though one of her own children were about to go under the knife. She hadn't cried when I had my tonsils out, though, so I was annoyed to think she'd get teary-eyed over a man we hardly knew. "I wish I could go to the hospital with you," Mom said.

"You can come tonight, after it's over."

"Is he going to be all right?" I asked.

From the look on Tillie's face, I knew it was the wrong question to ask. After a moment she let out the breath she'd been holding and said, "He will be if we pray for him, Roz. Anyone care to join me?"

Tillie moved toward her room, and Mom and I followed. Reaching her bed, Tillie eased herself down to her knees and folded her thick hands on top of the quilt. Mom kneeled beside her. Not wanting to be left out, I joined them at the foot of the bed.

Tillie closed her eyes but kept her face turned toward the ceiling. Speaking loudly, she said, "Heavenly Father, I need to talk to you about Lyle and what's about to happen down there at the hospital. Now, you know, Lord, that I'm old and ready to die. Soon as you call, I'm coming on up, and I'll be glad to finally get there and see the face of my Savior Jesus, and Ross too, in that order."

Mom and I both opened one eye and peeked at each other.

"But Lyle — now, he's got a whole boatload of good years left, and if you don't mind my saying so, it'd be a shame if you didn't leave him here for now and let him finish up his work. So if you're dead set on taking someone home today, Lord, I pray it's me and not Lyle. I'm asking you, Father, to let my son live. And I'm asking in the name of your son, Jesus. Amen."

"Amen," Mom echoed.

Tillie opened her eyes, nodded, and slowly pulled herself up.

"Can I make you some breakfast before you go, Tillie?" Mom asked.

"Just coffee, thanks, Janis. I want to get there as soon as possible. In fact, I'll call Johnny and have him go with me, or at least drop me off."

"Listen, take the car. I can walk to work."

"Thanks, but Johnny needs to know anyway, and he may very well want to stay at the hospital with me." She marched back out to the phone in the hall as Mom and I followed once again. "We can't have Lyle all alone at a time like this. The nurse said someone from the boardinghouse brought Lyle in and stayed with him through the night, but he had to leave for work this morning, so now nobody's there."

Tillie hurriedly dialed Johnny's number. She spoke with him in short, clipped sentences while Mom rung her hands, and I looked on anxiously. When Tillie hung up, she said, "He'll be here in fifteen minutes."

"I'll get your coffee," Mom volunteered. "And Roz, you go ahead and get ready for school."

"If you go see him at the hospital tonight, can I come?" I asked.

"Let's talk about that later," Mom said as she moved toward the stairs.

"He may not be up to seeing too many visitors at once, Roz," Tillie said. "But your mother and I will be sure to give Lyle your love."

That said, she dismissed me with a wave of her hand and went back to her room to get dressed.

Esther Kinshaw was called to watch Valerie and me while Mom and Tillie were at the hospital. Mrs. Kinshaw was our next-door neighbor, the one with the award-winning hot dish recipes and the twin granddaughters in Sausalito named after flowers. She was already there when I got home from school; she had, in fact, been there all day, Mom having called her over before she left for work in the morning. Mrs. Kinshaw met me at the door wearing an enormous bibbed apron over her floral print housedress and a delicate hairnet over her silver bouffant. One sure way to ruin a casserole, she told me, was to allow wayward hairs to slip in unnoticed. No cook was going to win any blue ribbons if one of the judges ingested a hair.

While Valerie napped, I sat at the kitchen table doing homework and watching Mrs. Kinshaw putter around the kitchen. "Did my mom say when she'd be home?" I asked.

Mrs. Kinshaw shook her head. "She just said I was to feed you supper, so I'm assuming it'll be sometime in the early evening."

"Did you talk to Tillie at all today? Do you know how Mr. Monroe is doing?"

"No, she hasn't called. But it's only his appendix, and Lyle is a strong little boy, so I don't think we need to worry."

I wrinkled my nose at her and said, "He's not a little boy, Mrs. Kinshaw."

She looked thoughtful as her hands kneaded a batch of biscuit dough. Then she laughed. "No, I guess you're right about that. But I've known Lyle since he was about so high" — she held a hand to her knee — "and sometimes I still see him in my mind that way." She sighed and clicked her tongue. "Seems like only yesterday Curtis and I moved in next door to Tillie and Ross. We were both young couples then with small children. My, how the time has flown."

I looked at the clock on the kitchen wall. Not quite four o'clock. Time was not flying for me. Mom hadn't even left work yet to go to the hospital. She didn't get off till five, and then she'd probably spend a couple hours with Tillie and Lyle Monroe before she finally came home. We hadn't had a baby-sitter in a long time, not since Minnesota. Ever since we moved to Mills River, Tillie had been around to stay with Valerie

410

and me.

Sighing, I went back to my long division. But I couldn't concentrate because Mrs. Kinshaw kept chattering on about Tillie and Ross and what wonderful neighbors they were and how they had such fine sons and it was just a pity Lyle had never gotten married, because he would have made such a nice husband and father. . . .

I didn't care. I just wanted Mom to come home. And Tillie too. I just wanted everyone to be where they belonged.

It wasn't until almost nine o'clock — and somewhere around chapter 52 of Mrs. Kinshaw's tedious life story — that Mom and Tillie finally got home. When I heard the key in the kitchen door, I flew to Mom and threw my arms around her waist, pressing myself happily against her stiff wool coat.

"Why, Roz," she said, "I expected you to be in bed by now."

Mrs. Kinshaw waved a hand and hooted in amusement. "I'm afraid we lost track of time, Janis, dear. Roz and I have just been talking away like a couple of chatterboxes."

Speak for yourself, I thought. Aloud, I said, "I'm glad you're home, Mom. How's Mr. Monroe?"

"He's just fine. He was sleeping soundly when we left."

"Thanks be to God," Tillie added as she slowly unbuttoned her coat. "Both Lyle and I are still alive and well. Lyle came through the surgery just fine and should be out of the hospital in a couple of days. As for me, I'm tired. I feel as though I've been broadsided by a train."

"It's been a long day for you, Tillie," Mom agreed. "Why don't you go on upstairs and get some rest."

Tillie nodded. "I'm not going to argue with you there, Janis. My feet are yelling 'Traitor!' and my bones are begging me to lay them down for the night."

"Well, you go on then," Mom said with a small, wan smile. She looked pretty weary herself. "Esther, thanks for taking care of the girls. Can I reimburse you for your time?" She unsnapped her purse and dug around for her wallet.

Mrs. Kinshaw shook her head. "I wouldn't hear of it, Janis. What are neighbors for, if not to help each other? No, I'm just glad to do it."

"Well, thank you. You've been a huge help. Can I at least walk you home?"

"You don't even have to do that, dear. I don't imagine I'll get lost between here and the house next door."

Mom wiggled out of her coat, then walked

to the hall closet to help Mrs. Kinshaw on with hers. As they stood at the front door a moment and talked, Tillie moved to the kitchen sink to get herself a drink of water. "Oh, Roz, I almost forgot," she said. When the glass was full, she turned off the faucet, took a long drink, and settled the glass on the counter. "Lyle said to tell you it was a friend of yours who drove him to the hospital and stayed with him last night. Nelson Knutson. He said something about your meeting this fellow at the library. Anyway, Lyle wanted you to know he thinks the world of Mr. Knutson now. He says Mr. Knutson stuck with him just like a brother right up to the minute he had to leave for work this morning."

"Are you talking about that man from the boardinghouse?" Mom asked, joining us in the kitchen. When Tillie nodded, Mom said, "Good thing he was around to help. Lyle says he's the only boarder at the house who owns a car. Or, at least one that runs. We'll have to thank him for what he did."

"I intend to do that very thing," Tillie agreed. "Soon as Lyle's out of the hospital, we'll go on over to Charlotte's and thank that young man for his good deed."

Mom nodded and kissed the top of my head. "We used to have a neighbor by the name of Nelson Knutson. Remember, Roz?"

Mom started putting away the clean dishes on the rack while Tillie said good-night and headed for the stairs. I stood dumbfounded in the middle of the kitchen, sure that the smallest move would leave me unraveling at the seams.

Finally I mustered up the strength to say, "Sure. I remember him. Well, I'm going to go to bed now, Mom. I'm really tired."

I slunk off and slowly climbed the stairs, wondering how Daddy was going to get himself out of this one.

CHAPTER 43

When I stepped into homeroom the next morning, Miss Fremont motioned me to her desk. "I just wanted to thank you for the chocolates, Roz."

Puzzled, I watched as she patted a large box of Whitman's with her fingertips. "Your uncle Nelson said they were from you and" — here her thin painted lips hinted at a smile — "from him as well."

I felt my eyebrows reach for each other across the bridge of my nose. "My uncle Nelson?" I asked warily.

"Why yes," she said. She smoothed her heavily teased hair and pushed her cat-eye glasses farther up her nose before going on. "Your uncle who sometimes leaves notes and whatnot in your desk."

"You know about him?" My heart speeded up and my knees felt weak.

"Of course. I was the one who told him which desk is yours. Such a nice man. To think he stops by early in the morning to leave you surprises. I wish every child had a family member like your uncle. You're very lucky, Roz."

I didn't know what to say. I looked again at the chocolates, my mind spinning so fast I almost felt dizzy.

"He left something for you in your desk today," Miss Freemont went on. "It's Valentine's Day, you know. You didn't forget, did you?"

"No." I held up a paper sack filled with prepackaged dime-store cards. "I brought a card for everyone. One for you too."

She nodded. "We'll exchange them at the party this afternoon."

I turned toward my desk, still trying to understand why my father would give Miss Fremont a box of chocolates.

"Roz?"

I turned back reluctantly. "Yes, Miss Fremont?"

She made a small line of her lips and looked around the room at the kids who were filing in, hanging up coats, putting books into their desks. "I was wondering . . ."

"Yeah, Miss Fremont?"

"Your uncle . . . I noticed he doesn't wear a wedding ring. But, well, I suppose he's married?"

The flash of hopefulness in her eyes made my stomach drop. Miss Fremont — sixth-grade teacher, stern-faced spinster, the butt of her students' jokes — had a crush on my father. I wanted to run from the room, screaming. Instead, I forced myself to stay, to swallow the bile at the back of my throat, and to whisper, "Yeah, he's married. But he works construction, so he doesn't like to wear his wedding ring."

The hope slipped off Miss Fremont's narrow face like drooping wallpaper. She tried to smile, but her trembling lips failed her. "Of course," she said quietly.

As though I felt the need to drive the knife deeper still, I added, "And he's got kids."

She sucked in her cheeks and lifted her pointed chin. "I wasn't aware of any Knutsons in this school."

"They're too young for school," I lied.

"I see. Well, you may take your seat, Roz."

She pushed the box of chocolates to the far edge of the desk as I moved away. I hung up my coat on the rack at the back of the classroom and took my seat. Slowly I lifted the lid of my desk to see what Daddy had left inside.

There, amid the pencils, erasers, and discarded gum wrappers I found another bouquet of Sugar Daddies, tied together with a red ribbon. It lay atop a heart-shaped Valentine's card, my name scrawled across the front in Daddy's distinctive handwriting. Miss Fremont stood and began to speak, but I wasn't listening. I opened the card and read.

Dear Roz,
   I am giving you all of my love on Valentine's Day. The time is almost here when we will be together again as a family. Do you know what February 29 is? Leap year day, a lucky day, a day for love. Only two more weeks.
                                   Love,
                                   Daddy

I was so excited I could scarcely sit still all day. Just two more weeks. If Daddy could avoid seeing Mom and Tillie at the boardinghouse in that time, we'd be home free. He'd make his grand entrance back into our lives on February 29, and then we'd be a family again. On top of that, I wouldn't have to keep my secret anymore. Letting go of the secret would be like letting out my breath after holding it beyond all human endurance.

After school I went to the public library

hoping Mara would be there. She'd left school before lunch because of a dentist appointment, and I hadn't seen her all day. I was eager to tell her the news. I scurried from table to table until I found her. Happy and relieved, I dropped my books and reached into my coat pocket for Daddy's note.

"Look, Mara."

"What's that?"

"Read it."

She did. When she finished, she raised her head slowly and looked at me. I pulled out a chair and sat down across the table from her.

"Daddy's coming home," I whispered.

"I see that."

"Well? Aren't you happy for me?"

She stared at me a long while, her jaw working as though she were chewing on her words. Then she said, "Yeah."

"It's what we've been praying for," I reminded her.

"Yeah."

I was trying to hold on to my excitement, but Mara wasn't making it easy for me. "You don't seem very happy for me," I said.

"It's just that . . ." She hesitated, her words trailing off.

"What, Mara?"

"It's just a feeling I've got."

"About what?"

"Your daddy. And this whole thing."

"You still don't think I can trust him, do you?"

"I don't know. Like I said before, I don't know your daddy."

"That's right," I said. "You don't know him. He's a good man. He took Lyle Monroe to the hospital and stayed with him all night when he didn't have to."

Mara nodded. "I know. You told me that."

"He's every bit as good as your father."

"I didn't say he wasn't."

"Then what *are* you saying?"

She gave me back the note and leaned forward a little. "I still think you should have told your mom."

"That would ruin everything."

Her jaw worked again. "Did you hear back from your uncle Joe yet?"

I shook my head, reluctantly, and flopped back in my seat. "I haven't mailed the letter yet."

Her eyes widened. "You haven't? What are you waiting for?"

"I don't know, Mara. I just . . ." I looked at the desk, the ceiling, the rows of books stretching out beside us. Anywhere but at Mara. "I don't know," I finished lamely.

"You're afraid of finding out the truth."

"No I'm not!"

"Yes you are."

Our eyes met then, locking angrily. After a tense moment she said, "Mail the letter, Roz. You still have two weeks."

I slipped Daddy's note back into my pocket, gathered my books, and stood up. "I've got to go."

Mara said something, but I didn't catch it, and I didn't look back as I headed for the door.

CHAPTER 44

On Friday afternoon when I got home from
school, I found Tillie in the kitchen making
a pot of chicken soup. "Is that for supper?"
I asked.

"Nope." Tillie shook her head as she
stirred rice into the pot. "It's for Lyle.
Johnny drove him home from the hospital
this afternoon."

"So he's all right?"

"He's fine. He'll need to rest a few more
days before going back to work at the
hardware store, though."

"I didn't know he was working at a hardware store."

Tillie nodded absently. "Just until he can
get a teaching job." She lifted a spoonful of
soup to her lips, blew on it, tasted it, added
more salt. "I thought a little homemade
chicken soup would help him get his
strength back. I'm going to take it to him
tonight. Esther Kinshaw is coming over in a

little while to stay with you and Valerie."

"What about Mom?"

"She's coming with me."

"She is?"

Another nod. "She'd like to see Lyle, and we'd both like to thank that Mr. Knutson for what he did. That is, if he's there tonight."

My heart dropped to my toes. In my mind's eye I saw myself running through the snowy streets of Mills River, beating a path across the miles from McDowell Street to Cisco Avenue so I could warn Daddy not to be at the boardinghouse tonight. But I couldn't run that far, not in the cold, not even without the cold . . . not even in a million years. If I could have, I would have called him at work, but I didn't know where he was working, or even whether he *was* working. But I had to warn him somehow that Mom was coming, because if I didn't . . .

"Tillie?"

"Yes, Roz?"

"I don't feel so good."

She wiped her hands on her apron and laid one cool palm across my forehead. "What's the matter?"

"It's my stomach." I clasped both hands

across my midsection. "I have a stomach-ache."

"Hmm . . . well, I can give you some bicarbonate of soda. That should help."

I shook my head. "I think I'd better lie down."

"It's probably just a little indigestion. What'd you eat for lunch?"

I tried to think back that far. Lunch seemed years ago. "We had . . . oh yeah, meatloaf and mashed potatoes."

"That explains it," Tillie said knowingly. "No telling what the ladies down at the school cafeteria put in their meatloaf. I've known the head cook, Thelma, ever since she was born. Did you know she failed home economics back in . . . now what year was that? . . . she was in Paul's class, I believe, and it was the year they were seniors —"

"Um, Tillie . . ." I interrupted, clutching my stomach more tightly. "If I don't lie down, I might throw up."

Tillie raised her hands in surrender. "By all means, then, go lie down. And here" — she grabbed a plastic bowl from the counter — "take this with you, in case you need it."

"Will you send Mom upstairs when she gets home?"

"Soon as she walks in the door."

I went to my room and got in bed, fully dressed. I knew I'd be there for at least an hour before Mom got home, but I had to make it look good. If Tillie believed I was sick, chances were Mom would too. When Tillie came upstairs a few minutes later with a glass of Coca-Cola, I pleaded my case by moaning.

"Merciful heavens," Tillie said as she placed the soda on my bedside table. "Thelma's really outdone herself this time. I wonder if any of the other kids are sick. Maybe I should call Mara's mother and see —"

"No, don't do that!"

"Why not?"

"Mara brought her lunch today. She didn't eat the meatloaf." I moaned again. "Just thinking about it makes me want to throw up."

"All right then, not another word. You just rest and try to sip that soda. The bubbles might calm your stomach a little."

I nodded agreeably and shut my eyes. Tillie left the room; I heard her heavy footfalls going down the stairs. When she was gone, I sat up and drank some of the soda. My eyes wandered the room, looking for a way to entertain myself till Mom got home. I settled for reading a book.

The time passed slowly, but I finally heard Mom's car in the driveway, her key in the back door. Then, after a moment, during which time I'm sure Tillie was telling her about my case of food poisoning, Mom came upstairs and found me moaning in the bed, covers up to my nose, plastic bowl on the floor beside me.

"Tillie tells me you're sick." Her voice was sympathetic. She sat on the edge of the bed and pulled down the covers so she could see my face.

I nodded. "I don't feel so good."

"Tillie says it was the lunch at school?"

"Yeah."

"Shall I call the doctor?"

"No. I don't think so. I'll be all right. But, Mom?"

"Yes, honey?"

"Don't leave me with Mrs. Kinshaw tonight. I don't want a baby-sitter when I don't feel good."

Mom thought a moment. Then she nodded in agreement. "Of course," she said. "I'll stay here with you. I can always visit Lyle later. He's probably not up for much company tonight anyway."

I smiled. "Thanks, Mom."

"Sure, honey." She kissed my forehead and stood. "I'll be back to check on you shortly."

I watched her leave, then let out my breath in a sigh of relief.

Tillie left me a bowl of the chicken soup, which I said I felt well enough to try to eat. I would rather have had the lasagna that Mom and Valerie were having, but it would have given me away. I ate the soup slowly, like someone unsure of whether or not it would stay down. When I finished I was still hungry, but I didn't dare ask for anything more.

After supper I spent the evening reading and sucking on Sugar Daddies that Daddy had given me for Valentine's Day. I ate four of them, one after the other, as I waited and wondered what was happening at the boardinghouse. After I ate them, I folded up the wrappers and stuffed them into my jewelry box, along with the rest of my wrapper collection.

It was close to nine o'clock when Tillie came home.

"Lyle's doing great," she told Mom. "Almost good as new."

"Thank God."

"Yes indeed," Tillie said. She smiled at me as I walked into the kitchen to join them. She took off her coat, kicked off her snowy boots, and wiggled into the slippers waiting for her by the door.

"When will he go back to work?" Mom asked. She was at the stove pouring Tillie a cup of coffee. She poured a little more into her own cup before joining Tillie at the table. I listened to them talk as I fixed myself a peanut butter and jelly sandwich.

"Midweek," Tillie said. "Probably Wednesday." She sipped the coffee, seemed to savor the warmth.

Mom nodded. "I'm glad he's doing so well. And did you get to meet Mr. Knutson?"

I drew in a sharp breath and stood motionless while waiting for Tillie's answer.

"Briefly," Tillie said. "He's a shy fellow, that one, and a man of few words. He looked like a hound dog when I shook his hand and thanked him for what he did for Lyle. He said he was happy to help out, and then he excused himself and was gone. But Charlotte, now, she thinks the world of him. She said he's always helping around the house . . . anyone needs anything, Nelson Knutson's the first one there to lend a hand. She said she wished she had more boarders like him. Unfortunately for Charlotte, though, he's given notice. Moving out at the end of the month."

"Oh? Where's he going?"

"Michigan, I guess. That's where he's from, according to Charlotte. All he told her was he's going back home."

Mom nodded. "I was thinking we could have him and Lyle over for dinner sometime, but maybe it's too late for that."

Tillie shrugged and took another long sip of coffee. "At any rate, he knows we're grateful to him, and that's what matters."

"Yes. And if he has family in Michigan, they undoubtedly will be glad to have him home."

I folded together the two halves of my sandwich and let out another sigh of relief. Daddy, aka Nelson Knutson, had proved himself. Lyle Monroe liked him. Miss Charlotte did too. They said he was a good man. He was always helping, always lending a hand and doing good deeds. He'd taken Lyle to the hospital and stayed with him so he wouldn't be alone. Tillie was pleased. Mom was pleased.

I was no doubt more pleased than anyone.

Taking a huge bite of my sandwich, I stepped to the kitchen table. Tillie looked at me and asked, "How's our little patient here at home?"

"All better," I said, the words muffled by peanut butter.

"I see you got your appetite back."

I nodded. "Yup."

I left Mom and Tillie to their coffee and carried my sandwich to my room. Once there, I pulled the letter to Uncle Joe out of my desk, ripped it into several pieces, and tossing them like confetti, I threw them into the trash.

CHAPTER 45

Mara and I called a truce when I told her what Miss Charlotte had said about Daddy. "Well," she relented, "if he really does go around helping people, then maybe he *has* changed."

"I'm sure of it, Mara." I gave her a vigorous nod as I dug into my banana split. We were sitting at the counter of the drugstore's soda fountain on Saturday afternoon. In spite of the frigid temperature outside, we'd decided to meet for ice cream. "I mean, everyone who knows Daddy likes him. And you know, Miss Charlotte doesn't allow for any drinking at the boardinghouse. If Daddy were drinking, she'd kick him out faster than you can say Jiminy Cricket. So he must be going to AA like he said."

Mara looked pensive as she spooned out a scoop of her butterscotch sundae. After a moment she said, "I'm sorry I made you mad the other day, Roz. It's just . . . I don't want to see you get hurt or anything. You're my best friend ever, you know?"

I smiled. "You're my best friend too. So let's just forget about being mad, all right?"

"All right." She nodded.

"After Daddy comes home you can meet him, and then you'll see. I bet he'll do all sorts of fun stuff with us, like take us to the movies and the county fair and . . . Hey, maybe he'll even take us up to Chicago, and we can meet up with *your* dad. Wouldn't that be something, the two of us together with our dads?"

I expected Mara to be excited, but instead she looked uneasy. "That *would* be something," she said.

"What's the matter? Don't you think your dad would want to get together with us?"

Mara shrugged. "I really don't know. It'd have to be in secret . . . you know, so his wife doesn't find out. It'd be kind of complicated."

I chewed my lip a moment. "Well, I'm just dreaming. What's that poem by that guy you like? The one about holding on to dreams?"

"Uh-huh. You mean Langston Hughes." She looked thoughtful as she paused to lick some butterscotch off the stem of her spoon. "Yeah, he said if you let your dreams die, life becomes a broken-winged bird that can't fly."

"Yup, that's the one."

Mara nodded slowly, then looked straight at me. "You know, Roz, I've been thinking about that."

"What about it?"

"Well, maybe it depends on the dream, you know?"

"What do you mean?"

"Sometimes it may be the dream that keeps you from flying, if it's the wrong dream to have."

Several long seconds passed before I said, "Sometimes I don't get you, Mara. I don't get what you mean."

"Never mind, Roz," she said, lifting her shoulders in a tiny shrug. "I'm just thinking out loud."

"I think you think too much."

We laughed a little at that, and Mara said, "Yeah, maybe we could spend a day in Chicago with our dads. That would be something."

"It sure would," I agreed. "Hey, when Mom comes to pick me up, do you want to come over for a while?"

Mara nodded. "Sure."

"You can call your mom from our house and tell her we'll bring you home later."

"All right."

"Or maybe you could spend the night. No, I know, maybe you could just live with us!" I said with a laugh. "Wouldn't that be fun?"

"Yeah," she said excitedly. After a moment, though, she added, "But I'd miss my mom and dad."

"Oh. Yeah, I know what you mean."

"So I guess I'll just go on living with them."

I nodded. We smiled at each other and went on eating our ice cream.

Even though Daddy was married, Miss Fremont still allowed him to come into the classroom to leave notes in my desk. I found one there on Thursday morning, February 22, exactly one week before leap year day. *Can you meet me at the café after school today?* he asked.

I could and I would. At the end of the day, I took the school bus to the public library, then walked from there to Hot Diggity Dog. The trek was no easy task, since I was headed into the wind. Nearly frozen by the time I arrived, I didn't bother to take off my coat when I slid into the booth.

"Cold enough for you?" Daddy asked with a laugh.

I was too cold to answer; I only nodded. Daddy hollered for Darlene to bring me some hot chocolate, which warmed my hands first and finally, slowly, my insides.

"Well, kid," Daddy said at length, "just one more week and we'll be together."

He held out a hand across the table, and I took it. In spite of the rough calluses crossing his palm, his hand felt warm and safe to me.

"I can't wait, Daddy."

"Me either, honey."

"Things are going to be good this time."

"You know it, kid. And look. . . ." With his free hand he dug into his shirt pocket and pulled out a small hinged box. "Look here at what I got for your mother."

He pulled his hand from my grip so he could open the box. The lid flipped up on the hinge, like a pried-open oyster shell. Instead of a pearl, though, there was ring inside with a large red stone, surrounded by smaller stones that looked like diamonds. I felt my eyes grow wide in amazement.

"It's beautiful, Daddy!" I said.

He nodded. A certain pride settled over his face. "Your mother has always wanted a ruby. That's what this is."

"A ruby? Wow. It's the prettiest ring I ever saw. Can I try it on?"

"Sure, honey. It'll be too big for you, but go ahead."

I pulled the ring from the box and slipped it on. Daddy was right; it was too big, but I held it in place by squeezing my fingers together. Turning it this way and that, I watched how the stones dazzled even in the dim overhead light. "Wow, Daddy," I said again. "Mom's going to love it."

"I think she will," he agreed.

"Is she supposed to wear it in place of her wedding ring?" I asked, "because she doesn't wear her wedding ring anymore."

Daddy looked pained at that. "Do you know what she did with her ring? Did she sell it?"

I shook my head slowly. "I don't know. I don't think she sold it. Maybe she just put it in her jewelry box."

"Well, if it's gone, I'll buy her another one." He tried to smile, but it was lopsided and brief. "This one isn't a wedding ring. It's more of a . . . I don't know . . . a promise ring, maybe. It's a token of my promise to make a new life for us."

I looked from Daddy to the ring and back again. "It sure is pretty, Daddy. You picked out the best ring ever."

"I'm glad you like it, honey. That means a lot to me. Maybe that means your mom will like it too."

"Oh, I know she will. You don't have to

worry about that. She'll think it's the prettiest ring she ever set eyes on."

Before I even knew she was there, Darlene was standing over me exclaiming, "Goodness sakes, honey! Where'd you get that ring? It's just beautiful."

"Dad — I mean, Uncle Nelson bought it —"

"Well, what's the occasion? Is it your birthday or something?"

I laughed. "It's not for me. He's giving it to Mo— he's giving it to his girlfriend." I looked at Daddy, but he had dropped his eyes. He was tapping the table uneasily with an index finger. "Aren't you, Uncle Nelson?"

Daddy reached for the ring and pulled it off my finger. "Let's put that away before it gets lost, Roz."

I looked back up àt Darlene. Her face had gone pale, and she had a look in her eyes that reminded me of Miss Fremont when I told her Daddy was married.

"How nice," she said, but her voice was as cold as the winter wind outside, and it made me shiver. Turning to Daddy, she lifted the carafe in her hand an inch or so and asked, "Another cup of coffee, Mr. Knutson?"

Daddy waved a hand over his cup. "No thanks, Darlene. I'm fine for now."

She went on looking at Daddy, clutching the carafe with whitened knuckles. Finally she nodded curtly and walked away.

"What's got her goat?" I asked.

Daddy shrugged, glanced at Darlene, back at me. "Women are funny, Roz. I never know what they're thinking. But anyway . . . listen, honey, I'm going to need your help getting this ring to your mom."

I nodded agreeably. "What do you want me to do?"

"Well, here's my plan. I want her to come downstairs on February 29, and I want her to find this waiting for her at her place at the kitchen table. That's the lucky day, you know. It comes only once in four years."

Another nod from me.

"It's the day I'm going to ask her to let me come home. I'm going to write her a letter explaining everything — how I've been going to AA, how I'm a different person, how I'm going to make it work this time."

When he paused a moment, I asked, "So what do you need me to do?"

He smiled and winked. "I need you to do two things, honey. The first is this . . ." He pulled a napkin from the dispenser and laid it in front of me, along with a pen he plucked out of his shirt pocket. "I want you to draw a picture of the inside of your house, you know, showing me where all the rooms are."

I took the pen, clicked it open. "How come?"

"Well, I'm trying to decide whether we'll keep this house or buy a different one."

"So we're staying here in Mills River?"

He nodded. "I kind of like it here. Don't you?"

I shrugged and went to work drawing the picture. "You want the upstairs too, Daddy?"

"Yes, downstairs and up. Everything."

"All right."

"That's good, honey. And don't forget to label the rooms, tell me what they are."

"Okay." I looked up a moment, an idea turning in my head. "You know what, Daddy? We could sell the house to —"

Then I remembered, and stopped.

"To who, Roz?"

Tillie, of course. She thought it was her house anyway. Now it really could be hers again, and Lyle could come live in it with her. But I didn't want to mention Tillie right then, because Daddy still didn't know she lived with us.

"Just sell it," I said. "You know, to whoever wants to buy it."

439

Daddy nodded slowly. "I've been thinking about that. I bet your grandfather made the down payment on that house, didn't he?"

I shrugged. I didn't know anything about that.

Daddy went on, "He must have. No way Janis could have bought a house on her own. So listen, Roz, we'll sell the house and buy another, one we all pick out together. Start all over with a clean slate, you know?"

I smiled and looked down at the napkin. "Do you want me to finish drawing?"

He eyed my floor plan, gave me a nod. "Yeah, go ahead. Now the second thing I need you to do is make sure the kitchen door is unlocked the night of February 28. That way I can slip in and slip out again real quick. I'll just slip in while everyone's asleep and leave this for her on the kitchen table, along with my letter and a dozen red roses. Do you think you can do that, Roz?"

I thought a moment. "I always go to bed before Mom does. Even if I unlock the door, she might find it open and lock it again."

Daddy leaned forward over the table. "Listen, honey, I really need your help here, so I'm going to ask you to do something that might be hard. Are you with me?"

I nodded.

"Good girl. When you go to bed, I don't

want you to fall asleep. I want you to stay awake somehow, and after your mother goes to bed, just go on downstairs and check and make sure the door is unlocked. Do you think you can do that?"

"I guess so. Maybe if I keep pinching myself, I'll stay awake."

Daddy smiled. "Don't pinch too hard. But try to stay awake somehow, because this is a big thing, Roz. It's a big surprise for your mother. It's the start of a new life. You believe me, don't you, honey?"

I smiled as big as I could. "Of course, Daddy."

"That's good, honey. I knew I could count on you." He patted my hand and slipped the ring box back into the pocket of his shirt.

CHAPTER 46

I did as I was told. On the night of Wednesday, February 28, I went to bed, but I didn't go to sleep. I sat up against the headboard and flexed my toes and pinched my earlobes and sucked on Sugar Daddies to keep myself awake.

It was more important than ever, I thought, for Daddy to come home right away, because I didn't want to lose Mom to Lyle Monroe. Lyle had come to supper that evening, and as he sat at our table eating and talking about his adventures in Bolivia, I noticed Mom listening to him with a new intensity, and I saw the way the two of them locked eyes and smiled like there was no one else in the room. Mom had never looked at Tom Barrows like that; mostly, he'd earned frowns of resignation. Now Mom's face registered a sort of shy anticipation, as though Lyle's brush with death had sparked off some sort of feelings between the two of them, and I realized that if my family was going to come back together, there was no time to lose.

Amid all the smiling going on, I smiled only once myself. There'd been a robbery at the boardinghouse, Lyle explained, "and several people, including Charlotte herself, are missing various items."

"Merciful heavens!" Tillie cried. "Did they take anything of yours?"

"No, Mother," Lyle said with a laugh. "I don't have anything of value, so I was kindly passed over."

"So what was taken?" Mom asked.

"Money, jewelry, a watch — items of that nature."

"And no one knows who might have done it?"

Lyle shook his head. "Charlotte thinks it's an inside job, though."

"Someone at the boardinghouse?" Tillie asked.

"Yes. The police think she may be right. The key suspect right now is the new boarder Charlotte took in last week, a fellow by the name of Louie something. The police questioned him and ended up letting him go. Couldn't find enough evidence to hold him. So Charlotte's asked Nelson and me to be extra vigilant, just to see if we can

443

pick up on any clues."

"Nelson Knutson?" I asked.

"Yes, your friend Nelson," Lyle answered.

That's when I smiled. I was proud to think Daddy had been chosen by Miss Charlotte to help solve the crime. If he could actually help in getting the robber arrested, Mom would be proud of him too.

Nine o'clock rolled around, and Mom sent me up to bed. When Tillie went off to her own room, claiming to be tired, I knew she was just giving Mom and Lyle time to be alone together. I didn't like that one bit, but I consoled myself with the thought that *this* was the night. Daddy was even now making plans to come with the ring and the flowers and the letter so that Mom would find them in the morning and take him back.

I wiggled my toes and hummed quietly to myself, even while sucking on a Sugar Daddy. Minutes slipped by, and then an hour, and then two. I was fighting sleep by then, growing drowsier by the minute. But I was determined not to fail Daddy. I sat straight up and dug my nails into the palms of my hands, hoping the pain would keep me awake. Finally I heard the front door open and close — that was Lyle leaving to catch the last bus back to Cisco. Then,

Mom's footsteps on the stairs. I lay back down and pulled the covers up to my chin in case she should check on me as she passed by on the way to her own room. But she must have been deep in thought, because she didn't stop. I saw her move through the shadows in the hall and disappear.

I waited another twenty minutes. And then quietly . . . very quietly . . . I tiptoed downstairs and unlocked the kitchen door.

As I slipped back under the covers, I looked at the lighted dial of the clock by my bed. Almost midnight. Almost February 29, the day that comes once every four years, the lucky day that would change my life and make everything right again. I was so excited I laughed, but just as quickly I put a hand to my mouth to stifle the giggles. I didn't want to wake up Mom or Tillie. Taking one last glance at the clock, I shut my eyes. Soon, in spite of my nervous excitement, I fell into a deep sleep.

I don't know exactly what kind of noise woke me. I'm not sure whether it even was a noise or whether it was just some kind of knowing. A knowing that Daddy was in the house, and yet a knowing too that things were not right.

My eyes flew open, and I rolled toward the clock. Almost three now. I lay in silence and listened. The house creaked. A car rolled by in the street outside my window. A dog barked loudly. Louder still was my own rhythmic breathing, fast and shallow. Where was Daddy and what was he doing? Was he leaving the ruby ring on the table right now? Why was fear unraveling in my chest and twining itself around my heart?

Then I heard it. Unmistakable. A kitchen chair bumping up against the table. Daddy was down there, stumbling about in the dark. If he wasn't careful, he'd wake everyone up and ruin the surprise. I crossed my fingers and willed him to finish and go away before he was found out.

But he didn't go away. From the kitchen his footfalls moved over to the hardwood floor in the hallway. His steps were loud and unsteady, just like on the nights he had come home drunk.

Just like on the nights he had come home drunk.

I sat straight up in bed and listened. He was climbing up the stairs, his footsteps muted now on the carpeting but still distinct. He was coming up, and that wasn't part of the plan.

My heart rate sped up, and my head felt

light. I laced my fingers together and squeezed until my knuckles ached.

But it's just Daddy, I thought. *It's Daddy. He won't hurt you. It'll be all right.*

The padded pounding of his feet came closer, and I knew he had almost reached the landing. I sank down and pulled the covers up to my nose so that only my eyes peered out. In the next moment Daddy was framed in my doorway, a dark silhouette in a darkened hall. But only briefly. He was only passing by. He moved down the hall toward the master bedroom. Mom's room, where Valerie slept too. Could Mom hear him coming? Did she think it was just Tillie returning from a trip to the kitchen for a midnight snack?

I pushed back the covers, held my breath, willed my frozen muscles to move. Quietly I tiptoed across the room. Even before I reached the door, I smelled the all too familiar reek of alcohol that had filled our house in Minnesota, the pungent sickening scent that was caught in the curtains, ground into the rugs, mixed into the very paint on the walls. Tonight it followed Daddy like a wake.

At the door I held my breath and peered out into the hall. Daddy had almost reached the master bedroom, where Mom and

Valerie slept.

I blinked and gasped as the light in the hall came on. In the same moment Daddy whirled around, faltered, steadied himself. I saw the gun in his hand. A look of surprise lay across his face like a mask, his eyes fixed on the figure before him. Tillie, ghostlike in her white cotton gown, was bearing down on him, the baseball bat held up over her head with both hands.

I screamed. The gun exploded. Tillie stiffened, stumbled, put a hand to her chest. The tip of the bat hit the floor, and Tillie leaned on it like a cane. The light came on in the bedroom behind Daddy, and the room grew loud with panic: Valerie's piercing screams, Mom calling Daddy's name. "Alan, no! Alan!"

Daddy aimed the gun again, pulled the trigger.

Nothing.

Again.

Nothing.

And again.

Nothing. Nothing but three dead clicks.

Tillie moved forward.

Daddy slapped the gun against his palm and swore aloud. He jiggled something on the barrel and pulled the trigger. The gun came to life, exploding once again and sending a bullet through the floor. Daddy reeled, righted himself, lifted the gun once more, but it was too late.

Tillie reached him now, the bat still clenched in her hands. She swung, hitting Daddy squarely on the side of the head. The impact hurled him into the bedroom even as it thrust Tillie up against the wall, where ever so briefly, she stood as though stunned, until slowly she slid down to the floor. One wide streak of blood marked her path on the wallpaper. A second widening circle of blood stained the front of her gown.

Mom bypassed Daddy, sprawled on the bedroom rug, and rushed to Tillie's side. "Hold on, Tillie. Hold on," she pleaded, her voice shaking. "I'm calling for an ambulance."

Mom grabbed the extension in the hall and dialed zero as I finally found my legs and ran to Tillie. I was trembling, every inch of me shivering with fear. Even the house itself seemed to vibrate with panic; the air felt thick with it.

Mom said something into the phone that I could scarcely hear over Valerie's shrieks. When she finished, she didn't hang up but left the receiver dangling by the cord, turning ever so slightly in the air like someone hanged. She ran to her room, and I called after her, "What are you doing?"

"Stay with Tillie," she hollered back. I waited a moment, but she didn't say more.

"Tillie," I whispered. "Tillie."

Her eyes were open. She settled them on my face.

I was crying now and breathing hard, gasping for air. *Don't die, Tillie. Don't die.*

She stretched a hand toward me, the hand that had gone to her chest when she was shot. I didn't want to touch it, didn't want to touch the blood. But when her warm moist fingers curled around my palm, I held on tight. "I love you, Tillie," I said.

She tried to smile. She gazed at me with eyes that seemed to be drifting, losing focus. "I love you too, Roz," she whispered. She looked away from me, beyond my shoulder, gave a small gasp. Her eyes widened, took on light.

She said my name again, but this time it didn't quite sound like Roz. It sounded like Ross.

I looked over my shoulder then back at Tillie. Her eyes were closed now, and her chin drooped toward her chest. A siren wailed in the distance. Valerie went on screaming. I saw Mom lean over Daddy, feel his neck for a pulse, lift the gun from the floor. She held the weapon in the palm of one hand as her other hand went to her mouth. She was weeping quietly, her tears capturing the overhead light and glistening on her cheeks. After a moment she stood and, aiming with both hands, pointed the gun at Daddy's head.

As I waited for her to pull the trigger, I felt Tillie's hand lose its grip on mine.

CHAPTER 47

Long minutes passed, one melting slowly
into the next, as I stood motionless in the
sterile room. Any noise around me — the
clanking of medicine trays in the hall, the
occasional voice over the hospital PA system, even the click and the hiss of the
equipment around the bed — became little
more than white noise to me, I was so lost
in thought. I was trying to make sense of all
that had happened since our move to Mills
River, and as insights came to me piecemeal
I worked to fit them into a meaningful
whole.

"You lied to me," I whispered to the figure
in the bed. "I can't believe you lied to me."

And yet, why was it so unbelievable? They
had all warned me. Wally, Mom, Tillie, even
Mara. They had told me Daddy couldn't be
trusted, and I hadn't listened.

Daddy lay there between the sheets, wide
bandages wound tightly around his broken

skull, reaching down even to cradle his chin. His face was drowning in a pool of white. White gauze, white linen. His eyes were shut, unseeing. His ears peeked out of cracks in the binding, but they didn't hear the words I'd just spoken. They couldn't hear anything now, hadn't heard anything for the past two weeks. The doctors weren't sure he would ever see, hear, taste, or touch anything again. They weren't sure he would ever wake up, but if he did, his brain had sustained enough damage to keep him bedridden the rest of his life.

It didn't seem like much of a life. Maybe Mom should have pulled the trigger when she had the chance. But she didn't. Had never meant to, she said, unless he woke up. But he didn't wake up.

I felt no pity. My feelings were of sadness and betrayal. And relief. And guilt.

"This is the first time I'm glad the old fool was drunk," Wally said when Mom called him long distance to tell him what happened. "It kept him from shooting straight. If not for Jim Beam, you might all be dead."

Maybe Jim Beam had ended up doing something right this time, but he hadn't worked alone. Daddy may have killed us all, if not for the element of surprise. He'd come up against what he hadn't expected, a powerhouse named Tillie Monroe who, with one swift blow, had sent him sailing into this lingering twilight.

Thank God for Tillie. Thank God she had come back to the house she had lived her life in and that she wanted to die in.

Still, in the midst of my relief, I was trying to lay my guilt to rest. None of it would have happened if not for me. I lifted my hands to the railing of the hospital bed and squeezed hard. I was the one who had been tricked. If tragedy had come to the entire family, it would have been because of me. While I was trying to figure out whether I could trust Daddy, I should have simply trusted Mom. She wouldn't have brought us to Mills River if it had been safe to stay with Alan Anthony. Why hadn't I thought about that? Why did I overlook what was so obvious?

I could only suppose it was because I wanted what I wanted. I wanted it enough to let myself be fooled, to believe in spite of everything that Daddy was trustworthy and the good life he promised was possible. I was a child, and yet I should have known. If only I had listened. If only I hadn't let the dream overshadow my common sense.

Mara was right. Sometimes it's the dream that holds you down and keeps you from flying, if it's the wrong dream. You have to let it go if you're ever going to soar.

Daddy had come to our house, just as he said he would, but his promises stopped there. He hadn't brought the ruby ring with him, or a letter, or a dozen red roses. The only thing he had brought to our house was the gun, one the cops said he'd purchased in a pawn shop in Chicago sometime around Christmas. The ring, which belonged to Miss Charlotte, was found in the glove compartment of his car, along with Mr. Wainwright's watch. A few other items were found at the pawn shop where Daddy had bought the gun, as he'd made several trips back there between Christmas and leap year day. Not only was Daddy a liar, he was a thief.

It was time to let go of the dream.

I clenched my jaw. I had something to say to this man, even though he couldn't hear it. But I had to say it anyway, for my own sake if nothing else. I leaned forward, unlocked my jaw, and sighed heavily. One tear trickled down my cheek. "I can't help it, Daddy," I whispered, "I still love you. Just a little. I can't seem to stop. But if you ever wake up, I'm not going to be able to believe anything you say. So I've come to say good-bye."

I dug around in my jeans pocket and pulled out several sticky Sugar Daddy wrappers, ones I had kept in my jewelry box at home. I slipped them into Daddy's unresponsive hand and curled his fingers around them. "Thanks anyway," I said, "but you can have these back."

"Are you ready, Roz?"

Mom was out in the hall now, framed in the doorway of Daddy's room. Beside her stood Lyle Monroe, clutching the handles of a wheelchair. And in the chair, wearing a brand-new hat and a new winter coat with a faux fur collar, sat the spitfire herself, Tillie Monroe.

I smiled at all three of them and nodded. "I'm ready, Mom."

"I'm ready too," Tillie said, adjusting her hat. "Merciful heavens, but it's hard to get a good night's sleep around here, what with all the prodding and poking and temperature-taking. They should have let me out a week ago. After all, it was just a flesh wound."

"Now, Mother," Lyle countered as he cast an amused glance at Mom, "a bullet that both enters and exits your shoulder is more than a flesh wound —"

"Well, son, having been the one who was shot, I should know. . . ."

As the three of them bantered about Tillie's wound, I took one last look at Daddy. I felt as though I should say something else, one last parting statement, but I had no more words.

I patted my jeans pocket, not the one I'd taken the candy wrappers from but the other one. Tucked deep inside was the necklace Daddy had given me for Christmas. That, I was going to keep. Not for any sentimental reason, but as a reminder. If I was going to survive in this world, I had to understand that not everything I wanted to be true was true, and not everything that looked good was good.

I moved to the hall and took Tillie's hand. "Come on, Tillie," I said, "let's get out of here."

Tillie squeezed my fingers and smiled. "Now you're talking, Roz," she said. "Lead the way. I'm right behind you."

EPILOGUE

Tillie lived for another three years in the house on McDowell Street, long enough to see Mom and Lyle get married and long enough to greet her grandson, my brother, Ross Monroe. Tillie said Ross looked just like his namesake, the grandfather he would never know . . . at least not this side of paradise. "But when I see him again," Tillie promised the baby, "I'll tell him you're here. He'll be proud to know that."

Certainly his other grandfather, Grandpa Lehman, was proud of him, calling Ross the gem that rose up out of the ashes, the little man who sailed in after the storm. Gramps had offered to move us out of the house after the shooting, "So you don't have to live with the memories," he said. But Mom said no, she wanted to stay. She had a feeling good things were in store for us there, and she was right, the birth of Ross some two years later being one of the happiest events.

Wally came home from Vietnam shortly before Ross was born. When he came back from his tour over there, he was a different person, and that in a good way. Much of the anger was gone, not because it had been spent on the battlefield, I think, but because the threat of Daddy had disappeared from our lives. Wally said he finally felt safe. No more North Vietnamese Army, no more Vietcong guerillas, and no more Alan Anthony. For the first time in a long time, Wally was at peace.

And so was Mom. I'll never forget the evening she called me away from my homework, asking me to join her downstairs in the living room. When I arrived, everyone else was already there: Tillie, Wally, and Valerie. Mom was on the couch with baby Ross in her arms, her husband, Lyle, beside her.

"What is it, Mom?" I asked.

"Are we in trouble or something?" Wally added.

Mom shook her head. "No, you're not in trouble. I just wanted to look at you. I just wanted to have you all right here in the same room at the same time."

"Okay." Wally shrugged, took another bite out of the apple he was eating. "As long as we're not in trouble."

Mom's eyes moved over each of us, one at a time. She gazed lovingly at the sleeping baby in her arms, then reached for Lyle's hand. "God has been good to us," she said quietly.

"Indeed," Lyle said.

We were quiet for a time and didn't even feel awkward about it. We shared an almost tangible gratitude that we were all there and all together.

Finally Tillie said, "This house is happy again. I can feel it in my bones. Can't you, Lyle?" She looked at Lyle, who smiled and nodded. "It was built for a family," Tillie went on, "and now it's satisfied."

We really were family now, as Tillie was Mom's mother-in-law and my brother Ross's grandmother. And my grandmother too, mother of my stepfather, Lyle, who I didn't think of as my stepfather at all but as my daddy. Now I knew how Mara felt about Willie Nightingale. He wasn't her grandfather but her father, her true daddy. Somehow, in a way we never expected, our Daddy Deal had been fulfilled and our prayers answered.

It was when I put Valerie to bed one night that I understood what Tillie had been trying to tell me on the day I got my tonsils out.

"Tillie, how do you know if you're going to end up in heaven?"

"Well now, that all depends on who your father is."

When Valerie folded her small hands together and said — she was saying it correctly now — "Our Father, who art in heaven . . ." I thought, *Oh. Of course. That's what Tillie was talking about.*

One more thing I should have seen earlier. But no one had ever told me God was a father. I had always simply thought he was God.

I had a suspicion, on the night she was shot, that Tillie had caught a glimpse of heaven. I asked her what it was she saw, and she said she couldn't tell me.

"But did you see anything at all?"

She looked past me and smiled, as though she were seeing it all again. "Oh yes."

"Why can't you tell me?"

Her eyes snapped back to me. "Because I don't have the words. I wouldn't be allowed to anyway, even if I did have the words. But I can tell you this much. I don't have to look back anymore. It's all ahead of me, all the lost moments of my life . . . they aren't lost. They've been tucked away for safekeep-

461

ing, along with so much more."

That's all she would say. No matter how much I pestered her, she said I simply had to be patient and wait until the day I would find out for myself.

"But don't worry," she added. "You can trust God for what's to come. He's a good Father. Unlike some."

Alan Anthony died in the summer of 1968, almost a year to the day we moved into the house on McDowell Street. Mom was already planning her wedding to Lyle when she came and told me Daddy was dead of sepsis. He'd developed a bedsore that got infected, and it was all downhill from there.

"I'm sorry, Roz," she said.

"I'm sorry too, Mom," I told her.

I allowed myself one good cry, and then I put it all aside, like closing a book when you reach the end and tucking it back up on the shelf. His memory faded over the years until it became little more than a distant ache.

Wally went off to college, Valerie started school, I became a teenager, and Ross had begun to walk and talk by the time Tillie stood up from the dinner table one evening and announced, "Janis, dear, you and Lyle can have the house now, free and clear. I don't need it anymore."

Mom looked up wide-eyed and sounded alarmed when she asked, "Why, Tillie? Where are you going?"

"Home."

"But this *is* your home."

"Not anymore, it's not."

That night Tillie lay down beneath her wedding quilt on her big brass bed and quietly slipped away. She got her final wish. She died in the house that she had built with her own two hands alongside her husband, Ross, the house that was happy when it had a family living inside.

Since then, the house on McDowell Street has always had a family living inside. I raised my three children there, and now my son, Ross Monroe Hillsdale, and his wife are raising their two children there. My son Ross was the second child in our family to be named for Tillie's husband. The third was my grandson, Ross Theodore Hillsdale. And so the Monroe and the Anthony families continue to grow and intertwine.

Mara visited often over the years, first with her children and later her grandchildren. After college she moved to Chicago and went on to become the well-known playwright Beatrice Nightingale. Her most famous play, *The Radio Man,* had a thirty-six-week run on Broadway. Not bad for a kid from a small unknown town in flyover country.

Since Tillie died, I suppose I've thought about her every single day. I think of the way she showed up in our lives unannounced, blowing in like a nor'easter and yet doing so in a way that brought our family together instead of ripping us apart. I think of her eccentricities, her iron will, her gentle kindness that caused people to love her, in spite of herself. I think of the way her cries of "Merciful heavens!" echoed throughout the house and bounced from wall to wall and from floor to ceiling. But that was the thing about Tillie; that was the legacy she left me. Without her, I might never have known what I know now: that heaven is indeed merciful, and all the hours and days and dreams we deem as lost are simply waiting for us in a place we'll someday recognize as home.

DISCUSSION QUESTIONS*

1. An age-old saying declares, "You can never go back home again." The meaning is clear: times have changed; people have changed; places have changed. Tillie returns to the house she and Ross built with their own hands. She considers the house hers, no matter if the title has changed to someone else. Have you ever attempted to return to a place you once considered yours (i.e. your childhood home, the city where you attended college, etc.)? If so, what sensations and emotions occurred? Was the attempt successful? Why or why not? Do you think the place had changed or you had changed? Or both?

2. Winston Newberry considered himself wronged by Tillie, who showed off his

* By Juanette Butts

Eiffel Tower–shaped birthmark. Winston waited countless years to enact his revenge. Have you ever believed someone caused you harm, whether intentional or not? Did you hold anger in your heart, waiting for the opportunity to pay the person back for what had occurred? Did you attempt to exact revenge? Did the attempt give you the satisfaction you anticipated? Who do you think suffered more: the alleged perpetrator or you? Would you change how you responded to the act if it were possible? Would your life be different if you had?

3. Wally adjusts poorly to Tillie's arrival. All he wants is for her to leave. ". . . if she came here to die, why doesn't she just go ahead and do it?" Have you ever felt as if someone or something invaded your life and you lost some — or all — control? Did you want the circumstance to resolve so you could regain control over your life? When you examine your life now, how do you think you would be different had the experience not occurred? Do you think your life would be better? Worse? The same?

4. Roz knows Mara lied about her father —

while conveniently forgetting she had lied as well. Both girls are afraid if the truth is known they might not be accepted. Fear of rejection is a powerful motivator to conceal aspects of your life you believe will cause others to either reject you or to end your friendship. Have you ever felt unable to be honest about yourself because you believed others wouldn't accept you? Did you share your secrets or keep them hidden? Do you think your relationships would have been impacted if you had told? Are your current relationships based on honesty?

5. Tillie tells Roz she is too young to understand that every moment can be an extraordinary moment. We tend to overlook the ordinary, not comprehending until time has passed just how life-changing everyday occurrences can be. Do you toss aside simple pleasures in anticipation of grandiose adventures? Do you ignore the blessings of where you are to seek imagined treasures elsewhere? Can you remember a time you considered an event inconsequential only to discover later it was a pivotal occurrence? Do you rush through today to reach tomorrow, or do you linger in order to cherish what God

has for you along the way?

6. When her father isn't in the diner, Roz runs away. She tells herself there is a safe place ahead somewhere, if only she can run far enough to find it. Have you ever been so burdened by trials and tribulations you wanted to escape? Did you believe if you ran fast enough, far enough away those troubles would never find you? Have you come to realize the majority of difficulties we experience reside within ourselves? Have you been able to resolve painful issues? Did you trust God to help you, or did you attempt resolution on your own? Which method works better? Why?

7. Janis expresses doubts that God is there. She doesn't believe he has any interest or control over what happens to people. She tells Tillie that God is very cruel. Tillie assures Janis that God has everything to do with what happens in people's lives. Without God, no one would have any hope at all. Have unexplainable circumstances caused you to question God's existence? Have you wondered if he cared about what was happening in your life? Have you thought him cruel for allowing painful occurrences to harm you? Have

you changed your opinion? Do you realize God does love you and hurts when you suffer?

8. Roz confronts her unconscious father regarding the lies he told her. She'd been warned by many but chose to believe him. Have you ever trusted someone despite others warning you the person was deceitful? Did that person's subsequent revelation surprise you? Were you able to admit your mistake, able to apologize to those concerned for your well-being? How long has it taken the guilt and heartbreak to ease? Do you feel able to recognize those intent on deceiving you? How will you handle the situation if it arises again?

9. Roz understands it was the desire for her dream to become reality that caused her to ignore reason and wisdom and allowed her father to manipulate her. Unimaginable tragedy could have occurred due to her choices. In returning the Sugar Daddy wrappers, Roz releases the dream she'd held so tightly. Have you treasured a particular desire despite family and friends advising you otherwise? Did you ignore your own common sense? Did the dream you harbored come to fruition, or did re-

ality force you to accept that what you wanted was unattainable? How difficult was it to release the dream?

10. Roz keeps the necklace her father gave her as a reminder "that not everything I want to be true is true, and not everything that looks good is good." She eventually came to understand heaven is indeed merciful and that all the hours, days, dreams deemed as lost are waiting in a place believers will recognize as home. Jeremiah 29:11 reads, *For I know the thoughts and plans that I have for you, says the Lord, thoughts and plans for welfare and peace and not for evil, to give you hope in your final outcome.* God has plans for our lives. However, we want what we want. Do you stray from the path he has designated for you to a path of your own making? Do you look at others and wonder if they also reject God's goals and lean to their own understanding? How difficult is it to relinquish your will for his?

ABOUT THE AUTHOR

Ann Tatlock is the author of the Christy Award–winning novel *All the Way Home*. She has also won the Midwest Independent Publishers Association "Book of the Year" in fiction for both *All the Way Home* and *I'll Watch the Moon*. Ann lives with her husband, Bob, and their daughter, Laura, in Asheville, North Carolina.